Miracles

The Out-Pouring Series

MARGIE MCCORMICK

WESTBOW PRESS®
A DIVISION OF THOMAS NELSON & ZONDERVAN

WestBow Press books may be ordered through booksellers or by contacting:

WestBow Press
A Division of Thomas Nelson & Zondervan
1663 Liberty Drive
Bloomington, IN 47403
www.westbowpress.com
844-714-3454

ISBN: 978-1-6642-2766-8 (sc)
ISBN: 978-1-6642-2768-2 (hc)
ISBN: 978-1-6642-2767-5 (e)

Library of Congress Control Number: 2021905470

Print information available on the last page.

WestBow Press rev. date: 3/19/2021

Contents

Preface

While walking through a library, I visited the teen/young adult section. I was looking for something inspiring for the younger generation that might rekindle a part of my youth. To my disappointment, the stories seemed so shallow or filled with mythical adventures, glorifying witchcraft, and in my opinion, the celebration of demonic powers.

I thought to myself, "Wouldn't it be great to have stories for young adults about one's relationship with God instead of magical nonsense?"

"Why don't you write them then?" I heard the Lord say to my spirit.

"Me? Write a book or even a series of books? I've never done that. I wouldn't know where to start." I reasoned with the Lord.

"I will help you." He spoke.

For months I tried to come up with a storyline, but I drew a blank.

Eventually, I told the Lord, "If you want me to do this, you are going to have to tell me what to write!"

By faith I believed He would. I prayed in the spirit in front of my computer and just started typing. Soon the words were pouring out of me and before long I had the opening scene written.

Every day something new would come out I had put no forethought into. I knew it had to be God's inspiration. I was amazed at the story developing in front of me.

Before long I had completed the rough draft. I asked several trusted friends and family to read the work and give me their opinions. I was given tremendous feedback that helped with the editing.

I must admit I procrastinated a lot and almost walked away from the project altogether. However, God was always whispering in my ear to finish the work he'd called me to do.

Just when I thought I was finished, I saw an offer from Jerry B. Jenkins, Best Selling Author of the "Left Behind" series, for tips and suggestions. Within minutes, I realized the editing process was far from over and began again.

My hope is many will read this story and find encouragement to follow their calling without further delay.

Some of the subject matter and wording may not be appropriate for everyone. I wanted those who have experienced hardship or trauma to know they have never gone so far, God can't help them, and are never too young for God to use them.

Acknowledgments

I would like to thank God for inspiration. Jerry B. Jenkins, Danielle DeRoche, Terri Crider, Jolene Tomaselli, Tanner McCormick (my Bubby), and Cindy Smith for their help and feedback. I want to give a special shout-out to those who gave towards the project: Wendy Dye, Heath Back, Lynn Gaston, and Rich & Kerrie Huff. I am grateful to every one of you and those who purchase the book.

1

The Miracle

Melanie guides the grocery cart through the produce section. Jake, her chunky twenty-month-old, points at the watermelons. "Wah-men."

He smiles in a strained manner and kicks his feet. Another speck of white is peeking through his swollen gums. Seedless watermelon had been her go-to for his previous tooth. However, the subsequent diarrhea was an unwanted side effect. Melanie tries to pass the melons as quickly as possible, distracting the baby by pointing out the mound of apples on the other side.

"Look, Jaky, red," she says.

Melanie looks up to see the aisle blocked by a pair of elderly women thumping cantaloupes and discussing the price of blueberries. She waits patiently for them to notice her, hoping they will allow her to squeeze by.

Before turning back to find another way around, she notices a teething ring hanging on a long plastic strip. It can be chilled in the refrigerator. That would be the perfect solution for her child's sore gums. It hangs close to the two women, now sniffing the cantaloupes. Although she can't get through the path with her shopping cart, she knows her long arms will come in handy, allowing her to reach the ring.

"Excuse me." She tries again with no response. Stepping away from the cart, she reaches out for the ring. She hears a thump on the tiled floor. Guess she'd be buying watermelon after all.

Melanie turns to look at Jaky with his big "I'm sorry" eyes, but when she looks to where he should be sitting, he isn't there. She scans the aisle for the person who must have taken him from his seat, but only the two elderly women share the aisle. As she steps around the cart, all the blood in Melanie's body plummets to her feet. Jake is lying on the floor; his head is turned in an unnatural position. A small trickle of blood seeps from his ear. His eyes are slightly open but there is no life in them.

Someone screams with such a sharp volume it hurt her ears. She stands there looking at her little boy, waiting for him to cry, to run to her for comfort. Suddenly, a man in a clean white button-up shirt with a yellow tie grabs her by her shoulders. He is saying something to her, but the loud wailing is drowning out all other sounds. She desperately wants the noise to stop; it's keeping her from thinking clearly.

A crowd starts to form. Thankfully the loud screaming stops as Melanie realizes she is out of air. Drawing in a deep breath, she sinks to her knees at her child's lifeless body. As soon as her lungs are sufficiently filled again she realizes the sound was coming from her. The screaming turns to heart gutting moans.

Jake must have stretched out to take a watermelon. She hadn't fastened the safety belt because one of the ends was broken. Why hadn't she chosen a different cart? Why didn't she just get him the stupid watermelon? Why had she walked away, leaving him unprotected? As quickly as the grief sets in, the guilt and shame flood her heart with stabbing regret.

Melanie puts her fingers under Jake's body.

"Ma'am, don't move him! We have called an ambulance and they are on their way!" someone, probably the well-dressed man, says.

Ignoring him, she picks up her baby anyway. There's nothing they will be able to do. In her heart, she knows that.

Melanie brings his small body close to her chest.

"Give him to me."

Melanie looks up through her tears at the teenage girl kneeling next to her.

"Please." the girl says.

The compassion in her eyes compels Melanie to yield.

As soon as he leaves her arms, a fierce ringing bellows in Melanie's ears. She feels as though her lungs are shutting down. She strains to draw air into them and pulls it in too fast, causing her trembling lips to vibrate against her teeth.

The ringing is soon replaced with the low hum of the teen speaking a language unknown to Melanie. Although she isn't fluent in any language besides English, she can usually detect the familiar syllables of French, Spanish, and Chinese. But this is unlike anything she's ever heard. It is rhythmic with repeating phrases.

The girl investigates the boy's face then lifts her voice. "I command this child's body to be healed and his spirit to return in the name of Jesus!"

Against all rational thinking, Melanie's hope begins to rise. Please, God, save my baby. An unimaginable future plays out in her mind of what life would be like without her child. How would Rodney take this? Would this be the final push towards divorce their struggling relationship would suffer?

"Little boy, I said live! In the name of Jesus Christ. Be made whole and live!" The teen touches Jake's forehead with one hand as she cradles him with the other.

Suddenly, Jake takes a sharp, deep breath. Melanie holds hers.

He gazes at the woman holding him, trying to figure out who she is.

Melanie's eyes grow wide and her back straightens. The crowded gazers collectively take a step back and hushed awe comes over them. The atmosphere changes. There is a thick presence amid them all, dense yet, unseen with the naked eye.

Jake takes in another breath and starts to cry. He raises his head searching for his mother. When he sees her, he reaches out and clutches at her with his tiny fist.

Moving with the toddler's momentum, the young lady hands

him across to his mother. Melanie buries her face into Jake's neck and starts sobbing again. This time in relief and gratitude to God. Yes, to God.... and the mysterious young girl.

"Thank you! Thank you! Oh God, thank you so much!" Melanie tries repeatedly to get her words to match the gratitude in her heart but, feels as though she falls short. She looks at the young girl, still kneeling close by.

"Are you a Christian?" the teen asks.

"I haven't been to mass since I was a girl," Melanie confesses.

The Sisters of Saint Mary's Catholic school were patient and kind with all of Melanie's classmates. They tried to instill the Word of God, but she had concluded the scriptures were simply made up by uneducated dreamers and had walked away from the faith.

"I... I've been wrong."

"He still loves you. He sent me here to help you find your way back."

A distant siren pulls the teen's attention behind her. She stands and addresses the crowd. "God sent Jesus to restore us to himself and to rescue us from sin, death, and hell. Believe and confess him as Lord and you shall be saved." The crowd listens intently.

"God loves you. Not just humanity, but you, individually. He knows you better than you know yourself." She looks at Melanie, still on the floor with Jake in her arms then back to the crowd. Some have tears in their eyes, some hang their heads, others seem spellbound – longing for more.

Melanie realizes she's been trying to fill the emptiness inside with other things, but only God can fill that void. "I believe and accept Jesus as my Lord and Savior." She looks up at the teenager and they share a smile, celebrated with tears.

Others in the crowd join in agreement, but one man, who had been hanging his head most of the time, stares strangely at Melanie. They make eye contact. He seems conflicted. Quickly he turns and walks away.

A teething ring comes into Melanie's peripheral vision. One of the ladies, who had been thumping melons, holds it out. "Were you wanting one of these?"

"Yes, thank you." Melanie wipes her face free of tears and takes the plastic ring.

The man in the white shirt and yellow tie motions the paramedics towards her. She struggles to stand. The time spent on the hard, tiled floor has left her feet numb and legs tingling with needles. One of the medics looks from Melanie to the store manager confused.

"Is this the child? Dispatch said..." One of the EMTs says. Both of them eye the manager questionably.

"He was." The manager struggles to explain. "He was...," He looks at Melanie trying to be sensitive to the situation, he lowers his voice to just above a whisper. "That child was dead I'm telling you. There is no way he should be moving right now. His head was..." He tries to demonstrate the awkward position the child was lying. With an exasperated sigh, his shoulders slouch in resignation to trying. "Look! I don't know what happened but just check him out and bill the store, please."

He turns his attention to Melanie. "Ma'am, please let us know if we can help in any way." He looks at the teething ring in her hand. "And please, don't worry about paying for that. Consider it a gift to the child." He looks at Jake and shakes his head still reeling from what he has just witnessed.

As the paramedics take Jake to look him over, Melanie looks for the teenager, but she's gone. Only a few lingered, talking about what they witnessed and felt.

"Ma'am, we should take him to the hospital just to be safe," one of the medics says. The store manager nods in agreement as does she.

2

Beginning of the End

Months before....

"No, no, no, no!" I toss shirts over my shoulder as I sift through the undesirables. Where is the blue designer T I'd scored at the thrift store last week? Or the other decent finds? "Where are all my clothes?"

I stomp towards the living room. "Mom! Where are all my clothes?"

Her mother's medicated stupor only adds to Cathy's irritation. "Where are my clothes?"

Regina lays over, grabs the back of her thigh to help pull her foot onto the sofa with a grimace of pain. "I was short. He only took a few. You still have plenty in there."

"Mom!" I growl in frustration. "He took everything that fits!"

Knowing it's useless to go on any further, I storm off back to my room. Noticing the time on the alarm clock, I rush to find something that won't get me killed today.

Standing in front of the bathroom mirror, I can't help but wonder why nothing ever works out for me. My whole life has been one disappointment after another. As I tug at the tight pink t-shirt with a colorful bear walking on its hind legs, I snarl at my reflection.

Up till now, I have avoided bullying. As I look at the psychedelic bear being deformed across my chest, I know this may be the day all that changes.

I throw my hands up in surrender and tell my image, "Just go with it. The bus will be here any minute and the other options are just too damaging!"

The bus horn can be heard echoing through the trailer park, so I grab my backpack and run out, leaving the door open. Mom will have to struggle to get up from the sofa to close it. Serves her right!

The bus driver patiently waits for me and a couple of others. My bad mood is only amplified when I see the homeschooled guy smirking at us from his front porch. As is my morning ritual, I give him the finger disguising it by appearing to scratch my face. And as was his morning routine, he smiles and waves at me like we are best buds.

On the bus, I approach my best friend, Elaine.

"Nice shirt," Elaine says.

"Silence!" I purposely sling my backpack against Elaine's head, pretending it was accidental as I join her on the seat.

"I've never seen that shirt before. Surely you didn't buy that for yourself. Who hates you that much?"

"Ha, ha, very funny. I don't remember where I got it. But everything else is dirty."

"Duh, do laundry."

"The washing machine is broken. The new one hasn't been delivered yet." I lie.

"Did you hear what happened in Chem last Friday?" Elaine's eyes glow with the latest rumor.

"No, and don't care." Normally I would have seen this as my opportunity to deflect the focus from my outfit, but I'm in no mood today.

"Oh, sure you do. It's about Trevor Hayes."

I have tried to pretend the football player is nowhere on my radar, but one moment of weakness in front of Elaine has ruined that plan. Trevor is almost six foot at fifteen. He has blonde hair and blue eyes. When I fantasize about him at night, I picture him as a fierce Viking that plunders my village and takes me as his slave to do with as he pleases.

"He broke up with Mandy Tucker, calling her a ...." Elaine's sentence is cut off by the sudden braking of the school bus.

"Reckless kids! Going to get someone killed!" Mr. Jones says. The bus driver puts the blinker on and moves over into another lane. As we pass the offending driver, all the kids stare out their small window at him. You can hear the music scream from the speakers of his black Dodge Charger. Long black hair whips out the window.

"Um, can someone say Satanist?" Elaine remarks about the driver before recognition flashed across her face. "Hey, that's that new guy!"

I see my opportunity to pull her focus from Trevor. "Who?"

"He's one of those Emo or Goth people. Calls himself Black Cup or Goblet. No, it's something dark. Dark...? Whatever, anyway I hear he sacrifices animals in his basement! Allison says all the cats have been mysteriously disappearing since they moved into her neighborhood." She gives me the spooky eye. "I also hear he's really smart and may be coming your way."

"Great, can't wait." I roll my eyes.

The bus bounces onto the pothole-ridden driveway of West End High School. It comes to a stop near the gym doors.

Elaine and I pinch each other on the upper arm, our way of saying, see you at lunch. We don't have any classes together. I tested high enough for the gifted program last year and enjoy a smaller class size. That suits me fine. The fewer people, the happier I am. I'm not a genius or anything, I just don't have all the modern technologies around to distract me from studying. I guess that's the one benefit of being poor.

I make my way to Mr. Groce's homeroom where I will stay for three classes: math, language arts, and science. I head towards my desk only to find the new guy, dressed in all black, sitting there. He takes a moment away from staring at his black nail polish to peer at me through the part in his hair. I notice he is wearing eyeliner and can't help but roll my eyes as I choose another seat.

Mr. Groce calls everyone's attention. "Ok, ok, be quiet, now. We have a lot to go over and we have someone new joining us."

He looks at the student manifest trying to read the name correctly. "Um, Jon..."

"Dark Challis." the guy in black interjects.

Mr. Groce looks at him over the top of the clipboard, looks back at the paper. "Ok, whatever."

Dark Chalice? Seriously?

"Dude! You named yourself after a black goblet?" A guy in the front of the class asks, laughing, producing a ripple effect to most of the others.

"No, my last name is Challis. C.H.A.L.L.I.S., you waste of air!"

Mr. Groce clears his throat to reign the class back in.

I personally never saw the appeal to being emo or goth. In middle school, I had a friend who got into that stuff. Some mascara-wearing guy came up to her in the gym one day and told her, "Our soul shades match, wanna do nothing sometimes?". I was totally confused but she seemed to think it was the greatest thing she'd ever heard. The next thing I know, she's wearing all black, listening to songs about how terrible life is, drawing demonic-looking cats on everything, and insisted I call her Scourge. Her family moved away shortly after that.

When lunch period arrives I find Elaine to confirm she got the new guy's name almost right. She laughs and tries the think of jokes but can't come up with anything clever.

"Hey, Challis, you take your coffee black too?" I hear someone yell out to the new guy as he takes an empty seat a few tables down.

He ignores the hecklers seeming unphased.

The mocking most likely would have continued but, Rebecca Sprule, a more suitable target walks in and he is forgotten.

For the fourth time, I catch Elaine staring at my chest. "What is your deal? Do you have some lesbian fantasy I need to worry about?"

"Oh, you wish! I can't stop staring at that poor misshapen bear on your shirt. The poor creature is crying out for mercy! If your boobs get any bigger, he'll be pulled limb from limb!"

"Shh!" I warn her. "Don't bring attention to the shirt. I'm halfway through the day without anyone noticing."

Elaine huffs a cynical laugh. "Hardly! Every dude in this place has been staring at your rack all day!" She leans over and whispers. "Look! Even Dark Cup is looking."

With one eye peeking out from behind a curtain of black hair, his stare isn't at eye level. He looks away quickly after being caught. I scan the room and realize she's right. Every so often, I catch another guy looking at my chest.

Elaine punches my thigh and whispers again excitedly. "Hey, I'm not sure, but I think Trevor Hayes just took a pic of you with his cell."

He is tapping on his phone. Her desire for anything to gossip about has her seeing things.

"As if!" I say but as a precaution against someone getting the idea, I hunch over and put my arms in front of my chest.

Back at home, I sketch a picture of a horse or at least try to. This one looks better than the others, now at the bottom of my trashcan.

"Cathy!" Mom calls out.

I roll my eyes and set the notebook and pencil aside. I take my sweet time down the narrow hallway of the trailer, realizing I'm hungry as I pass the kitchen. If you like beets and ketchup, there is a meal waiting, otherwise, you're out of luck.

"Cathy!"

"I'm coming! Give me a minute!" Knowing she can't see me; I extend my middle finger and mouth a cuss word or two.

She survived the accident that killed Dad. I guess I should be glad I still have one parent left, but I often imagine what life may be like if Dad was the one to survive.

"What?" I snap at her as I enter the room.

"I need you to make me something to eat. I'm hurting too bad to move."

"Yeah ok, well we need food before I can help you there."

She searches her purse for the EBT card. She hands it out to me. "See how much we have left."

Using her government-provided cell phone, I call the balance inquiry number.

"Your EBT card balance is zero dollars and seventy-three cents." the digital voice says.

"There's not enough," I say as I toss the card onto the bed in her direction.

"What did you buy? We should have at least thirty or forty dollars!"

"Don't blame me! You're the one who let Judy use the card as payback for the light bill. Remember, she paid the past due last month so it wouldn't get turned off."

She holds her hand out for the phone. I fling it in the same manner as the card.

Before she even dials the number, I know who she's calling. "Why are you calling him? We need food, not pills!"

His line rings.

"Mom, seriously? He gives me the creeps. I don't want him here!"

"Yo!" He answers and she puts a finger to her lips telling me to hush before she responds.

I walk heavy-footed through the trailer, making sure she hears my anger with every step. I throw open the door then slam it back again.

I head for the junkyard. Halfway there, shielded by the tall grass of the field that separates Jiles' Scrapyard from the trailer park, I sit hidden from view. I'm so tired of going over the what-ifs in my mind. I wish I could leave and start over somewhere else. I will not ever let my kids live like this. I get to my feet and finish the distance to Greg's place.

I pull back the loose fencing and wiggle through. The old man used to try to run me off, but when I kept coming back, he gave up. One day, he watched from the dusty window of his office, as I piddled around picking up cigarette butts and snack wrappers to throw in the makeshift garbage can, made from an old paint drum. I picked up some aluminum cans acting like I didn't know they were piled up purposely for recycle. I was hungry and thought maybe I could sell a few to get enough money for a candy bar. I didn't know at that time you had to have a lot of cans to even amount to a dollar. He'd stepped out of the small shack

"Hey!" he said. His voice gruff.

I'd dropped a can and looked at him, waiting to be run off again. Instead, he held out a garbage bag and told me to load the cans in the back of his pick-up truck. When finished, I turned to find him holding a five-dollar bill out to me. I looked at the money flapping in the wind and then at him in confusion.

"Well! Take it! Nobody works at my place for free. You trying to get me in trouble, girl?" he had demanded.

I snatched the money from his hand and immediately ran to the grocery store down the street. I bought four dollars and sixty-eight cents worth of candy bars, which I ate in about two minutes.

I keep coming back but, not just for the work. I like the way the place smells of old oil and gasoline. I feel at peace sitting in the back seat of the old Buick that's been warming up in the sun. There are no kids outside of these windows squealing at being found and tagged "it". No angry girlfriend letting the whole trailer park know her man is off-limits and she'll gut any other woman that looks at him. No mother down the hall stoned out of her mind.

Ole' Greg and I have become sorta like friends although he only calls me girl. I don't ask him about the young man in uniform, a younger version of himself is posing with, in the dusty framed photo, and he doesn't ask me where my dad is or why my mom has never come looking for me.

He tells me fifteen-year-old girls should be hanging out at the mall with other girls, giggling about whatever they giggle about these days.

"I don't giggle, Greg." I tell him while sweeping the office floor.

He straightens in his chair to make a point. "I've seen you girls in the mall walking in a group so tight you nearly trip over each other's feet, saying stuff like, totally." Greg flaps his right hand out in a single wave with a goofy look on his face, trying to imitate his version of a silly teenage girl.

I stop sweeping and prepare to make a point. "First of all; you have never seen me hanging out at the mall with any girls like that. Secondly, how long has it been since you've seen this gang of females? Nobody has said 'totally' since like, forever."

"Aye, you know what I mean." He groans as he pulls himself up from the grease-stained chair from behind his cluttered desk. He reaches into his back pocket and I know he's getting ready to pay me for the next-to-nothing work I've done. I don't like to seem desperate, so I turn my attention back to sweeping and try to act unexpectant as he hands the twenty out to me. It's too much for what little I did, but I know by now not to argue. I quickly take it and slip it into my pants pocket.

"Thank you." I say quietly.

"I gotta lock up early today. So, you best be heading on to the mall with your spending money." He winks at me.

Instead of heading home, I walk toward the grocery store a mile away. The sun is low in the sky and I need to hurry. It's dangerous on the road after dark. All the druggies start making their nightly run to the meth house on Bowdon Lane.

I gather things that will stretch, avoiding meat. After calculating the taxes in my head, I know there is just enough to cover it. I see an open cashier, but an old woman steps in front of me from out of nowhere. She smiles at me as she sets the gallon of milk and bottle of honey on the conveyor belt. I smile back and unload my items behind hers.

The sliding doors open, catching my attention. I see the flock of giggling girls Greg could have easily been referring to. They sound like a bunch of cackling chickens. In the few seconds, it takes them to walk through the doors and down the produce aisle, out of my sight, I swear I hear them say, "I'm so shook.", a hundred times. Under my breath, I whisper, "Totally", and smile to myself.

"That'll be twenty-nine-eleven." the cashier says.

That sounds like a lot for what little the woman was getting. The green numbers displayed on the small screen read $29.11. I look down at the conveyor belt and notice my items are gone.

"Oh, ma'am, I think you rang up my stuff with hers," I say.

The cashier looks frustrated and starts to remove the bread from the grocery bag hanging from the arms on the carousel.

"No, no, it's ok. I'll pay for it. But could you put her things in separate bags, please?" The elderly woman asks the cashier sweetly.

"Yeah, I guess so." the cashier says. She rolls her eyes.

"Ma'am you don't have to do that, it was my fault for not paying attention." I turn to the cashier and see her name tag reads Heather. "I'm sorry, Heather." I tilt my head like a child, hoping for sympathy as I hold out my money.

The little old lady reaches over and touches my hand grasping the twenty-dollar bill. "No, Sweet-heart, the Lord told me to pay for it."

She continues like it's the most normal thing in the world for the Lord to speak to her. "He loves you very much and has great plans for you." She smiles and side-glances at the screen showing the dollar amount. She taps the screen. "Jeremiah twenty-nine-eleven, you should read it. It's written for all God's children just like you."

She turns her attention to the cashier handing her cash and coins that are exact, almost like she'd expected that total from the start. I didn't see her reach into her pocket for the money and she isn't carrying a purse, which also seems strange.

Taking the receipt from Heather, she looks at me so kindly. "Do you have a Bible, Sweet-heart?"

"Um, no ma'am."

"Come outside with me, dear, I've got an extra one in the car."

She doesn't even wait to see what I will say. She gathers her bags from the carousel, and I take mine with a glance at Heather, the cashier. Heather looks just as bored as before and seems not to care one bit a minor is about to follow a stranger to their car. Of course, I don't blame her. Oddly, I don't feel threatened in the least. I could probably knock the old lady down with barely any effort if it came to that.

I speed up to match the pace of this strange woman. She looks as though she's a hundred and two but walks like she's twenty. I think for a second to just take off across the parking lot with my free items and leave her to give the extra Bible to someone else, but I don't. I guess it's the least I can do since she paid for my supper.

She opens the door behind the driver's seat, leans inside, and reemerges with a thick black book in her hand.

"Ma'am I...."

"My name is Lettie, dear. Now here." With her hands holding mine on the Bible, she looks me straight in the eyes. They seem to pierce through me, and a warmth drapes over me like oil flowing down the crown of my head to my feet.

"Cathy, read this for what it is; it holds your life and future. Don't read it like it's just a book because it isn't. It is alive with the very words of God. Through it, He will speak and if you will listen and obey, He will protect you and you will do His mighty works."

The odd warmth leaves me speechless.

"Now, you get home safely." She says it more like a command than a request.

Still feeling heavy from whatever that was, I start walking towards home. I only take two steps when it dawns on me, she had called me by my name. I turn with the question, "How....".

She's gone. No car. No old lady. Nothing. Just a few other cars parked further down. There is no way she could have gotten in her car, started it, and drove away that fast!

I stand there a moment trying to figure out what just happened but reminded of my surroundings when a loud pickup truck screeches to a halt in the parking space beside me. The passenger gets out of the truck, still rocking from the abrupt halt. She yells a few cuss words at the driver before slamming the door. She twitches and blinks oddly past me. I quickly realize it's getting late and not safe for me to be hanging around.

About three trailers from our own, I see Pete's green van sitting in the driveway. I can't stay at the junkyard tonight; I'd bought things that need to be refrigerated so; I halfheartedly head home. Before opening the door, I take a deep breath. In my mind, I see the layout of the trailer and plan the quickest route to my bedroom. Head down, Cathy, no eye contact, no talking, just b-line-it down the hall and close the door. He'll be gone soon enough; I pep-talk myself.

I swing open the door, walking quickly, as I had planned. I make it to my bedroom, shut and lock the door behind me, cut on the light, and empty my hands onto the floor. Taking the step and a half across the room, I drop to my mattress that sits without a frame and stare at the old beige carpet. My heart is pounding so hard I feel it in my neck, temples, and even in my toes. What in the world!

I stuck to my plan. I didn't make eye contact with anyone but in my peripheral vision, I think I saw....

I grab the small trashcan from beside my mattress. I'm glad I always take the time to line the can with a left-over grocery bag because it makes cleaning easier. I stare at the wadded-up papers that were my attempts to draw a horse. Involuntarily my mouth opens wide and I vomit all over them.

Pete was here longer than usual but, he left about an hour ago. I still haven't left my room. I look over at the bags of grocery items still sprawled where I'd dropped them. I am not hungry anymore, but some things need to be put in the frig or it will spoil. I look over at the trashcan. I haven't tied the bag shut because if I start chucking again, I need it open and waiting. It reeks and I want to get it out of here, but I don't want to go out there. I don't want to see my mom's face. I don't want to see the couch. I will never sit on it again!

Although it was from the corner of my eye, I'm sure I saw Pete on the couch with my mom kneeling on the floor in front of him. If she was doing what I think she was doing, I know what she's now trading for pills. Just the thought of it makes my stomach turn again.

My heart isn't pounding out of my chest anymore, it just feels very heavy. I feel like something inside me has broken. Tears start rolling from my eyes in a flood. I think about Dad. What would he think? What would he do if he could see her now? Did he know she was capable of something like this?

The flood of tears causes my nose to run; I need a tissue. Just walking toward the door makes me feel weak. I look down the hall making sure he's gone. The living room is dark. I'm guessing Mom went to her bedroom to crash. I move swiftly to the bathroom, closing the door behind me. After blowing my nose, I go back to my room and pull the bag from the trashcan. I work up the courage to take it and the food to the kitchen and recycle one of the empty grocery bags.

I make a conscious effort to divert my eyes from the living room. I stand at the refrigerator with the door open. Using the light, I force myself to look over at the couch.

By now, I'm familiar with the squealing power steering when Pete's van turns left. I see headlights glide across the window as it pulls into our driveway. I slam the frig door and rush back to my room, locking the door, turning off the light, so they'll think I'm asleep. I stand with my ear against the door and hear them laughing as they come inside. It sounds like they brought more people with them.

"Don't start without me!" Pete's voice sounds close. Fear rises in my chest as I hear his heavy steps approaching the bathroom which is only one step from my door. I hear the bathroom door open, but I don't hear it close. Everything around me intensifies and I listen for even the smallest sound, my heart thuds with slow purposeful beats. Through the thin fabricated door, I hear him breathing. I look down and see the shadow of his feet standing just outside my door. The handle turns slightly until the internal locking mechanism catches and won't go any further.

I hadn't noticed I was holding my breath until I hear the bathroom door close. A moment later, the toilet flushes, and I feel the slight vibrations of his footsteps as he heads back to the living room. I take a deep breath in and walk backward in the direction of my mattress.

I step on something and jerk nervously. Moonlight streams in and falls on the Bible I was given earlier today.

Knowing I won't be able to sleep for a while, I sit cross-legged in bed at an angle where the outside light falls on the book. The blue cover is plain. The words, Holy Bible, Contemporary Version, and a cross, emboss the front. I open it right in the middle.

Psalms seventy-one CEV: I run to you, Lord, for protection. Don't disappoint me. You do what is right, so come to my rescue. Listen to my prayer and keep me safe. Be my mighty rock, the place where I can always run for protection. Save me by your command! You are my mighty rock and my fortress. Come and save me, Lord God, from vicious and cruel and brutal enemies!

I stop at the part numbered, four. The words seem to sing my own life right now. I've never thought about calling out to God. I've never considered if he is real. I remember the lady told me; "Jeremiah twenty-nine-eleven, you should read it." I turn to the front of the book for the contents page. Flipping through, I find Jeremiah chapter twenty-nine and verse eleven in the CEV.

I will bless you with a future filled with hope, a future of success, not of suffering.

I close my eyes, still throbbing from crying earlier, "God, if this is real, if you are real, please let me know. Please tell me what to do." Fresh tears make my sore eyes sting. I clench them tightly and lay back on my pillow. With only a few more sobs I feel myself settling into sleep.

When the dream started, I was reliving a favorite memory of mine. I was eleven and Dad was still alive. The three of us were at the park downtown having a picnic. Mom was setting sandwiches on the old blanket from home. I was sitting next to Dad with my ear against his chest, listening to the deep vibrations of his voice as he talked about his day. I would rub the embroidered patch that read, Lewis and breathe in the smells of gas fumes, oil, and sweat from a hard day's work. It doesn't sound appealing to most people, but that scent was what I grew up with. That was my safe place, my happy place.

The grass around us is lush and green. The sky is clear blue, and the sun's heat is cooled by a gentle breeze.

From behind, I hear a voice carried by the wind, "Turn and see," The voice says to me.

Without hesitation, I stand to my feet and turn completely in the opposite direction. The grass behind us is dry and dead. A black cloud looms in the sky and the wind becomes stronger. My hair whips into my face and dust sting my eyes. I close them for a moment. When I open them again, I am surrounded by teenagers of all ages. They seem to be asleep on their feet. I gently push through the crowd till I am at the front of the large group.

"I have called you to be a light in the darkness." The voice declares over us.

What I thought was a cloud, is a wall of darkness that consumes everything in its path. It grows darker, moves quicker, and I realize it is coming right for the park. I hear my mother start to cry so I turn around. Over the shoulders of those around me, I see her kneeling on the makeshift picnic blanket. Dad! Where's Dad? I can't see him. I try to push my way through the crowd again, but they stand firmly in place.

I panic and feel the familiar grief again. Dad! I try to speak but I can't make the words form; only slurred syllables come out. Still fighting my way through the mob, I see Mom overwhelmed with sorrow as she looks where Dad had been sitting. Her soft cries turn into blasts of unnatural sounding alarm.

Finally, I break through the crowd, but jerk awake and see only my bedroom. The alarm clock roars at me in the same tone as Mom's screams from the nightmare. I reach over and slap the top of the plastic box.

I sit up and think about the dream. I wouldn't call it a nightmare. Yes, it ended that way but the first part… it was different.

3

Spirit, Soul, and Body

Rebecca Sprule slams into the locker next to me shaking me out of my thoughts. All-day I've been thinking about the dream I had last night. I was so unfocused I had to step out of my comfort zone and ask the Dark boy next to me to repeat our homework assignment because I had missed it.

"Oh, I'm sorry Drool-el," Mandy Tucker says exaggeratedly, "did I trip you?" A few chuckles come from those staring now.

Rebecca stays leaned up against the lockers trying to make herself small. She's an unfortunate one that gets a lot of grief from bullies. Rebecca had tried to strike up a conversation with me once, but we didn't mesh. I don't dislike her; I just had a hard time relating to her. She seemed interested in my life and asked a lot of questions. I don't like talking about my life, so the conversation didn't go far.

Mandy continues to make little puns about Rebecca's name, weight, and whatever else she can think of to get a laugh from the spectators. Why she enjoys this so much, I have no idea. Mandy has a lot going for her. She doesn't need to make anyone feel small. She is gorgeous and most of the other girls feel small in her presence already.

Suddenly, from out of nowhere, Rebecca gets bold and slaps

Mandy across the face! I didn't hear what was said just before, because I was trying to mind my own business.

A collective gasp comes from the crowd. Rebecca backs up against the lockers again seeming to regret her decision. Mandy's face turns a violent red, but not from Rebecca's hand. The slap seems to be a meager show of resistance and had only caused Mandy some shock and embarrassment.

Then it was on! Mandy attacks Rebecca with punches to the gut. Rebecca topples over. The beating continues with blows to her head. She tries to shield herself and even makes a couple of attempts to fight back, but without time to recover from having the air knocked out of her, it's obvious she is losing this fight.

The crowd gets tighter as people coming down the hall want to see what's going on. Whether it was just not my day or because I was so close to the action when it all went down, somehow, I was suddenly involved. The rushing crowd pushed me right into the path of Rebecca's flailing fingers and some of my hair got caught in her grasp. My head gets pulled down into one of the brawler's knees. My nose feels like it was hit with a mallet and tears explode from my eyes.

"Hit her again!" I hear someone say followed with a lot of oos and oh's.

I taste the blood running from my nose and that is it! I have had enough!

"Stop!" I push Mandy in one direction and Rebecca in the other. Mandy loses her balance and falls to her skinny tailbone. Rebecca slams against the lockers once again. The bell chimes telling everyone to get to their next class and the crowd disperses quickly, leaving us three staring at each other.

Mandy's hair is a mess but seems no worse for the wear. Rebecca, however, is sobbing. Her hands lay atop each other, covering her mouth. Drops of blood fall onto her shirt. I see, what will be, a horrible bruise on her upper cheek tomorrow. The white part of one eye is full of blood.

I pull the collar of my t-shirt up to my throbbing nose. I decide against going to my next class looking like this. You don't stay invisible long after an event like this. I head for the nearest exit. The alarm will sound when I go out the door, but I don't care. By the time an adult arrives to investigate, I'll be long gone.

It's a long walk from school to home, but it gives me some time to reflect. Mostly I think about how much I hate my life. As soon as I'm old enough, I know I'll leave home but where will I go? I don't have any family other than Mom. Feeling lousy, I talk out loud to myself. "It's pointless."

I look over and see the grocery store as I pass by and I think about the old lady. The Bible verse she spoke to me says it's not pointless. According to it, God has a plan for me. I shift my backpack from one shoulder to the other and feel the added weight of the Bible inside.

I'm almost home when I see Pete's van in the driveway.

Nope. Not today.

Making a slight adjustment, I head across the field to the junkyard. Although, I'm sure Greg doesn't mind me hanging out there anymore, sneaking through the fence will keep him from aiding and abetting. Reaching the Buick, I toss my backpack inside and crawl in on my hands and knees, resting my head on the book bag. I lay there looking through the hole in the back seat that leads to the trunk and reach inside feeling my way past the photos too painful to look at, the diary I never know what to write in, to the Twinkies that are nice and warm from the heat of the sun on the metal above them. I pull myself up and take the Bible from the bookbag and open the twinkie.

I stare at the headers of the Old Testament and New Testament on the contents page of the Bible. Well, I think, this is all new to me so let's go with the New Testament. I see the first section is called Saint Matthew. I take mental note of the page number and thumb through it till I get there.

The Ancestors of Jesus

Jesus Christ came from the family of King David and also from the family of Abraham. And this is a list of his ancestors. From Abraham to King David, his ancestors were: Abraham, Isaac, Jacob, Judah, and his brothers (Judah's sons were Perez and Zerah, and their mother was Tamar), Hezron; Ram, Amminadab, Nahshon, Salmon, Boaz (his mother was Rahab), Obed (his mother was Ruth), Jesse, and King David.

I scan down the page and see a lot more names hard to pronounce. I'm only two verses in and I'm already frustrated. I soldier on determined to see what this is about.

Verse eighteen; This is how Jesus Christ was born. A young woman named Mary was engaged to Joseph from King David's family. But before they were married, she learned she was going to have a baby by God's Holy Spirit.

"Uh, yeah, I'll bet that was hard to explain," I say. My mouth is full of the last bite of the twinkie.

I continue to read the story, becoming more interested and seeing for the first time why people decorate their yards with manger scenes. I'd always wondered how camels and men in long dresses tied into Christmas. The baby lying in a box with hay made sense now too.

Soon the story skips Jesus' childhood and goes to him getting baptized by some guy in camel clothes who ate bugs. I close the book and look up at the roof of the car. I try to make sense of what I just read. It all seems very confusing to me. Now I have more questions, instead of the answers I was looking for. I think about the old lady telling me not to read it like it's just a book because it isn't. It is alive with the very words of God.

"I'm trying lady, I am but I think I'm going to need help," I say.

For a long time, I just sit there in my thoughts. I tend to over-analyze things. Mom used to say I could think a thing to death. After a while, I see the yellow top of a school bus pass by just over the fence. School is out. No need to hide any longer. I wonder if Pete is still at our house and I decide to wait it out a little longer just in case.

Later, I remember it's Tuesday and a church van usually drives through the trailer park around five to offer a ride to any kids who want to go to church.

I scoot across the bench seat dragging my backpack behind me then tucking the Bible inside before making my way to the trailer park. Just as I get halfway across the field, I see the church van heading towards the exit. I start running hoping by some miracle they see me before they leave. I need answers and this is my best option right now.

When I get to the folding doors, I tap to get the driver's attention. He opens the door and smiles a big grin. "Something told me to wait a little longer," he says.

I take a seat across the aisle from the boy that lives at lot fifteen. He smiles at me, but I stare out the window trying not to make eye contact with anyone. I think about what the driver said and tuck that away with the other weird stuff that's been happening lately.

When we pull up to the church, all the little kids get so excited they get up, pushing past one another to be the first one off the bus. The driver chastises them with a smile letting them know he is not mad, but they must return to their seats until the van has stopped moving.

It isn't much different inside. They act like this place is filled with cotton candy and chocolate fountains. You can hear them cheering loudly through the building. I follow everyone else, not knowing where I should go. A cluster of kids who have reached the double doors down the hall, open them as instruments start playing. The stage is lit up and kids jump to the live music playing. It isn't dark inside like a bar or concert, but it's... well...cool. I don't know the song they are playing but it is catchy.

Someone touches my hand and I instinctively pull back.

"Oh, I'm sorry," shouts a young woman with mocha-colored skin. Stretching out her hand, she speaks over the music. "My name is Vanessa. I'm one of the youth directors here. I haven't seen you before, are you new?"

I pause for a minute rethinking if I want to do this. I shake her hand. "Cathy."

She leans in and turns her ear toward me. "Sorry?"

"Cathy!" I say a little louder.

She smiles but looks at me oddly. "Are you ok?" she asks.

"Yeah, I guess." I shrug. I'm sure she notices my awkwardness.

I don't know the social protocols of a church. What's expected of me?

She leads me to a seat at the front, just behind her and some other young adults. They must be other youth leaders. My attention is caught by the guy from lot fifteen, waving at me with a huge grin on his face. I sheepishly wave back and refocus on the music.

The infectious celebration oddly puts me at ease and soon I join in with the music.

"I'm gonna clap my hands," followed by all the kids singing out, "My hands!" while clapping twice to the syllables of the lyrics.

"I'm gonna stomp my feet!" says the band.

"My feet!" The audience echos.

"I'm gonna shout for joy!"

"Joy, joy!"

"Come on everybody and sing! We're praising, praising the power down."

"Praising the power down!", the kids sing.

When the singing is done, the band continues to play softly in the background. An elderly man goes up on the stage, holding a microphone, and introduces himself as Elder Andrew Shook. He presents the youth directors and promises an exciting night. Vanessa stands up along with the other leaders who line up in front of the congregation. The main speaker instructs age group five through seven to follow Ms. Jane. The short blonde waved her hand high in the air as all the kids clap and cheer. Then Mr. Paul, for ages eight through ten, does the same wave. The kids respond with the same clapping and cheering. I don't want to seem rude, so I clap along, though I draw the line at cheering. Then he announces Miss Vanessa, who waves excitedly for age group eleven to fourteen. I stop clapping knowing this means I've got to be introduced to another new person.

"Mr. Jeff for ages fifteen to eighteen. And finally, follow me and Mrs. Shook, for ages nineteen and above," says Mr. Andrew. A petite lady behind him waves her hand.

I follow the crowd as we all stand and begin to file into our age groups. As I approach the man who looks to be in his mid-twenties known as Mr. Jeff, I stumble over some kid who decided to tie his shoes in the middle of the aisle. Instinctively I reach out to grab anything to steady myself and am rescued by a hand with polished nails; black polish to be exact.

I swear, using the name of Jesus and looking at the little kid as he runs off to his class as if nothing happened.

"I don't think they like people using his name like that. They call it vain or something." My rescuer says softly.

I turn to thank the person for their help and advice. I'm shocked into silence to see it is Dark Challis.

Before I can say thanks, he is striding ahead, following the rest of those in our group.

Most of the chairs are stacked against an unlit corner of the large room. Ten or so have been arranged in a semi-circle with a single chair facing the ten. Mr. Jeff stands at the door and greets us as we come in.

"Hey, Steve! Good to see ya, buddy." He high-fives the first guy in which I recognize as the homeschooled guy from the trailer park.

The next girl in holds a cell phone in the air. "Wait till you see my new iPhone, Mr. Jeff, it does ev-ver-ry-thing, I mean like everything!"

"Great Shaday, but not in class ok. Let's save that for the end." Mr. Jeff says with his high five left hanging in the air.

"Hey, welcome, man." Mr. Jeff says enthusiastically keeping the high five in the air to still no reciprocation from the goth guy. He steps into the room and heads straight for the chair meant for the youth leader.

"Don't leave me hanging, young lady, I'm starting to think I'm losing my street-cred," he says.

I give him a weak high five as quickly as I possibly can and feel like a moron for doing so. He leans over and whispers. "Everything ok?"

I nod my head. Wow, these people are concerned if I'm ok with being here. I find that strange.

"Matthew, my main man." Mr. Jeff says to the guy behind me.

I hear their hands meet in a high five.

"What? You're not going to try to get out of class?" Mr. Jeff asks Matthew.

"I'm good." I hear him say to the youth leader.

Steve and the other girl sit a couple of chairs apart. I go for the chair farthest away on the end. The guy behind me sits next to me even though there are chairs available to separate. He looks over and smiles at me.

Mr. Jeff closes the classroom door and joins us. He doesn't mention the intruder in his seat, just nonchalantly chooses another and begins the discussion.

"Since some of you are new to the class, how about we all introduce ourselves. My name is Jeffery Pike. You can call me Jeff, Mr. Jeff, Brother Jeff, or any other respectful variation. I would like to know your name and what brought you here tonight. Steve, let's start with you."

He takes a deep breath and rubs his palms on his blue jeans. "I'm Steve… do we need to say our last names Mr. Jeff?", he asks before continuing.

"That's up to you but try to keep it brief, ok?"

The teen nods. "I'm Steve Zablockis, I'm sixteen. Although I've lived in America all my life, my parents are from Latvia. I was homeschooled so my mama and I could take care of my papa because he has advanced Parkinson's disease. I'm here because I love Jesus and want to be a preacher one day." He looks to Mr. Jeff to see if that's enough information or if he needs to continue.

Shaday looks at me. "Steve likes to brag he's already finished with school."

"That's not what I'm doing. Just giving my story, ya know." Steve tries to look innocent, but I think Shaday is right. That's the vibe I've always gotten when he watches us all load onto the bus in the mornings. Why else would he get up that early and watch us?

"Thank you, Steve. Shaday, why don't you go next. "Jeff nods her way.

Shaday flips a long braid away from her face. "Ok like, I'm Shaday Jackson. I'm sixteen. And, uh, I live with my Grammah

Cora cause… I just do." She looks at Mr. Jeff out of the corner of her eye then continues. "I got a job baby sittin' my sister's kids while she at work. I guess that's it. Oh, and I'm here 'cause I love Jesus too." Shaday looks to Mr. Jeff to pick the conversation up from there.

"You're up Matthew." He points to the blond-headed guy next to me.

"I'm Matthew Mitchell. For the newbies here, my dad is the Pastor." He says this as if we should be impressed. "I'm sixteen, I am homeschooled too by my mom, and being the PK is what brings me here tonight." He side-glances at me. "But this class is starting to look a whole lot more interesting." He winks and looks at my hair.

I look away and see Mr. Jeff is waiting on me but I've got the deer in the headlight look on my face, so he moves on.

"How about you, young man, what's your story?"

For a moment it seems Dark is too impressed with his nail polish to answer, but he shifts in Mr. Jeff's chair and begins. "My name is Dark Challis. I'm sixteen and I was forced to be here by John and Susan who are afraid I killed all the neighborhood cats."

Maybe the rumors are true then.

We sit in a weird silence for a minute until Mr. Jeff finally responds. "So, should we just call you Dark?"

Matthew laughs.

"Whatever, I don't care. Just pretend I'm not here." Dark says. He crosses his arms and turns sideways in the chair facing the door.

Mr. Jeff looks unaffected and comes back to me. "And how about you, young lady?"

Still watching Dark, it takes me a minute to register it's my turn. The one eye of his I can see moves up and focuses on me, yanking me back to my surroundings. I clear my throat. "My name is Cathy Maze. I'm fifteen." I shrug, not knowing what else to say.

"We know John, Susan and missing cats brought Dark here. What or who brings you here?" he says.

I bite my lip and glance over to the dark guy to see if he reacts. He does not.

Speaking in public has never been my strong suit. They all talked about their family. I suppose I should do the same. "My parents didn't force me here. I just live with my mom. My dad passed away a couple of years ago. I came here because I have some questions, but it can wait till the end of class."

"No, no, let's hear it. Maybe one of the questions could be our topic tonight. I was going to talk about Noah's ark, but a rescue boat full of animals seems like a sensitive subject now." That one got a sideways death stare from Dark.

"I started reading the Bible yesterday, but it's hard to understand. I mean, I know what the words are saying and stuff but, I don't know where it's all coming from and how it applies to me." I start there. The woman disappearing and the bizarre dream can wait, I decide.

"That is a great question, and I can work with that. Thank you for providing me with a topic I know a little something about. If I had a chalice, I would toast you." Mr. Jeff exclaims humorously emphasizing 'chalice' and even miming the act of toasting.

That was the last straw for Dark. He stands and peers at Mr. Jeff with disdain. We all freeze except Mr. Jeff; he looks just as calm as before. Dark squeezes his fingers into a fist and opens his mouth to speak, but before one word could be spoken, he is interrupted by the loudest fart I have ever heard. One big blast of air and it was done.

"Excuse me." Steve apologizes.

Everyone burst out laughing except for Dark who stomps towards the door. Mr. Jeff runs to catch up to him. "Sorry, sorry, sorry, Dark, don't leave man. It's all good. We just aren't used to such seriousness here." He reaches out to touch Dark on the shoulder but thinks better of it. "Please? I'm sorry, please forgive me. I won't say those things again. We like you and want you to stay."

Really, Mr. Jeff, I think. We like him. Who is this we you are referring to?

"Whatever, man!" Dark huffs as he walks back to the chairs, this time taking one he should have taken to begin with.

Mr. Jeff reclaims the seat facing all the others. "Ok, the quick answer to your question is, you must be born again to properly understand the Bible. You make Him Lord and put it into practice."

That does not help me. Now I have another question. "What is being 'born again'? And what does it mean to make Jesus the Lord?"

"Hmm, let me ask you some questions so I know where I need to start. Have you ever been to church as a kid? Do you know any Bible stories?"

I shake my head. "No, not really. I went to a Vacation Bible School when I was ten, but I didn't know what they were talking about then either. Up until now, I thought they were just making up stories to entertain us."

"Have you ever had a concept of God, or Jesus, His Son?"

"I've heard people talk about God and Jesus, but it is usually when they are upset about something; like when people cuss or say the names like that." I glance at Dark thinking back to before the class.

"Well, let me be the first to tell you God is very real, and Jesus is still alive."

I stop him before he can move on. "I thought Jesus lived hundreds of years ago or longer."

"Two thousand years approximately." He smiles cleverly.

I give him a skeptical look.

"Bear with me a moment as I explain. I'll try to be brief." He takes a deep breath. "Ok, Jesus did die. He took the punishment for our sins and was crucified to bear the curse for us. When He died, He was in hell for three days then rose to life again by God's Holy Spirit. He is still alive to this day, sitting with God and acting as our high priest."

"To be born again, you believe God is real and He rewards you when you seek Him diligently. Then you believe in your heart and confess with your mouth that Jesus is Lord. When you do that, you become a new creature. The old you that was dead, becomes alive with the Spirit of Christ and all things become new. It's a spiritual rebirth."

"When you become a Christian, you don't make stuff up and call that Christianity. Everything a follower of Christ believes should be coming from the Bible. That's why we study it, to renew our mind to the truth. Am I explaining this well enough for you?". His expression is pained.

I nod.

Mr. Jeff continues. "God made us like Him. He is the Father, the Son, and the Holy Spirit. They are three but one at the same time. A lot of people don't know this, but you are a three-part being. So, when God said let us make man in our image and after our likeness, He made mankind a three-part being: spirit, soul, and body. Your spirit is the eternal part of you that responds to God. You have a soul, that is your mind, will, and emotions. And finally, you live in a body. Are you with me so far?"

"I think so, but can you explain the spirit part again. I know I have a mind and emotions, so I get the soul part. And I know I have a body-"

"Yes, you do.", says Matthew. When he realizes he spoke aloud he tries to play it off by saying, "Um, praise the Lord, tell it like it is sister." He looks at Mr. Jeff and is met with a warning look from the teacher.

I continue, "Like I was trying to say, isn't the spirit and soul just two words for the same thing?"

"No, they are different. Although your spirit and soul are both eternal and never die, you are a spirit. You possess a soul. In the world of psychology, scientists have labeled the soul as your conscience and the spirit as the sub-conscience. But really, God created your spirit to communicate with him. It was supposed to be the main way we functioned, just using our body and mind as tools in the material world to translate what we saw in the spirit or heard from God. The main difference between the two is the spirit is who you are. Your soul is a tool you use to communicate."

Still trying to take in everything, I go back to something he said. "What is the curse you were talking about and how did Jesus take that?"

With each question I have, his face seems to light up even more. I think he may be enjoying the Q & A.

He smiles. "Well, in the beginning, God put mankind in charge of the earth and said we could have anything we wanted except for one thing. He told Adam he could eat from any of the trees in the garden except the tree of knowledge. He warned him in the day he ate, he would die. It is evident He didn't mean a physical death because, when they believed the lies of Satan and ate the fruit, they didn't die physically but spiritually. By doing this, the whole world came under a curse, and mankind was enslaved to the devil."

"Why did God not want them to have knowledge?" I ask.

"It wasn't that God didn't want them to know things, He just wanted them to get the knowledge from Him. God is absolute good and perfect love. He knows everything! There is no better place to get knowledge than straight from the Father. We have all seen what can happen when people get information too early or too late or from the wrong person. Just because you can know something doesn't mean it will benefit you."

"I thought knowledge was power," Dark speaks up from under his hair.

"But power in the wrong hands causes terrible damage. For example, do you think it's important for a person living off the grid to know how to start a fire?" Mr. Jeff asks.

Most everyone nods in agreement.

"Do you think it's important for a two-year-old to know how to start a fire?"

"No!" Steve spoke up.

"Nuh-uh! My sister's youngest, Cleo, he found some matches and set his bed on fire one time. Like to have burnt the house down!" Shaday says.

Mr. Jeff nods, knowing he's got his point across. "Yes, exactly. We all need knowledge but most of it needs to be structured in such a way that allows us to mature and have knowledge mixed with wisdom. The devil lied to them and said God was trying to hold something back from them that would make them like God. But they were already made in His image and after His likeness. The devil is still trying to deceive people by getting them to try to be like God, without God."

"So, as the result of Adam and Eve believing the lies of the devil and acting on what he said, they aligned themselves with him instead of God and caused the curse to come on the planet. Every human born after that is now in slavery to Satan. Rather than speaking to the earth, and bringing what was desired, they had to work with their hands and be subject to the curse. Or another way to say it; they stopped using their spirit to control their soul and body, and they became twisted. Now, most people are controlled by their flesh and emotions while their spirit lies dormant in a kind of death. Jesus bore the curse for us so we can be free of it."

"Because Jesus has come and taken all the punishment for sin and defeated the devil, we can come back to God and do things His way. When you accept Him as Lord, His Spirit comes into your spirit and makes it alive and receptive to God again."

"But if Jesus defeated the devil, why isn't everything back to the way God made it, to begin with?" I ask.

The teacher smiles and points at me. "That's an exceptionally good question. God gave the earth to mankind for a set time. Mankind made a decision that cursed everything. The devil took away our right to choose, Jesus gave it back. Although God is all-powerful, He doesn't oppress us with it, but truly makes us free by giving us a choice. He operates by faith and laws. There are natural laws that govern the planet and us, but through faith, we can change things. He won't take back the dominion He gave to mankind. Instead, He made a way for those who willingly choose Him, to operate in The Blessing and outside of the curse. It's kind of like a legal loophole. Though the curse is still here, we can now work around it through Jesus. This is a great picture of just how much God loves us."

I thumb through the pages of the Bible in my lap. I feel

overwhelmed. It would take me forever to learn what Mr. Jeff just told me. I feel discouraged.

"That Bible you're holding is not just a normal book like you pick up at the library. Don't think you have to read it in a hurry to find out all there is to know. It tells us God's thoughts and ways. And when we read it, it causes faith and our minds to rewire, so to speak, to do things His way. Romans 12:2 in the King James Version, tells us to be transformed by the renewing of our minds to prove God's perfect will. And Colossians 3:10 KJV, says this new man is renewed in knowledge like our Creator. Learning how to do things God's way is a lifelong journey and the Spirit of God will help you."

Mr. Jeff looks at the time on his cell phone. "In these last few minutes, would anyone like to be born again right now?"

No one speaks up. I sit silently in my chair despite feeling like I've just heard some amazing things and I have no reason to believe they are not true.

"Well, it's time to stop for tonight. I hope that helps to answer your question. If you want to know more about being born again and filled with the Spirit, meet me in the lobby." He says to us.

As we leave the room, Mr. Jeff shakes our hands or tries, Dark is still not having it. "Thanks for breaking wind… I mean, the tension, Steve," he says.

"Sorry, Mr. Jeff, you know I have a sensitive stomach. I tried to hold it in, but I just couldn't." Steve turns and looks at me, the last to leave the room. "I'm so sorry, Cathy, I hope I didn't make you never want to come back."

"No, it's fine, Steve. Don't worry about it." He doesn't seem as smug to me anymore. I wonder if I will react differently to him in the mornings now. Will we really become friends?

I try to imagine hanging out with a guy as a friend and it seems too weird.

We all make our way down the halls back into the main entrance.

"Hey, you live next door to me, well, almost, right?" Steve asks me though he knows the answer.

"Um, yeah, kind of," I say. I hope he doesn't come over. If he saw my mom in one of her drugged-out stupors, I would just die!

Click

Shaday's iPhone flashes as she takes our picture. "Girl, I can do your make-up for you if you want me to. You want me to bring it next Tuesday? My friend T.T. is white and I have some foundation I use on her we can use on you, ok? See you next Tuesday!" She jogs away, getting into an older model car that smokes and chugs as it pulls away. I didn't have a chance to say, 'No thanks, I don't wear make-up'. If I do come next week, guess I'll be getting a make-over.

Matthew chimes in at this point. "I don't think you need a makeover just a tissue and some tender lovin' care," he says. He almost slobbering on himself.

"Ok, lover boy. Your dad is waiting for you. Go on now.", Mr. Jeff tells him then says to me, "Don't pay any attention to him. You're the first new female to grace our presence in a while and he had some new lines to try out."

I smile but I'm not sure if the youth leader just said Matthew was desperate or I'm not that pretty and he'll hit on anyone new. Neither one sounds encouraging, though I can't say I disagree with him. I've always known how plain I am.

As I'm getting onto the church van to ride back home, I see Dark getting into an expensive-looking car with a woman who has the same black hair. I'm struck by how beautiful she is and during the van ride back home, I wonder if Dark also looks like her underneath all that hair.

When the van pulls into the trailer park I look to see if Pete's van is still there. It's not and I feel relieved.

"Hey, it was great having you there tonight. I hope you will come back next Tuesday, oh, and Sunday too. My family drives on Sunday but I can call the bus line to have them come get you if you want me to." Steve waits for me to answer.

"Sure." I have nowhere else to go and if I'm going to find out what this is all about, I'm going to have to go somewhere. Might as well be there. I turn to go to our trailer then think of something else. I whirl around. "Hey, what time Sunday?"

He shrugs. "I'll have to get back with you." He waves and turns to go again.

I use my spare key to unlock the door and go inside. I head through the dark hallway to the bathroom to pee and wash my face before bed. I flip on the light and look in the mirror. To my horror and utter embarrassment, I see dried blood caked around my nostrils and a tiny patch of hair missing where my hair usually parts. I hadn't looked in a mirror since the fight at school and I had completely forgotten about my injuries. I looked like I had been mauled by a bear. No wonder everyone kept asking if I was ok and Shaday offered to give me a makeover. Yep, Matthew must be desperate, I conclude.

What a horrible day!

I clean up and go to my room. No need to turn on the light, I'm going straight to bed. But just inside, I step on something soft. When the light comes on, I stand there and just stare at my clothes scattered everywhere. It looks as though they were ripped from the hangers. Drawers lay thrown aside with their contents strewn around. My blankets were piled on the floor where my mattress used to lay.

My mattress, she has traded my mattress. And she had clearly looked for other things of value. I was upset at first but knowing what I had left of worth was hidden in the Buick gave me some comfort. I turn the light off and lay on the carpet where my bed used to be. In the dark, I try to figure up how many years, months, weeks, days, hours, and minutes until I turn eighteen. I don't think I can wait that long. I consider what my options are until sleep comes. Then the dreams started again.

4

Born

"I think you should go for it," Elaine says as she talks with her mouth full of chicken fingers.

I nibble on mine, making sure I savor them. It may be my last meal for a couple of days.

"I don't know. Don't Christians have to be, like, good all the time and never do anything fun? I don't have a boyfriend right now, but I want one in the future, you know." The hum of the cafeteria continues but my focus turns to Trevor Hayes and then surprisingly to Mr. Emo himself. Trevor is laughing with his teammates oblivious to my existence. However, Dark Challis and I make eye contact. I should look away, but I don't for some reason. We stare at each other for only seconds, but it seems like longer. Elaine's voice brings me back to the conversation at hand.

"My family are Christians. We go to church all the time. Well, not all the time but on special holidays and such. It's no big deal. You just sit there until it's over and you're ok with God."

After hearing the youth leader talk about making Jesus Lord, I don't think Elaine is the same kind of Christian as the people I talked to Tuesday.

"The Satanist is looking at you!" Elaine says in hushed alarm.

"What?" I ask confused.

She signals in the direction of Dark Challis.

"He was at that church thing last night, so I don't think he's a devil worshiper," I tell her; instantly regretting it.

Elaine's eyes widened excitedly. "Really? What did he say or do?"

"Nothing just looked at his nails and got mad when the leader of the class poked fun at his name and stuff."

"Wait, why would someone like him be at church?" she asks suspiciously like I might be making it up.

"How should I know? I didn't talk to the guy." I finish off my fries and lick ketchup from my fingers.

"If he shows up again, you should ask him if he worships the devil." She looks way too excited in my opinion.

"If I go back."

"Oh, you will. You're too curious not to." She laughs as if she knows me so well.

Does she?

The worship band is rocking it tonight, but I haven't slept much this past week because of Pete's more and more frequent visits. Just as I start to nod off, someone plops down beside me, and I rouse slightly to move over.

"You are even prettier when you're sleepy," I hear Matthew say.

I look up to tell him I'm awake but realize he's very close to my face. I lean back and look confused at him. What is he doing? Is he trying to kiss me?

"You can lay your head on my shoulder if you want to," he says.

I back away. This guy acts like this place is his own personal Christian Mingle app.

"Laying it on a little thick, aren't you?" someone to my right says.

I look over and see Dark Challis sitting there. Shaday and Steve are just down from him standing and clapping to the music.

"What?" Matthew asks.

"You heard me. I think you need to lay off." He tucks his hair behind his ear and gives Matthew a menacing stare. The black eye liner around his eyes makes the green pop out. They create such a contrast to all the black, it's fascinating.

"I think she can tell me for herself if I need to lay off man," Matthew tries to sound brave but looks unsettled by the dark stare.

Before I have a chance to interject my thoughts, Andrew Shook takes the stage and directs any new people to the youth leader they are to follow to class.

On our way to the room, Shaday catches up with me.

"I'm so glad you are back girl. I do not want to be the only female in a room with the Scarecrow, the smooth-talking Lion, and the black metal man if you know what I mean," she laughs.

"Does that make me the witch or the dog?" I ask, assuming she is Dorothy in this scenario.

Ha, ha, ha, girl, you are funny!" she says but never answers my question.

"Ok, ok, let's get right into it," Mr. Jeff says. He rubs his hands together. "It doesn't look like anyone new joined us so let's pick up where we left off last week." This is only my second time with these people, but he seems even more excited than last week.

I go to take a seat closer to Shaday instead of Matthew and realize that means I'll be next to Dark. Whatever at least I won't get hit on every five seconds.

Matthew looks disappointed when I don't take the seat on the end next to him again.

"I want to give everyone a fair shot at topics so, Dark, is there anything you would like to suggest as a topic tonight?" Mr. Jeff asks.

Dark is slouched in his seat with his arms folded. He reaches up with one of his hands and runs his fingers across the top of his head and through his hair making his whole face visible for the first time. He has a masculine jaw and a sharp nose. Combined with those bright green eyes, he is very handsome and yes, he does favor the woman in the car, which I'm assuming is his mother.

"Sure," he says. "What's the point?"

"Can you clarify that for me?" Mr. Jeff asks.

"What's the point of Jesus dying for us, when life hard and nothing is any better?" Dark asks. His tone is defiant.

Mr. Jeff thinks about that for a moment. I think about it too. I decide that's a good question. I'd like to know why life is so hard if Jesus came to make it better.

"Life can be difficult because we still live in a fallen world that is cursed and what He did doesn't automatically fall in your lap. God gives everyone a free will and allows them to choose who they will serve." The youth leader gives us a chance to consider that.

"But Christians don't have it so great either," Dark says. "What about Christians in other countries being decapitated? What about the Christians in America who die from cancer or get divorced or," he pauses, "commit suicide?"

We all look at Mr. Jeff, sure he's been stumped.

"You can only have what you believe. The Bible says God has made a way for our escape. Not that difficulties won't come, but we can make it through if we trust in Him and put His word into practice. Can you see that?" he asks Dark.

"I don't know." He shakes his head, not looking convinced. "If someone dying from cancer has tried everything known to do and they are still no better, then what's the point?" Dark continues the same narrative.

"The point is, there is hope to those willing to believe. I've known of people healed of cancer and other sicknesses. Some of them through medicine and some of them through faith in what Jesus did on their behalf. But, even if a person doesn't quite get to the point of total belief in their healing and they die, if they know Jesus as Lord, then they go to Heaven for all eternity. That, my young friend, is the point to all of this; being with Him here and there.

I interject. "If Jesus paid the price, as you call it, then why do we have to believe?"

"I believe it's accurate to say God designed redemption to come through faith because it satisfies His desire that we have the freedom to come to Him and not that we are forced into it. God knew in advance Adam and Eve would have that choice to make.

He could have simply not given them access to the information. Why do you think He did allow them the choice to obey or not? And why do you think they chose to believe the serpent over God?"

We all look at each other except Dark who just stares into space.

Matthew is the first to respond. I guess he'd already heard this one. "I think they didn't believe what God had said because the other explanation the devil gave seemed like the easiest way to become like Him."

"I can see that," says Mr. Jeff. "What they were failing to understand is God wasn't withholding knowledge from them at all. He just wanted to be their source for it. By taking it upon themselves to gain knowledge without God, costs them everything. So, that still brings us to why did God put the tree in the garden, to begin with? Him being God, He knew what would or could happen."

We all seem stumped.

"Love," says Mr. Jeff. "God giving us the choice to believe is the purest form of Love. Think about it, you wouldn't want to have to force your parents to love you. If you make them, it isn't genuine. And by creating us in His image and after His likeness, giving us the ability to choose to believe could be our strongest God-like power."

Shaday speaks up. "But not everyone can choose to believe. My parents used to say they loved me all the time. But they did things that took them away. So, I'm sorry, I can't believe they love me."

"I empathize with what you've gone through, Shaday, but when talking about believing in God, versus people, the choice is different. He never leaves us or lets us down. And you do have the choice to love them, regardless of their actions, because of the love of God in you. Though you can't control what they do, you can control how you respond."

She shakes her head, unconvinced.

Before anyone can refute him, he continues to answer Dark's questions. "Let's take divorce. Why do people get divorced?" He looks around and waits.

I decided to give it a go. "Because they fall out of love."

"But if you are a Christian, love is a commandment from God, not just something you feel or don't feel, it's an act of your will. God's kind of love is fully committed even when it's hard. The Bible tells us we know how to love because He first loved us. So, if a person gives up on their marriage, it's because they don't believe they have the ability or they choose not to. In a lot of cases, people put the responsibility for their happiness in the hands of other people. As soon as their spouse doesn't stimulate that feeling of happiness anymore, they walk away. But if they would believe God is their source of joy and not their spouse, that unmet expectation wouldn't be an issue. You see, it all comes back to what you choose to believe."

"But even Jesus said you could get a divorce if a spouse was unfaithful," Matthew says looking proud of himself.

"Yes, but He also said Moses allowed for that in the law because their hearts were hardened, but from the beginning, it was not that way. But let me clarify. I believe the Bible teaches us to value ourselves. We don't let people abuse us. So, if a person is being physically abused, or there is ongoing or unrepented adultery or they are abandoned by their spouse, then that person has every right to get a divorce. I heard a minister call it the three A's; Abuse, Adultery, or Abandonment. But too many times, people give up on their marriage because their heart is hardened, and they don't want to forgive or keep trying."

Although his analogy is about marriage, I think about my relationship with Mom. I've always laid the blame at her feet. I've excused my feelings towards her because I believe she isn't being the mother I deserve. But what about me? If Jesus commanded us to love not only when it's easy but simply because God loved us first, then how should I change the way I talk to her. Moments replay in my head of times I've talked down to her or dissed her. I swallow hard and feel sad inside.

"Let's talk about your other point; martyrs." Mr. Jeff looks at Dark. "Those being martyred for their faith have decided Jesus is worth dying for. And just because they die does not mean they were without peace. I believe you can be at a place in your faith that no matter what may happen to you physically, you are confident God is with you every step of the way. And if you think about it, they get to be with Jesus in Heaven a little quicker. Isn't that where we all eventually want to be? And to add to that, being a Christian doesn't guarantee you won't face evil. It just means, unlike those without Christ, you are not alone to fend for yourself, you have God."

"What about people who commit suicide?" Dark asks.

On that question, Mr. Jeff takes a while to answer. The tension thickens the air.

His voice softens and his speech is slower, more purposeful. "Usually, people who go that far don't believe there is a way out or another answer. But that's not true. I would venture to say most people who commit suicide are not born again, but if they are, they have allowed life's problems to look bigger than God Himself. There again, they have a belief problem. They are believing there is no hope." Mr. Jeff looks at Dark intently.

With a slight adjustment in posture and a tilt of his head, a cascade of silky hair falls forward, covering most of Dark's face again.

Shaday amends the question, "Do they go to hell?"

"Hell was created for the devil and his followers. Anyone who accepts Jesus as their Savior does not go to hell, no matter what they do or don't do. Remember what we talked about last week. Because of the fall of man, everyone is born a slave to Satan. But knowing Jesus as Lord and Him knowing you, has rescued you from slavery and hell. We all make mistakes and do foolish things, but Jesus took the punishment for the sins of the whole world on Himself. If He took the punishment and you accept that gift of grace, as the Bible calls it, then it would be unjust for you to be punished too. But anyone who rejects Jesus was headed for hell already, whether they commit suicide or not."

"You mean, I can do anything I want to do as long as I believe Jesus died for my sins and I'll still go to heaven?" Dark asks incredulously.

Mr. Jeff smiles knowingly. "No, as a matter of fact, Paul dealt with this in early church history. He talks about grace and sin quite a bit in Romans. What I'm saying is, if you truly make Jesus Lord, you will become born again and you won't find pleasure in sin anymore. You will want to live holy before God. Anyone that says they are a Christian, but has no problem doing things the Bible teaches is wrong, needs to question if they really gave their life to Jesus, to begin with. When you get born again and the Holy Spirit comes to live inside, your new nature will desire what's right. When you do what is wrong, you'll have an uneasy feeling inside, we commonly call conviction. The Holy Spirit will lead you if you let him. You will either believe the truth and repent or you will reject the truth and suffer death. Because we are spirit beings and will never cease to exist, a Biblical definition for death could be defined as not fulfilling one's purpose. A lot of people talk about an empty feeling inside they can't seem to fill. We were created for God. Without Him, life doesn't seem worth living. The eternal good news is there is hope if you'll believe."

Mr. Jeff gets quiet. We all look at the floor. For me, I'm thinking about my dad and mom. My dad indeed did die and didn't get to live out whatever purpose he had. Or maybe that was his purpose to that point, I don't know. But I do know Mom is living a kind of death, not fulfilling her purpose. And that brings me to myself. What is my purpose? I think about the scripture the old lady told me to read; I know the plans I have for you, God said.

"Let's get down to the bottom line here." Mr. Jeff breaks the silence. "There are so many promises in the Word of God you guys don't know yet. But that is the beauty of living the Christian life. You have your whole life and walk with the Lord to learn about Him and who you are in Him. With that said, is there anyone here who would like to begin their journey with Christ?"

Although I'm sure Steve, Shaday, and Matthew are already Christians, Mr. Jeff looks their way to include everyone. I feel a push deep inside me. I'm torn by my desire to raise my hand and the fear of what others may think of me. I don't like drawing attention to myself but what if there isn't another opportunity? I don't know how many chances God gives out.

Almost like he could read my mind, Mr. Jeff says, "You know, none of us are promised a tomorrow. I just want you to ask yourself this question; If I died tonight, do I know I would go to heaven? If you cannot answer yes, with one hundred percent confidence, then don't wait. Just raise your hand."

I cannot answer yes to that question and I don't want to take the chance. I lift my fingers first, letting them guide my arm in the air slowly.

Mr. Jeff smiles at me then looks at Dark, but he doesn't look up from the floor.

Mr. Jeff stands to his feet and moves towards me. "Come on guys, let's pray with Cathy."

Matthew, Shaday, and Steve walked over to my seat. Mr. Jeff holds his hand out to me. I take it and stand.

"The Bible says those who come to God must believe He is, and He is a rewarder of those that diligently seek Him. Paul also wrote if we confess with our mouth and believe in our heart, Jesus is Lord, we shall be saved. Cathy, you can talk to God in your own words or I can lead you in a prayer if you'd like," he says.

"I'd like you to help me," I tell him. I'm shaking and I don't know why. I feel the oddest sensation.

"Ok, just repeat after me. Father, I come to you in the name of Jesus. In Your Word it says You so loved the world, You gave Your only begotten Son, that whosoever believes in Him should not perish, but have everlasting life. It says in John, KJV, as many as receive Him, you give them the power to become children of God, even to them that believe in His name. I know I could never be good enough on my own to earn salvation. It's only by grace that I am saved through faith and not of myself. It is the gift of God: not of works so I can't brag on my self-efforts. I believe in my heart You raised Jesus from the dead and I confess He is my Lord. I turn away from the devil and sin. I am a new creation, alive in You. I invite you in, Holy Spirit, amen."

I repeat all he says. I think about each word as I say it, and

I mean it with everything in me. The shaking is replaced with happiness I've never felt before. Love fills my heart. I feel like I could run all the way home and only touch the ground a few times for traction.

I look up at Mr. Jeff. He's crying and I realize, I'm crying too.

"Welcome to the family, Cathy," he says.

Completely against my usual behavior, I wrap my arms around his chest and hug him tightly. I feel the others come in close and participate in a group hug. Our embrace is interrupted by the sound of the classroom door closing. We all look to see who has come in but there is no one there. Mr. Jeff looks behind me to where Dark was sitting and his expression changes slightly. I turn my head to see what Dark is doing. The chair where he was sitting is now empty. We realize the noise we heard was Dark walking out.

Shortly afterward, Mr. Jeff's alarm goes off and it's time to leave. When we make it to the vestibule, Mr. Jeff announces to the other leaders I have given my life to Jesus and they light up like he's just told them I won the lottery and I'm sharing it with them. Honestly, I feel like I have won the lottery.

The bus, Steve and I ride, has a flat tire, so we have a little wait time while it's replaced. We sit on the benches in the open foyer with the other leaders and talk about where I go from here.

"It is so important you read the Bible every day. Now that you are a citizen of Heaven, you need to learn what is yours," the leader named Paul tells me.

I look at him confused. Mr. Jeff sees my face and adds, "Sometimes we'll say things in such a way you may not understand at first, but as you start reading the Word, you'll see what we mean. Also, we are here to answer any questions you have."

The woman I'd met last week named Vanessa says, "We also like to assign you an accountability partner, someone you can contact if you're having problems or can contact you if you seem to be falling back. I would like to volunteer to be your partner if you are ok with that?" she asks. She looks at Ms. Jane and Mrs. Trena Shook, which I'm guessing could be my other options besides Vanessa.

"Yes, I'm ok with that," I say. I need all the help I can get.

We hear a horn, and our attention is turned to a familiar car parked out front. From a shadowy hallway, Dark walks out into the dim light of the lobby and out the door to his mother, waiting for him.

Around the same time, the church van pulls up and blows the horn for its assigned riders. As Steve and I say our goodbyes and head out the door, I hear Mr. Jeff ask the others to pray for Dark. I couldn't hear everything they were saying but I can tell Mr. Jeff is concerned about him. This is the first church I've been a part of. I don't know what they do to kids who turn down the opportunity to have Jesus. I hope they will give him more time. Maybe he's like I am; unsure of how things work.

For the next few weeks, I pour over the Bible. I bring a notebook with me to church on Sundays and Tuesdays to write down references to scriptures that will help me. Some of them are very straight forward and I get it right away but other times, the passages seem so deep and I struggle to grasp them. But I don't worry about it. Miss. Vanessa and Mr. Jeff tell me I've got plenty of time to learn.

"Trust in the Holy Spirit to lead you in the Word and what to focus on. You will get there, I promise," Vanessa tells me all the time.

Every Tuesday when we meet, Dark Challis comes back. Mr. Jeff often extends the opportunity for anyone to make Jesus their Lord, but Dark hasn't taken the offer yet. We don't talk at school. I catch him looking at me sometimes or we look at each other at the same time. It's weird and kinda weirds me out like we are on the same wavelength or something. I told Elaine I became a Christian, but she reacted like I'd told her I'd brushed my teeth that morning. It was like, no big deal. Of course, she did throw in, "Knew it. Told ya you would."

The Bible study is usually started by a question I have about something I've read during the week before or heard Pastor Mitchell say in Sunday service.

"I'm having a hard time understanding some of Jesus' methods," I say.

"Ok, let's hear it." Mr. Jeff invites me to share.

"So, in John chapter six, Jesus starts talking about being the bread of life and they will have to eat His flesh and drink His blood. That makes some people upset and they either get mad or confused and leave. I can't say I blame them. I mean, surely cannibalism is not something we have to do as believers." I think about that for a second and then ask, "... is it?" My eyes get wide and wait for him to answer.

Mr. Jeff smiles, "We do eat His flesh and drink His blood."

My mouth opens in protest but before I can voice it, he continues. "When we take communion using bread and juice, that is a representation of the body and blood of Jesus. He was speaking figuratively and spiritually and like most things He said, they took it from a natural viewpoint. When we take communion, several things are being symbolized. I don't think we have the time to go into every reference in the Bible to when bread and wine were used in a type and shadow of Jesus. Also, I'm not here to give you all the answers, nor do I have them all. Some of these things you will come to understand as you let the Spirit lead you through the Word. But a few verses up from where you are referring, Jesus says He is the manna or the bread of life. If you go to the Old Testament, you find accounts of the manna. Ask the Holy Spirit to give you wisdom concerning what Jesus was talking about and why. The old testament gives us types and shadows of Jesus."

"But why didn't He just come out and tell everyone what he was doing and why? Wouldn't they have received Him better?" I ask. Feeling like I don't have the answer I need.

"These people were steeped in religion. Most of the ones who put up the most resistance were religious leaders who'd been studying the law all their adult life. They should have known Him. The fact they didn't show what He said was true: You confess me with your lips, but your heart is far from Me. And remember, it was not only humans who were hearing His Words, it was the forces of the enemy as well. The Bible tells us if the darkness had known what Jesus was doing, they would have never crucified Him, and God needed that to happen to finish redemption. That's one reason Jesus spoke and did only what God told Him, He was keeping the plans hidden from the devil."

"Redemption? What is that?" I ask.

"In the King James Version of Galatians 3:13 says, 'Christ has redeemed us from the curse of the law, having become a curse for us.' Another way of saying redeemed is rescued."

I nod without looking at him while my pen scribbles as fast as I can write.

Shaday raises her hand. "Is that why He always talking in riddles?"

"The Bible calls them parables because He took natural things to explain spiritual ones. But parables are not the only way God reveals things to us. Does anyone know another way?"

"My dad is always telling me praying in the Spirit is where we find out things we don't know. Or something like that," Matthew responds.

I admit I'm a little jealous of Matthew. He has been hearing the truth all his life. I can only imagine how differently I would have dealt with Dad's death if I'd known the peace of God then. Abruptly, I wonder if Dad knew Jesus. Did he go to hell? I decided I may not want to know the answer to that question and put it away.

"That's right. Praying in the Spirit builds you up on your most holy faith. It edifies and enlightens you, and you can be confident when you pray in the Spirit, you are praying out God's perfect will for your life. Who knows better how to pray for you than the very Spirit of God?" Mr. Jeff holds out his hand like he's just presented us with a silver platter of goodies.

"I don't think I can trust someone who won't be plain about what he is or isn't," Dark speaks. "If God wants to help us so badly why doesn't He just show us Himself already and stop making us guess?" He remains in his reclined position with his arms crossed.

His posture stinks of arrogance. The nerve of him to talk about God withholding information when he's doing the same thing!

"And what about you?" I ask. My tone is haughty. If he can dish it out, he should be able to take it. "Here you are talking about God not being upfront and you don't even tell people your real name. Look at the image you're portraying!" I think I must have gotten overly passionate about my argument. Mr. Jeff steps in.

"Let's remember we are here to talk and not accuse," he says. The alarm on his phone sounds. "Wow, it always seems to go way too fast."

Dark peers at me through his curtain of hair. I don't care!

Still seething inside, I bypass the usual discussion in the vestibule and head straight for the church van. I sit there as the others load, staring out the window at the ground. I'm not sure why I'm so upset. Tonight's class was informative, and I have a lot to think about for the week. But there's a nagging in the pit of my stomach.

I see Dark walk past the van and get in the driver's seat of the Charger parked next to us. He starts the engine and loud metal music screams from the speakers. He puts it in reverse and begins to back out. I can see from my higher viewpoint in the passenger van. Just as he passes where I'm sitting, we make eye contact.

Once he is out of sight, I lay my head on the seat in front of me. Why am I so angry? Why should I care if he tells us his real name? My emotions are all over the place. I used to not care how people lived their own lives.

On the way home it occurs to me, Dark's mother didn't bring him or pick him up this time. That means he came on his own. Maybe his parents are not making him come anymore but he is choosing to come. At that, I smile and feel better.

5

Superhero

"It's muh birthday, it's muh birthday." Shaday sings, snaps her fingers in the air, and does some fancy footwork as she walks into the Bible study class.

"Girl – look what I got for my birthday!" Shaday says.

She jerks her arm out in front of me making sure her wrist is inches from my face. Multicolored lights appear on the Apple watch telling me the time and date.

"Where did you get that?" I asked.

"For my birthday, girl, I told you." She pulls the device back towards her face as she taps and swipes across the face of it.

"I mean, who gave it to you?"

"A friend of mine," she says.

It seems to me she is hiding something. I remember her showing off a brand-new iPhone when I came for the first time. Since that was about six months ago, I know it wasn't her birthday then as well. I couldn't imagine she had earned enough money babysitting to have bought it for herself but who knows.

"How long have you been babysitting for your sister and how many kids do you watch?" She doesn't answer right away. "Do you need a partner? I could use a phone too. And it doesn't even have to be an iPhone. Just – any phone will do."

Before she has a chance to answer me, Mr. Jeff clears his throat.

"Hey guys, I have someone I want you to meet." He turns his attention to a young woman, I was too distracted to notice coming in. She doesn't look young enough to be a student.

"This is Teresa." He pauses for a minute and they share a smile with 'love' written all over it. "She and I are getting married!"

Four of the five of us jump up and start congratulating them. Dark turns from sitting sideways in his chair, looking at his nail polish, leans back, and crosses his arms.

"Oh, my…," Shaday begins but knows Mr. Jeff will be on her about taking God's name in vain, so she amends to, "goodness. Have you set a date?"

Mr. Jeff lets Teresa tell. "We've been engaged for some time we just haven't said much to people because we were not sure when we wanted to get married but…" She looks at Jeff to finish.

"Well, we have decided to go ahead with a small ceremony next month," he says. He smiles a broad grin.

"That is awesome, you guys!" Steve congratulates them.

"Hold on now, that's not all." His expression turns from one of romantic bliss to something a little more serious. "After we get married, we will be leaving." He looks at each one of us for a moment.

"Well, duh!" Shaday flips her hair. "Most people do go on a honeymoon."

"Yes but that's not all. We want to do some mission work abroad before we start a family," he tells us.

We are speechless. I assume the others are having a hard time imagining the Tuesday night Bible study without Mr. Jeff like I am right now.

"Wha-, who…, who will teach the class?" I ask. A touch of panic is starting to creep up on me. I have so many more questions.

"Well," He starts like he's not sure what will happen. "I would like to leave you guys with a replacement but if no one has stepped up for the honor, then the church may combine your class with the adults Mr. Andrew and Trena Shook teach." He looks at Teresa.

I'll bet this is her doing! Mr. Jeff wouldn't just leave us like that! I think.

"The Lord will make sure what needs to happen, does." Teresa's quiet-mousey voice is sticky sweet.

OH, STOP TALKING, TERESA! I think to myself.

"I want to spend a little extra time with you guys before we leave so I've asked the Pastor if we can have a retreat." He looks excited.

"Seriously?" Steve and Shaday say in harmony.

"What kind of retreat?" I ask. I'm not stupid. I know what a typical retreat is but how do church people do them? Is it the same?

"Oh! You'll love it, Cathy." Shaday almost squeals. "We go out to the woods and camp out and roast hotdogs over a fire. We do all kinds of stuff!"

"This one will be a little different than ones we have had in the past, guys." Mr. Jeff tries to keep us properly informed which is difficult to manage with their enthusiasm. "It will only be us and Miss. Vanessa's class. None of the younger kids are going."

"Even better!" shouts Matthew.

"Calm down, please." Mr. Jeff gestures putting on the brakes with an understanding smile. He is excited too, I can tell. "Activities will be limited because it will only be for one day and night. Not the usual three-day outing."

"Still, I am so ready for some time with my peoples," Steve says, trying to sound cool and failing.

"I'll be there too." Teresa pipes in.

Big whupty-do! I think.

Mr. Jeff kisses Teresa on the cheek and she leaves the room with a cute little wave and high-pitched goodbye. "Nice to meet you all."

He tries to pick up with the class as usual, but it's no use. Everyone except Dark is chatting about our plans.

"When we goin', Mr. Jeff?" Shaday asks.

"In two weeks. We'll leave out on Friday evening and come back Saturday evening so we can all be at church Sunday morning.

It felt as though the next two weeks took a year to come. I was able to get Mom to sign the permission slip, although, I don't think she knew what she was signing. She won't notice I'm gone all night because it's becoming a frequent thing lately. Pete has been staying at our place more often. Even when he's not there, I lock my bedroom door. When he is there, I sneak out and go to the junkyard to sleep in the Buick. I don't trust him one bit.

Dark even turned in a slip, which surprised me. Lying in the back seat of the Buick one night, looking at the stars, I tried to imagine him sitting around a campfire singing Kumbaya, but I just couldn't get the image playing in my head.

A couple of days before the trip, Vanessa asked me if I had everything needed, such as a sleeping bag and proper clothes for hiking through the woods. I did not, so she took me shopping. It's the first time someone has bought me something new since my dad died. Since then, all my clothes have been hand-me-downs from people who took pity on me or things I could steal from the Goodwill donation box.

The day has finally come! We all load up in one of the church vans; ten teens and four adults. It's a fifteen-seater, still, we are crammed in here like sardines. Shaday and I sit next to each other while Dark sits directly behind me. The whole ride, I feel his eyes boring a hole in the back of my head. Matthew and Dark are separated by Steve who tries endlessly to have a conversation with Dark but to little response.

Matthew leans forward for the fourth time since the van left the church parking lot and asks, "So, what are you lady's talking about so secretly now?"

I roll my eyes trying to exercise patience. The book of James says we should let patience have its perfect work, but mine is about worn out.

"Boy, if you don't stop rakin' on my nerves, I'm gone turn you from the Pastor's only son to the Pastor's only daughter!" Shaday growls at him.

All who hear it burst into laughter. He is finally quiet for the rest of the trip.

One by one we step out of the van and stretch our legs, looking at the forest in front of us. Brown and white signs hang neatly, warning hikers and campers about the presence of wildlife and the possible danger.

The most prominent sign: DO NOT FEED THE BEARS!

Matthew suddenly appears beside me and puts his arm around my shoulders. "Don't worry, I'll protect you," he says.

I shrug his arm off me. Shaday and I look at one another and start laughing. If only he knew how ridiculous he sounds.

I sigh deeply as we follow everyone else in collecting our gear. "I wish Elaine could have come. I want you two to meet."

"Why didn' she? Mr. Jeff don't care. Matter of fact, he woulda said the more the better." Shaday flips her braids to the side as she saddles herself with a thick backpack.

"Yeah, I know but it was her parents who wouldn't let her come. Something about the kind of church we go to. She wouldn't give me a clear answer but said they don't believe like we do or something like that."

"Mm-hmm, oh I know what they mean! It's the tongues baby."

My face contorts wondering what that has to do with anything. "Are you saying they don't speak in tongues?"

"Uh ah girl, some church folks don't think it's real or the devil makes you do it."

"What?" The thought seems unthinkable to me. Although I have never spoken in tongues, I've heard others at the church do it. It is strange, but I think it's because I don't fully understand it yet. Still, I don't get an evil vibe from it.

"Oh yeah, I asked my Gramma about that, you know – like, if it was the devil and she say, 'I been to them clubs' honey-child and ain't never seen them drunks talkin' in tongues!'" Shaday stumbles and grabs my arm to steady herself as she laughs at her impression of her grandmother. "My Gramma Cora is a sight, girl! She was wild in her day."

"I don't understand," I say. I shake my head and step over a fallen tree limb. "Why would they think the devil makes you do it?"

"Well, I went to church wit G-momma when I was little before her breathing got so bad. Some of them services be wild! People running around the room and jumping over benches. Sista's be dancing till they weave fall out and falling on the floor twitchin' like they being electrocuted."

My eyes get big. "Is that normal or are we normal?"

"Mr. Jeff!" She calls out ahead. "We got a question."

He stops with Teresa and waits till we catch up to them. Shaday retells her experience at the other church and asks my question for me.

"Both are normal. I'll use the analogy Shaday used about being electrocuted. If you take a nine-volt battery and put your tongue on the connectors, you feel a small tingle of energy. But, if you touched a live power line, the energy would make you jerk, stiffen, and would probably kill you."

"Ha, yeah no joke," Steve says.

Mr. Jeff looks back and smiles at Steve. "So, let's don't try that, right? Ha, ha! Anyway, the power of God can come in different measures as the people are willing to receive."

"I think some people be fakin' too," Shaday says.

"Well, ok so, sometimes people can get carried away in emotion, but I would be careful about judging who is real and who is faking, as you put it. When I was a kid, I laughed at a man who would spin in circles every time he felt the Spirit strongly. Then one day in a revival meeting, I danced in one spot for two hours. I remember dancing because the joy I felt was so pure and strong, I was overflowing and had to let it out. But I had no concept of time. People who genuinely feel the Spirit in that measure, crave it again and again. It's amazing!"

One of the kids from Vanessa's class changes the subject. I zone out and think about what I would do if I started dancing in front of the whole church. I can't imagine it without blushing. I would die of embarrassment!

We follow the trail to the clearing they seem familiar with. I stare up at the tall pine trees admiring the picturesque view of sunbeams streaming through the limbs. Then I close my eyes and focus on the sounds of the woods around us. I filter out the clatter of orders being given as the adults start unpacking the large tents.

It occurs to me I've never been camping or hiking. The city park was the closest I'd ever been to nature.

With my head leaned back and eyes closed, calm washes over me, causing me to relax a little too much and I sway almost losing my balance. Reflexively my arms spread out to regain balance and I open my eyes to see if anyone saw me almost fall. Scanning the group, everyone seems too busy to be looking my way and I feel relieved until I see Dark is staring at me. Embarrassed, I turn quickly and walk away to check out more of the site.

They would all probably think I was a dork if they knew how giddy all the sights and sounds are making me. I feel serene hearing the dried leaves crunch under my feet. I touch every branch and admire the various vegetation. The further I walk, the more I discover something new I've never seen before. I'm not a recluse, but I've been so distracted about Dad, Mom, and how trapped I've felt, I haven't taken time to enjoy the little things.

I'm brought back to the present by a sound to my right. I stop in my tracks and listen to the noise again. Some twigs snap and a little black bear cub peaks its head through some bushes. I squat low and wiggle my fingers, calling the cub to me like I would a dog.

"I wouldn't do that if I were you."

I jerk to my feet, startled, and in turn, frighten the cub away as well. I look back at Dark standing several feet behind me. He's an odd sight for sure. In these surroundings, you would expect to see a person in hiking gear or like the rest of us, in jeans and layered tops for changing temperatures. The all-black ensemble with matching long hair and nails is such a contrast to the natural tones surrounding us.

I start to ask him why he is following me but quickly realize I've strayed from the original path and gotten turned around while deep in thought. I'm lost. We are lost. I think.

"Which way did you come from?" I ask. I try to play it cool.

"The same way you came. It's not a good idea to go off into the woods alone, you know." He looks so bored as he chastises me.

Not knowing what else to say, I reply, "We should probably go back then."

I walk a couple of steps closer to him, hoping he will just take over and turn in the right direction. Instead, he focuses on something behind me.

"Don't move," he says. His voice so low, it's almost a whisper.

I don't listen. I turn my head, looking over my shoulder, and see the biggest creature I have ever laid eyes on! It's the bear cub times ten! I've seen movies and television. I've watched nature shows and I know you are supposed to just be still or play dead or something. But when you see a bear up close, you kinda forget what you've heard. And when it stands up on its back legs and roars at you, you forget all that nonsense!

I let out a shaky yelp and take off running as fast as I can. I realize my mistake in doing this right away. I'm not on any sort of path, so I'm having to pick my knees up high to clear fallen branches and rocks. I can hear the bear gaining ground behind me.

A flash of black sweeps around the front of my face and I am knocked to the ground. I try to scream but a hand covers my mouth and Dark whispers breathlessly in my ear. "Shhh. Be still."

Back a little further than I thought, I hear the bear grunting followed by the cub's cute protest. It must have been Dark gaining ground on me and not the momma bear after all.

We lie there for some time until we can no longer hear the massive paws crushing foliage beneath them.

I suddenly become aware of Dark's body on top of mine and his breath in my ear. He moves quickly to get to his feet and holds his hand out to me. I take it without a word.

We both avoid eye contact as we try to find our way back to the camp. After a while, we smell smoke and hear the faint sound of voices. It's just in time too. The sun is getting low in the sky and the idea of the two of us having to stay warm under the night sky is... well, actually not so terrible sounding now that I imagine it.

Stop it, Cathy! I think to myself. *What is wrong with you?*

Just before we get to the camp, Dark clears his throat, getting my attention.

"I'm going to walk over there." He points over my shoulder through the woods.

I wrinkle my face and tilt my head. "Why?" I ask.

"It's just better if I do." He walks away before I can ask any more questions.

He must not want to be seen with me. He doesn't want people to think he likes me. A mix of pain and anger prick at my emotions but I control my facial expression as I step from the woods into the clearing. Why should I care? I don't like him either!

Shaday runs up to me. "Where have you been? I was getting worried! I didn't mention to anyone that you were gone, and they didn't seem to notice either." She waits for an answer.

I tell her the only thing I can think of. "I had to poop." As soon as I hear myself say it, I instantly regret it but there it is. I can't take it back.

Dark walks out of the woods further down the clearing than I had.

"Well, look who decided to join the group again," Matthew says.

"Matthew." Vanessa chides, giving him a warning look.

Mr. Jeff stands and walks over to Dark. They talk quietly for a moment then join the circle. We roast wieners over the fire extended at a safe distance by long metal skewers. No plates, no condiments, and only bottled water to wash it down with. It was the best meal I've ever had!

Once everyone has had their fill of hotdogs, Mr. Jeff begins to talk to us.

"Guys, the four of us want to share some things from our hearts with you. We know you are in a challenging period in your lives and sometimes it's hard to know who to trust and who to believe. Parents may be demanding you listen to them. Advertisers try to lure your attention towards sports, music, fame, and many other things. Even we are trying to get your attention." He gestures towards himself and the other three adults. "It would be easy for me to say you should listen to us because we genuinely believe we have found the answer to an outstanding life; His name is Jesus. Most of you have already taken the first step and excepted Him as Lord, but with all the chaos in the world, sometimes we lose focus on who He is. John 10:10, KJV, says, the thief does not come except to steal, kill, and destroy. I have come that they may have life and that they may have it more abundantly. I wish I could stress how important it is you know Jesus more personally as the days and years go by. And more importantly, that He knows you. Of all the voices you will hear in your life, they will all fall into one of two categories. They will either be influenced by God or the enemy. Pick the voice you know loves you, the Lord Jesus."

Mr. Jeff smiles and looks to Teresa to go next.

She smiles back at him bashfully and begins to share in her mousy tone. "I don't have a lot to say, just a little something to go along with what Jeffery said. As you go through life, trying to decide if the voices you are hearing are from God or the enemy, ask yourself these questions. Am I in the right place, at the right time, for the right reason, and with the right people? If you cannot answer yes to all those questions, go home. For some of you, your home may not be a safe place. But I can say with certainty everyone at church is willing to be your family when you need them." She looks at Venessa and Vanessa's boyfriend, Buddy, with a tender smile.

Vanessa waits for Teresa to continue. After several moments of silence, she is the last to catch on Teresa was done and passing the proverbial baton on to her.

She jerks her back straight and her shoulders back. "Oh, it's my turn, ok!"

Chuckles come from most of her students as they recognize a trait of hers, just as I have noticed in our time together as mentor and friend. She tends to be oblivious to social cues. When she realizes she missed one, she responds almost startled. It's cute.

"Yes, my turn, ok. Let's see…" She looks up trying to recall what she'd planned to say. "I've been thought of as quirky my whole life. Many times, the way people responded to me made me feel insignificant. The Holy Spirit has been showing me these few years into adulthood just how much He values me. I want you guys to always remember how much you mean to God. When something happens that makes you feel unvalued or of a lower class than someone else, just remember He doesn't see you that way."

She pulls out a folded piece of paper from her pocket, opens it, and reads. "Romans 5: 7 and 8 in the New Living Translation say, Now, most people would not be willing to die for a person who is especially good. But God showed His great love for us by sending Christ to die for us while we were still sinners." She refolds the paper and puts it back in her pocket. "In this life and the next, you will forever be loved. Never forget that." She pats Buddy on the leg, letting him know it's his turn.

He looks nervous. "I'm not a youth leader like Jeff and Vanessa and I have a hard time communicating sometimes. Bear with me as I give this a try." He clears his throat. "The best advice I can give any of you is to keep coming to church. Life gets harder and harder out there and if you are not allowing the right people to speak into your life, it will be extremely easy to fall into temptation." A flash of emotion darkens his face for a split second. "Here is a scripture that helps me. Matthew 26:41, the New International Version, Watch and pray so that you will not fall into temptation. The spirit is willing, but the flesh is weak. Anyway, I hope that helps you." He looks at Venessa then at his shoes.

I glance over at Dark. He too is staring towards the ground, off into another world. I gaze a little too long and realize it when I see Matthew watching me. He looks angrily from me to Dark.

With a little more discussion, sleeping arrangements are announced. The ladies in one tent and guys in the other. No one seems to be tired except for one girl named Destiney. She boasts as more of a morning person and climbs in the assigned tent for the night. The rest of us play games. Someone brought a deck of cards and several gather around watching Mr. Jeff and Buddy play war. Vanessa and Teresa discuss wedding plans while keeping an eye on the rest of us who have walked down to the small pond not too far from the campsite. A second fire has been built near the edge of the water for two reasons. It's supposed to ward off animals and when it's time to go to bed, we can put it out easily with the sandy dirt from the water's edge.

Steve and Shaday sit near the fire and each other, staying warm and talking. I walk close to the water and watch the moonlight dance on the small ripples the fish make on the surface.

"Why is it the bad boy always gets the girl?"

I look over my left shoulder at Matthew, who isn't looking at me, despite having just asked me a question.

"What do you mean?" I ask. I know very well what he is implying.

He looks at me very differently than he has all these weeks before.

"He's no good, you know. He's probably a Satanist and just wants to do all kinds of perverted things to you."

"I don't know what you are talking about." Deny, deny, deny. That's my strategy. Not that it's too hard to do. There is nothing between Dark and me. He was even too embarrassed to be seen coming out of the woods with me.

"Oh, please. I see the way you two look at each other." His words stink of jealousy.

"Matthew, if you are saying something is going on between me and Dark Challis, you are so wrong. I mean, I can't even tell you how wrong you are." I laugh sarcastically but inwardly I ponder what Matthew just said. Does Dark look at me... that way?

"Well, this is my last attempt. If you say no, I won't bother you again." He pauses, looking as though he is expecting the worst.

"Will you go on a date with me?" he asks.

I don't answer right away although I knew the answer even before he asked. I wait a moment, trying to think of a nice way to put all his flirtatious behavior to rest.

I sigh. "I don't see we would make a good fit, you know. You're a nice guy and all-."

Matthew turns and quietly walks away before I can finish my sentence.

I sigh again, more deeply this time. I turn my focus back to the water, kind of glad that's over.

I hear leaves rustle on the other side of me in the woods. I stare intently trying to see if it's that bear. I realize this is stupid because if it is the bear, there is no way I would see her in the dark as black as she is. I slowly start backing up. I feel like all the blood has drained to my feet and my fear is intense.

"It's just me." I hear Dark say from the shadows, his black clothes keeping him camouflaged in the dark.

"What the..." I almost cuss but caught myself. I look over my shoulder to see if anyone heard me, but thankfully, I'm too far away.

"I spoke up because you looked terrified. You thought I was that bear, didn't you?"

"You would have too! You could have let me know you were there."

"Oh, but then I wouldn't know just how wrong Matthew is about his assumptions."

I couldn't tell for sure, but he sounded almost hurt.

I turn my attention back to the water. "Well? Are you going to come out of hiding or not?"

"For what reason?"

"I don't know. Maybe to talk or just hang out with other people."

"Aren't you afraid I might sacrifice you to Satan?"

I roll my eyes. "No. Do you think I stare at you with puppy love longings?"

It was meant to be as cynical as his question but came out sounding like I was hoping he did.

After more uncomfortable silence, I ask, "Are you still there?"

"Yes." He steps from the darkness completely and comes toward me. He sits on the soggy ground and looks across the water.

Not wanting a wet seat, I find a near-by rock and squat there. We sit in silence for a little while listening to the crickets and frogs calling out to prospective mates. Occasionally, Steve will laugh at something Shaday tells him, but we are too far away to hear their full conversation.

"Why do you wear black all the time?" I ask.

"I guess for the same reason you wear blue all the time. I like the color."

The statement takes me off guard a little. I'd never noticed most of my clothes are blue, but now I think about them, they are.

How odd he would notice. A lot of my clothes are hand-me-downs but the few I did pick out on my own tend to be some variation of the color.

"It's not the same. I wear blue a lot but it's not the only color I wear, and I don't dye my hair blue."

"I don't dye my hair either. This is my natural color," he says. He speaks without looking at me.

"What about the nail polish?"

"What about it?"

"Why?"

He looks at his nails. "It keeps me from biting them."

"Really? Hmm, maybe I should try that," I say. I look at my nails.

More silence.

I redirect the conversation. "What was Mr. Jeff saying to you when you came into the clearing earlier?"

Dark picks up a water-logged stick and rubs its smooth sides.

"He, uh... he was telling me it wasn't proper for us to be alone in the woods together. I told him, I stayed back to make sure you didn't get lost. I'm not sure he believed me but after watching you for a while he must have concluded nothing happened. Why? Did he say something to you?"

"No," I say.

"Figures," he says. The slight shake of his head makes him look offended.

I try to look at him without being obvious. I take notice of how sleek his hair looks in the moonlight. I imagine running my fingers through it, testing its silkiness. He glances at me, so I pretend I'm staring beyond him at the water. I want to ask him if he thinks I'm plain or maybe decent-looking? But I'm afraid of what he may say. Still, why does he seem to dislike when Matthew hits on me?

"What happened to your dad?" he asks.

Ug! That dreaded question. Most everyone that tries to have a conversation goes right for that one. I don't know why. Other kids have lost parents before. Why can't they just leave it at that?

"He was killed in a car accident. I don't know what caused it. My mom won't talk about it."

"Did becoming a Christian help you? You know, with the grief."

I think about that for a minute.

"Yeah, I think it has. But until you asked, I hadn't realized that."

"How did it help?"

"Well.... I haven't thought about him as much lately. I've been reading the Bible every free minute I have and then thinking about all I'm learning the rest of the time. It's been consuming my every thought."

"And that's good... not thinking about him?"

"Yeah, because of the way I remembered him. The memories carry a lot of pain and unanswered questions." I twist some grass around my fingers, pull it from the ground, and toss it inches away.

"Just because you've been distracted doesn't mean it's helped you though."

I can't tell if he's digging for reasons or trying to disprove how I feel.

"It has helped because I don't dwell on what I don't know. It used to bother me I didn't know how the accident happened or how he died. You know, like, was it painful for him, or did he die instantly? Putting my focus on God has helped me to realize my life is more than just about losing my dad. For the first time in a long time, I feel hopeful for the future. I don't feel stuck in my life anymore."

I hear the words I'm saying and realize for the first time this emotional change has been taking place without me noticing it. I hadn't thought about the changes in how or what I thought about. My statement comes out so confidently, but I listen to myself, feeling like I'm just now being informed.

"Really though, what's the deal with all the black?" I return to the topic.

"When I was a kid, I was really into superheroes, so I wore a lot of bright colors. But my dark hair stuck out against the colors. Other kids would say I looked more like a villain than a hero and

I guess I got tired of hearing it all the time. When I wear black, I blend in and it's more comfortable."

I can relate to wanting to blend in. I think about him rescuing me from the momma bear. Was there still a part of him that wanted to be a super-hero?

"I think you bypassed blending," I say. It was not meant to be funny but for some reason, it struck me as such.

I bite my lip and look at him. He stares at me then cracks a smile. It was small and quiet, but we share a moment.

"Hey, guys! Can we get everyone to come over here? It's time to wind down so we are going to pray before turning in." Mr. Jeff calls out to everyone.

Dark stands swiftly and holds his hand out to me just as he did in the woods. It's such an old-world-gentleman thing to do and seems strange to see him do it. I take his hand and quietly say, "Thank you."

Even quieter, he replies, "Welcome." Then he walks quickly away from me and joins the other guys near their tent.

Mr. Jeff prays for all of us to have a safe and comfortable night's sleep. He asks God to give the angels charge over us, which I assume means something like our safety. God is thanked for the day of fellowship we had, and everyone is prompted to reply, amen. Which we do.

Inside the large tents, we are laid out close to one another. I haven't slept with another person in the room with me since I was a kid. This feels awkward to me, but I push the weirdness aside and tell myself to get over it. These are the sleeping arrangements and that's just the way it is. I can't help but wonder if this feels strange to Dark too?

There is some nervous chatter among both groups as we all tried to find a comfortable position without laying on someone's hair or grossing people out with our pit stank. I marvel at Destiney, the girl who'd gone to bed early. She is sound asleep and doesn't even budge as other girls crowd around her. Eventually, it gets quieter as we start to drift off.

In the not-too-distant woods, we hear coyotes barking and

howling and suddenly everyone is wide awake again. You can feel the tension as we listen for anything getting closer. Mr. Jeff announces to everyone to remember we are surrounded by angels and will be perfectly ok. A few twigs snap, close enough to the camp to make us question that, however.

Out of nowhere, the silence is broken by the sound of someone passing gas loudly. It's followed by Steve saying, "Sorry guys. This happens when I'm nervous." There's a couple of giggles followed by all the guys breaking out in complaints.

"Gross!"

"Oh, my goodness! That's rank, Steve!"

"Sorry. I'm sorry. I can't help it." He pleads as he lets go of another blast of wind.

All the girls are snickering. Another fart rings out, this time in our tent.

"Whoops! Must be contagious, Steve, now I'm doin' it!" Shaday yells out.

It takes almost an hour for us all to stop gagging and laughing. However, no one is thinking about creatures in the woods anymore and soon we all drift off into peaceful sleep.

6

Dark Confessions and Coincidences

Monday at school.

"I hate you couldn't come with us," I tell Elaine.

"My mom is such a spaz! I swear, I never get to do anything." Elaine finishes her carton of milk. "So, was the Dark One there?" She moves her eyebrows up and down.

"Yeah," I say. I try to keep my tone as bland as possible.

"Well?"

"Well, what?" I don't want to talk about him to Elaine. I feel like I'm betraying some kind of confidence. Besides, he hasn't said two words to me all morning. I smiled at him when he came into homeroom and although he smiled back it was hardly noticeable. I got the feeling he wasn't interested in any more chit-chat.

"Come on! You slept in the forest with the Gothic Vampire of West End High. Did you wake up with puncture wounds anywhere? Were you lured into the foggy night by a strange spell where you fell victim to his gorgeous eyes?"

"Whoa! Who's been looking at his eyes, hmm?" I turn the table on her.

"Eh, he's cute in a horror movie kinda way."

"I don't even know what that means."

"I'm so bored. You gotta tell me something juicy happened."

"Well, I was almost mauled by a bear."

I tell her about the incident leaving out Dark Challis' part. In this version of the story, I told her I tripped and played dead until the bear left.

As Tuesday comes, I feel rushed to learn what I can. This will be the last class with Mr. Jeff. He and Teresa are getting married Saturday and leave for their honeymoon then subsequent mission assignment. I still have Vanessa and the other youth leaders to talk to, but Mr. Jeff always seems so excited to hear and answer my questions.

Much to my irritation, Teresa joins the class with Mr. Jeff. I try to ignore her presence and ask a lot of questions about the Holy Spirit. Since the retreat, I've been thinking a lot about it.

"I thought the Holy Spirit came to live inside of you as soon as you were born again." I interrupt the love-sick back and forth the two of them are having about the subject. As irritating as it is to watch, secretly, it's what I want someday with a guy. To be able to share, not only my body and soul with someone but also my spiritual growth sounds so romantic.

"He does. When you are born again, He comes to live in you. When you receive the baptism of the Holy Spirit, He rests upon you. It's like if I filled a glass with water, then set the filled glass into a tub of water. It would be both filled and baptized."

"How does it happen?"

"The same way you were born again." Mr. Jeff replies, "by faith."

"So, tell me again, why do I need to be baptized in the Holy Spirit if He's already living inside me? Isn't it more important for Him to be in me than on me?"

Mr. Jeff seems lost for words.

Teresa takes his hand. They share a wordless connection. It's like watching two halves of a whole connecting before my eyes.

"The gifts of the Holy Spirit are expressions of His character." She smiles at Jeff then looks at me. "It's like how you show others you love them. I can tell Jeff I love him all day long but if I don't put action to my words, they are useless."

"Yes!" Mr. Jeff says. He squeezes her hand then picks up where she left off. "The Holy Spirit is your helper. His expression of love to you and through you brings everyone affected into a more perfect image of Christ."

Shaday now speaks up. "What about tongues. How does it help anybody if they don't understand what I am saying?"

"Tongues is your heavenly language. Although there may be times when the Holy Spirit uses that gift to give a message, it's mostly for your benefit. Have you ever been going through something so bad you didn't know how to pray?" Mr. Jeff asks the group though he looks at Shaday.

"I guess so," she says, shrugging.

I know exactly what he's talking about! Things at home are getting worse and I'm not sure what to do.

"When you pray in tongues, you are teaming up with the Holy Spirit and praying God's perfect will. I can tell you from personal experience it gives you a big boost in confidence when you believe you are saying exactly what's needed and the devil can't get in the way! And praying in the Spirit builds you up on your most holy faith according to the Bible."

"Ok! I'm in, sign me up," I say. I lay my Bible to the side and standing up. "Do that thing where you pray and touch my head. I need these gifts like right now!"

Mr. Jeff laughs at my wording, but he knows I mean it. I'm ready.

"Cathy, repeat after me. Father, I believe Your Word."

I repeat.

"I ask You, Holy Spirit, to fill me to overflowing with Your mighty gifts."

I repeat.

"I receive all the gifts of the Spirit as You need me to use them."

I repeat.

"Now just thank Him, Cathy, and praise Him, knowing He gives us the desires of our heart, especially when it lines up with His promises."

"Thank You, Lord," I say repeatedly. "Praise You!" I continue to worship. I feel His joy rising in my heart and my tears flow freely now.

Soon, after pushing aside the shyness, I lose myself in praise. Jeff, Teresa, and Steve join me. I run out of words but the joy inside me feels like it needs to burst out. I open my mouth without giving a thought to my next words, my tongue lets go. Syllables pour from me like water gushing from a hydrant. In my mind, I'm praising Him but from my mouth flows a language I've never heard.

I open my eyes and look at Steve who is also speaking in tongues and sobbing at the same time.

Mr. Jeff grabs Steve and hugs him. I'm guessing by the way they are responding; this is a first for Steve too.

With tears in his eyes, Mr. Jeff says, "Wow, what a going away present!" He wipes at his face, trying to catch up with the flow of tears. "This is awesome, you guys."

"Jonasan Challis," we hear Dark say.

His head is in his hands and for a moment, I wonder if it was him speaking.

"What was that Dark?" Mr. Jeff asks.

He moves his hands and looks up at Mr. Jeff with tears in his eyes. "My name is Jonasan."

Jonasan recovers his face with his hands and speaks from behind them. "Today after school, I wrote a note to my parents telling them I was sorry for ending my life. I was planning on saying goodbye to... someone tonight before doing it. I just don't want to feel anymore."

It's like all the air was sucked out of the room. None of us know what to say as we listen to him pour his heart out.

Mr. Jeff crosses the room and sits on his knees at Jonasan's feet.

"I have been praying so hard for you man." Mr. Jeff tells the now sobbing young man in front of him. "The Holy Spirit told me Satan was after the gifts and anointing you have been given by God. The enemy is trying to stop you from becoming the great man of God you are destined to be."

Anyone looking at this emo guy would have never thought of him as a man of God, but having spent the last few months learning God looks at us with the purest love and the destiny He has planned for us, I know it's very possible, even for Dark, I mean, Jonasan.

"Jonasan, I'm asking you not to take your own life, but to give it to Jesus. Let Him take your life and do something with it." Mr. Jeff begs him.

Jonasan nods.

As they pray together, I think back to the night we talked about suicide. Was he asking for himself? Did he wonder if there was any point to his life? A lot of his demeanor now seems to make a lot of sense.

Mr. Jeff spends the rest of the class trying to encourage us God has an amazing future in store for us, just as wonderful as the opportunity he was soon to venture out into. We all cry at some point with Mr. Jeff as he tries his best to prepare us. He prays with each of us and speaks words inspired by the Holy Spirit.

We all smile and leave the class feeling a little lighter and hopeful for the future, but still a little sad at the idea of not having Mr. Jeff here anymore to guide us. Who would, rather, who could fill his position? The thought is incomprehensible to me.

I feel Elaine's elbow stab sharply into my ribs. The jolt of pain is enough to pull me out of shock.

"Uh, yes, Cathy, the name. I mean, that's my name. Me." I stare up at Trevor Hayes like a noob.

"Nice. I was wondering if you would like to go to the dance with me?"

"Me?" I point to myself.

"Yeah, you." He smiles and his pearly whites twinkle.

"Um, I guess I could."

"Dope! What're your digits so we can text?" He pulls his cell phone out of his back pocket and prepares to enter my number.

I look at Elaine in panic. I don't have a phone, but I don't want to tell him that!

She looks at me with wide eyes, just as surprised as I am he is asking me out.

"I'll tell you what, just give me your number and I'll call you later, k?" I try to play cool, but I have no idea what I'm going to do.

"Sure." He puts his cell phone back into the designated pocket.

I balance my books trying to get notebook paper. But he takes the ink pen from my hand and writes his number on my wrist. He leans in close, "Don't forget and wash it away. I'll be crushed if I don't hear from you."

He smiles seductively. I pucker my lips as I stare at his. He turns his head and watches Mandy Tucker and her followers down the hall. They snicker at something she says.

He looks back in my direction. "Don't pay attention to her. She's just mad cause she got curved." He smiles again and walks away leaving me in a surreal state.

I turn to Elaine. "What just happened?"

"You were asked to the dance by Trevor Hayes!", she says. She looks just as shocked as me.

Sunday, after church service, I tell Vanessa, "I need a prom dress and was hoping you have one I could borrow."

"Prom? Oh wow, that's been a minute. I'm not sure if my old dresses will still be in fashion but I can bring them to church tonight so you can try them on. Who asked you?"

"His name is Trevor Hayes and he's gorgeous!" I emphasize the last word. "But it's not prom, just a dance."

"That's cool. How long have you been seeing him?" she asks.

"Well, that's the weird part. As far as I know, he didn't even know I existed until he asked me to go with him to the dance."

"That sounds a little strange to me Cathy. What do you know about this guy? Is he a Christian? If you haven't spent any time together, why would he suddenly want to take you to something like this? I mean, when I was in school, these dances and who you took was a big deal! You didn't just ask anyone."

Her words sting. I know I'm not pretty and someone like Trevor

Hayes asking me out is like a once-in-a-lifetime thing, but it hurts for her to point it out. I stay quiet for a minute trying to find a way to answer her questions, but all I want to do is cry and leave.

"I know it's strange but not out of the realm-of-possibility someone would find me interesting enough to want to get to know me." I swallow the lump of self-pity back down.

"Oh, honey, I didn't mean it like that. As a matter of fact, just the opposite! You are more beautiful than you know. But not every guy has pure intentions. This is a dangerous world. Besides, the Bible says we shouldn't be unequally yoked together...."

She continues to try to explain what she meant, but I zone out and internally pet my wounded pride. A narrative of 'who does she think she is' plays in my mind.

"I need to go; the bus is waiting for me."

I didn't return for the evening service.

I'd tried to vent to Elaine about it at school, but she doesn't know Vanessa and assumed things about her character that doesn't line up with how I know her. And she kept telling me the mean things Mandy Tucker and others were saying around the school. That just made me feel worse. Tuesday night at Bible study, Shaday didn't show up, so I couldn't talk to her about it.

"Hey, Cathy!", Vanessa calls after me before I get to the lobby after class. "I brought a couple of dresses. I can take you home and let you try them on if you still want to look at them."

I shrug.

"Look, I didn't mean to hurt your feelings Sunday. You're my sister and because of your circumstances, I think you need someone to have your back. You know, someone to help watch out for you." She sounds sincere.

In my heart, I know she believes that. I'm just not sure I do. I can't remember the last time someone cared about me like that.

"Let me take you home tonight and you try them on, ok?"

"Ok."

"Great! I have a few things to do here and then I'll be ready to go." She rushes off.

"Cathy!" I hear Steve call out to me.

He and Jonasan walk over to me. "The bus driver is ready to go."

"I'm riding with Vanessa tonight. I'm trying on some old prom dresses of hers."

"Ok, I'll go let him know." Steve jogs off outside to the bus we usually ride together.

"Prom dresses?" Jonasan asks.

"Yeah, I need one for the dance next month," I say.

"Who are you going with?" His tone is even but his forehead wrinkles slightly making him look concerned.

"Trevor Hayes."

Steve returns. "Ok. I let him know," he says, out of breath.

"Aren't you riding the bus?" I ask.

"Nah, Johnny here is going to take me home in his cool car." Steve looks excited.

"Don't... call me that." Jonasan rolls his eyes and looks around.

"Sorry, I forgot."

I smile. "What's wrong with Johnny?" I ask.

"I just don't like it." He looks serious so I decide not to tease him about it. "Oh, I almost forgot," he pulls a cell phone from his pocket, "I got a new phone and don't need this one anymore. Do you want it?" He holds the device out to me.

"Oh man, I need a cell, but I can't get it activated right now, so it would be pointless," I tell him.

Vanessa approaches. "Ok, I'm ready," she says.

Jonasan continues. "It's already activated and paid up for a year. I got a new one and don't need it anymore."

He continues to hold the device out. I take it.

"Wow! Thank you," I say.

"Did you get a new number too because they usually transfer the sim card to your new phone?" Steve asks.

"No, I still have the same number." He says out of the side of his mouth to Steve. Then speaking to me again, "Here's the number for that phone," Jonasan says. He takes a piece of paper from his pocket and hands it to me.

"Well, that would be a whole new-," Steve says.

Jonasan interrupts him. "Hey, let's go for that ride now, Steve." He grabs Steve's arm, pulling him away.

"What was that about?" Vanessa asks.

"I think Jonasan did something nice for me and he was trying to downplay it by acting like it was no big deal." I smile looking at the device.

I'm nervous to allow Vanessa into the trailer but she already knows about the situation with Mom. I've prepared her as much as I can for anything she may see or not see. I told her about not having a bed. She offered to get me one, but I assured her I was fine without it.

"Mom would just trade it for pills anyway. It's cool. I kinda like the floor. It supports my back," I say.

I don't have a full-length mirror at home, so I rely on Vanessa's opinion about whether the blue or green dress looks best on me. I feel better in the blue one. I pull and tug on it, maneuvering my hips and breast inside the dress till it feels like it's straight.

"How do I look?" I hold my arms out and spin around slowly.

"That one is kinda tight. You sure you don't like the green one?" she asks. She pinches her chin.

"It's not I don't like it, it's just a little too big on me." I don't add it also looks like a bedazzled church dress.

The one I'm wearing has a blue sweetheart neckline bodice with tulle at the top, the only thing keeping my boobs from poking out. It flows gracefully in a handkerchief-style hem, bordered at the hips with an iced-out band.

"What's up with you having two prom dresses in different sizes?" I ask this casually while unzipping the dress.

"I had a little bit of a food problem when I was a teen. I would binge and purge a lot. I was on my way to a full-on eating disorder when Jesus rescued me."

I stop and look at her. "Well, they are not that far apart in sizes, and the green one wouldn't have made you fat by any stretch. Why did you think you needed to do that?"

She laughs but with a note of sadness. She picks up the green dress looking it over before putting it back on the hanger and in the garment bag.

"I had my own, Trevor Hayes once. His name was Billy Tuttle. I let his opinion and the opinion of others, who didn't care about me, cause me to make poor choices." She looks a million miles away as she zips the bag up.

"But you don't know Trevor is going to be like that."

"I was just pointing out the similarity of both situations. Like how they both asked us to the prom out of nowhere, and we know nothing about his character. Now I've learned a thing or two about God's Word and the Truth, I can see how the enemy was using Billy to try to destroy my self-worth and the value God sees in me. I just don't want to see you go through the same thing."

She looks at me thoughtfully then continues. "I meant what I said. You don't know how pretty you really are."

I almost laugh at the comment but stop to consider it.

"And I would venture you don't know your value to God." She smiles sweetly at me.

"What do you mean?"

"I grew up without a dad at home. A lot of my friends did too. I didn't see it then but looking back on how we treated ourselves and the things we were willing to do for love, or what we thought love was, we were starving to know who we were. God designed family in such a way that allowed everyone to support and depend on each other. Men and women have different strengths and weaknesses. And children are not just there to learn, they can be a profound help to parents who will allow themselves to see their kids as their brothers and sisters in Christ first. But the enemy hates God and so he hates the family and the strength it has. So, he works tirelessly to break up the family unit and once he has separated them and they are vulnerable, he bombards them with lies. Jesus called His disciples, fishers of men. The devil goes fishing too: he throws out lures to try and snag you into traps. I'm not trying to say Trevor is a lure the devil is using, but we have to be careful by knowing the character of people before we put ourselves in a position of trust."

"It's just a dance," I say.

"For a lot of young people, it starts as just a dance or just prom. The next thing they know, they are being pressured to make life-changing decisions with their body."

"So, are you saying I should tell Trevor I can't go to the dance with him unless he can prove to me, he isn't being used by the devil?" I speak a little snarkier than I'd intended.

"Well, maybe not in those exact words. I'm just asking you to go into this with your eyes open to who God made you to be and don't let people try to pull you away from that."

I put on an old t-shirt and shorts while she hangs the blue dress in my closet. She starts to drape the green one in its garment bag over her arm, but she pauses.

"I'm going to leave both the dresses here in case you change your mind about which one you want to wear."

I shrug, but I highly doubt I will ever wear the green one. It's damaging beyond words.

After she left, I lay on my pallet and think about what she had said. I think she's overreacting but if she's not and Trevor does want to have sex with me, what will I do?

I toy with the idea as I fall asleep.

I get to the cafeteria before Elaine so, I send a text to Trevor.

(Me) Hey, it's Cathy. This is my #

He's across the room with other guys on the football team. He reaches into his jacket pocket and looks at the screen. He seems confused at first, then looks around the room until he sees me. He winks sending chills down my spine.

The phone beeps.

(TH) TBH thought U threw me a curve. We on?

(Me) Absolutely! Will meet U @ gym Fri, K.

(TH) U wearing something sexy?

The text throws me. I feel a small knot in the pit of my stomach.

(Me) Have 2 wait N C 😉

"When did you get a cell?" Elaine asks as she throws her leg over the cafeteria bench.

I turn it over, so she doesn't see the text then slide it into my bookbag.

"A friend gave it to me." Saying that makes me think of Shaday. I haven't been seeing her lately and it's got me worried.

"So?" she asks. She looks at Trevor across the room. "Did you call him?"

I spoon some apple sauce into my mouth. "Mm-hm, kind of."

She squeals loudly and draws attention from several sitting around. I punch her leg and give her a look.

7

Dancing and Dodging

The music is loud, and the school gym is decorated with vines, fake plants, and trees. Three smoke machines are blowing full blast. The committee told the school board it was a jungle theme, but word around school is it's a homage to smoking weed.

I stand just inside the doorway in Vanessa's blue dress. I practically ate nothing for a week so I wouldn't have to squeeze into it. Elaine helped me with my hair and makeup. Our efforts paid off if I say so myself, I look dope as a movie star.

"You look so hot!" I hear Trevor say behind me before I see him.

I turn around, already blushing.

"You look good enough to eat," Trevor says. He wraps his arm around my waist and pulls me tightly against him.

I feel cringy and pull back. What is wrong with me? This is what I've fantasized about many times. The hottest guy in school is drooling over me, but all I can think about is Vanessa's voice in my head. All I can feel is shielded and on guard. I'm torn inside between liking the attention and feeling incensed he is taking such liberty with my personal space.

He leans in to kiss me, but I jerk back and quickly say something to distract him. "Wow, you look nice. That's a cool tie." I fan my face. "I'm thirsty. Are you thirsty?"

I see the impatience in his demeanor. I don't want to make him mad. I don't want him to think I'm frigid.

He lets go of me and heads for the table where the punch and plastic cups are laid out. I look around for Elaine. Having just gotten her license, she drove us here, but forgot her camera and had to go back for it. Although she doesn't have a date, she agreed to take pics of me with Trevor. I want proof to show my grandkids I did have a hot date at one time. She should have been here by now.

The flashing lights reflect on the smoke and it's hard to see much of anyone. Besides, everyone is so dressed up they look different. Still, I strain to see if Elaine is here somewhere.

I wring my hands, still wondering what's wrong with me when I hear Mr. Jeff's voice in my head.

"When you get born again and the Holy Spirit comes to live inside, your new nature will desire what's right. When you do what is wrong, you'll have an uneasy feeling inside what we commonly call conviction. The Holy Spirit will reveal sins' true death nature. You will either believe the truth and repent or you will reject the truth and suffer death."

But I'm not sinning as far as I know. Then I hear mine and Vanessa's conversation playback to me.

"It's just a dance."

"For a lot of young people, it starts as just a dance or just prom. The next thing they know, they are being pressured to make life-changing decisions with their body."

"Here." Trevor holds out a cup of punch to me.

I drink the sweet liquid quickly, trying to think of what to say. Words are not coming and before I know it, I'm swallowing the last of the punch. Small grains of undissolved sugar cause the last sip to go down roughly.

"Thank you. That was just what I needed." I tell him as he takes the cup and tosses it in a nearby trashcan.

"Now, let's dance," he says. He grabs my hand and leads me out onto the floor.

I'm not much of a dancer. I do the best I can without looking like a total loser, but I know I look stiff. Trevor keeps pulling and rubbing up on me trying to loosen me up. It must have started working too. After the third song, I start feeling looser and freer with my body. Trevor pulls me close to him and buries his face into my neck, despite the fact the song is not a slow one. He starts kissing my ear lobe and my neck, sending goosebumps down my body. The flashing lights and smoke start to swirl in magical motion.

I close my eyes feeling dizzy. Suddenly, our embrace is broken. I open my eyes to a blurry Jonasan. Although he is several inches shorter than Trevor, he confidently stares him down.

"What's going on?" I ask. My speech is slurred.

I didn't think Jonasan knew Trevor, but they seem to share a moment of recognition.

"Not going to happen, Hayes!" Jonasan says.

"Hey, don't fight over me boys. I'll dance with both of you." I point to them both but my vision doubles and suddenly there's two of each of them. "Or all four of y-"

I hit the dancefloor hard with my tail bone and continue to fall over to my side, unable to control my limbs. Just as I disappear into the fog, I see a flash of black and can just make out a fight has started. I'm so confused, my mind is hazy, and I can't seem to make sense of what's happening.

Even lying still on the floor, my vision is pulsing with my heartbeat making the dizziness worse, so I close my eyes again. I remember hoping no one steps on me, hiding in the fog this way. Then I feel myself become light, and a floating sensation washes over me. I hear sounds of heavy breathing, the opening of a door, clicks, dings, and the closing of another door. A calming peace comes over me just before I pass out.

The first person I see when I wake up is Vanessa. For a moment, I'm trying to figure out why she's at our school dance. Then I begin to take in my surroundings and realize I'm in an emergency room.

My head is pounding, and I feel the bile rising in my throat threatening to explode forth.

"I think she's coming around," Vanessa tells someone.

I try to open my eyes wider than a slit, but the light causes sharp pain deep in my skull.

"Uh." I manage to get out before my stomach releases, and I jerk forward with the force of my constricting muscles. My eyes are closed tightly so I can't see the trajectory of the vomit, but I feel the blankets weigh down on me and hear a splashing noise on the tile floor.

"Ok, I'm going to be sick. I can't..." Buddy says just before the scraping sound of the metal rolling hooks suspending the moving curtain.

"Oh, turn off the lights please!" I manage to say.

I hear a chain being pulled over my head and the stinging brightness fades. It's then I'm able to look around and see Vanessa and Jonasan on either side of the bed.

"What happened?" I ask.

"You were drugged," Vanessa says.

"How?"

"Trevor Hayes put something in your drink." Jonasan sounds disgusted.

While I process how he could know this and try to quiet the pounding in my head, I hear the curtain yanked back again as a nurse comes in. Lights from the nurses' station spear deep through my lids and bring back the wave of nausea.

"Has a parent or guardian arrived yet?" the nurse asks.

"I spoke with her mother, but she's disabled and unable to come here," Vanessa says. I'm guessing that's a nice way of saying Mom was stoned or passed out.

"Since that is the case, I will have to get a hospital advocate to come to talk to her and sign."

With consent to treat given, I am sent home after a few hours, a couple of bags of fluids, and something for the hangover later. Vanessa wanted her and Buddy to take me home, but Buddy was nervous I might puke in his truck so, Jonasan volunteered to take me.

The ride home is quiet. I want Jonasan to fill in the missing pieces for me, as my recollection is still fuzzy, but I put my focus on breathing evenly and not allowing the swaying of the vehicle to cause another tide of puke.

In true gentleman fashion, he quickly circles the parked Charger to open my door and help me inside the trailer. When the door swings open, the stench of cigarettes and alcohol blast me in the face. Beer cans and drug paraphernalia litter the place. Only Vanessa had seen where I lived, and it was semi-clean that day. As I stare at the mess, the smell attacks my weakened stomach and I hurl without warning.

I feel Jonasan pull my hair away from my face and pat my back. I am mortified!

"Go, please, go!" I beg him.

"But..."

I run to the bathroom humiliated and angry. I cry and scream through gritted teeth. I am beyond words or thoughts of reason and planning. I am at my breaking point emotionally. With no shred of dignity left to hold on to, I become numb. I peel off the vomit-soaked dress and turn the shower as hot as I can stand it. After washing, I let the water run over me until it turns cold.

I hadn't brought nightclothes in here with me, so I wrap a towel around myself. I look down the hall and listen, trying to make sure Mom and Pete are still gone. It's quiet, so I walk into my dark bedroom and flip on the switch. The light reveals Jonasan sitting with his back against the wall. I jump and clinch the towel tighter.

As soon as he realizes I'm in nothing but a towel, he covers his eyes. "I'm so sorry! I wasn't thinking about you not having a change of clothes in there."

He stands and feels the wall towards the door with one hand while keeping the other tightly over his eyes.

"Why are you still here? I told you to leave!"

His voice is muffled through the closed door. "I wanted to make sure you were ok."

Now that I'm dressed, I open the door to confront him. "I don't need your help!"

"Well, sorry! I'll go." He turns to leave.

Before he reaches the end of the hall, the front door swings open, Mom and Pete come inside.

"Cathy? Are you here, baby?" Mom calls out, her speech slurred.

I rush forward and grab Jonasan's arm. I suddenly feel like a child in need of a protector. My face revealing my desperation, I beg, "Don't go."

Mom rounds the corner and sees Jonasan and I standing close to each other.

"Oh! You've got a friend over."

Pete walks up behind her, his brows furled. He looks me up and down. "Looks like she just got out of the shower. He's more than a friend if you ask me." Pete looks very displeased.

"Now stop it, Pete. She hasn't had time to be messing around. Look, the living room is all cleaned up and if she took a shower, that would have all had to happen since we've been gone to the store." She looks at me. "Thanks for cleaning up, baby."

Beyond her, I see the mess has been cleaned up. A trash bag stands leaned against the wall filled with the stuff. I look at Jonasan. I squeeze his arm privately to say thank you.

"We're going to sit in his car and talk for a while, Mom. He might take me to Vanessa's house too if that's ok with you." Before she's answered, I go into my bedroom and start putting on warmer clothes and shoes. With Pete here again, I'll be sleeping at the junkyard.

"Sure, sweetheart."

"Thanks, Mom," I say loudly.

"What? She's young, let her have her fun," I hear her telling Pete. "Look at it this way, if she's away, we can play." Mom's drunken state makes me cringe.

I pull on Jonasan's arm again as I pass him in the hall. I practically drag him out the door. Once inside his car, I apologize.

"Sorry, you had to see and hear all that. I did try to get you to leave though."

"I've seen worse than that before. I used to hang out at places like this."

I look at him incensed, knowing he's lying. Elaine had told me he lives in Hill Top Meadows. Only the rich live in that neighborhood. And what parent is going to buy their kid a Charger if they are delinquent?

"You don't believe me?"

"Not for one second."

"How do you think I knew Trevor had slipped you something?"

I had wondered that. "I guess you saw him do it."

"No, I know Trevor, well, know of him. I used to hang out with his kind. I guess you could say his cousin was my girlfriend." A look of sadness comes over him.

"What do you mean, his kind?"

"Well, let's just say I've seen enough to get people in a lot of trouble. As long as they stay away from me and those around me, I let them be."

I shake my head and peer at him.

"Why didn't you warn me?" I feel my temper rising.

"Like you would have believed me! You just got done saying you didn't. 'Not for a second', if I remember correctly."

"Some Christian you are!" I feel a tug of regret when I say it.

"Wow! So, here we go. I guess all religious people are the same. You talk a good talk, but as soon as someone is different than you, you turn on them and bite!"

"Well, if I'm so vile to you, why does it seem like you are always watching me, trying to save me or something?" I yell.

"It's obvious you need someone to watch after you! I don't go tromping through the woods to outrun bears for fun! I don't give out cell phones like candy! I don't go to stupid school dances to watch the girl I love rubbing up on another guy! I know things you don't know and I'm trying to protect you!"

Did he say he loves me? Instead of probing him about that question, I choose another.

"Who appointed you my protector?"

He just shakes his head in frustration.

"Once again, you wouldn't believe me." His tone is softer now.

"Persuade me then."

There is a long pause but I'm patient.

"One night after Bible Study, this was before the retreat thing, I wasn't going to go back to church. I had decided I was going to end things; you know. I got the note ready and the way planned out, but before I could do it, this huge guy shows up in my room. He told me God had sent him to tell me He loved me and had a plan for my life. I thought I was tripping, but I hadn't taken the pills yet. He took me to the clearing in the woods where the retreat would be. I mean, like, teleported me there! He showed me stuff that would be said and done so I would realize he was real. He said I needed to help you in any way I could; to protect you because you are a front runner in the coming move. Whatever that means!"

"When did he tell you to love me?"

Just now realizing he'd let that slip, he surrenders to it. "He didn't. I discovered that all on my own."

We sat in silence for what seemed like forever.

Slowly, he reaches over and slightly touches my hand with his fingertip. I tilt my hand towards his touch. Our fingers gently slide together before they intertwine. With my hand in his, I feel at home. I feel safe.

We didn't say anymore. We just sat there for hours, holding hands.

When I climb onto the bus Monday morning, I'm met with a strange silence. Usually, the other kids are chatting about the weekend and catching up with their friends. I ignore the anomaly and look in our usual spot for Elaine, but she isn't there.

Man! I wanted to tell her about Trevor and Jonasan and how over the weekend I went from being asked to the dance by the most popular guy in school to possibly being the girlfriend of the most goth-looking guy (although he and I didn't talk about being a couple now).

In my first class, I'm disappointed to see Jonasan isn't at school either. To add to the weirdness, people continue to act strange around me. It doesn't take long to understand the events of the school dance had gotten around, and I was the topic on everyone's lips today. To add insult to injury, Principal Dye calls me to his office over the intercom. I try to bravely walk past the hushed whispers and giggles but am caught off guard by the phrase "Tease", thrown out as I walk past some football players.

Still stunned and confused by the lude comment, I enter Mr. Dye's office where I see two other men. The Principal instructs me to sit as he tells me the two men are detectives.

"Miss. Maze, I expect you to answer the detective's questions with truthfulness." He turns his focus from me to the men, "Detectives...". He motions in my direction and sits back in his swivel chair looking stern.

"Miss. Maze, we understand you were at the school dance Friday night, is that correct?"

"Yes sir."

"You were in attendance with a...", the balding detective flips through a notebook, looking over his notes, "Trevor Hayes, correct?"

"Yes sir, but I wasn't there long. I had to leave because-"

"Just answer the detectives' questions, Cathy. You and I will discuss other school issues later.", Mr. Dye instructs me with a raised eyebrow.

I nod but feel uneasy about his wording.

"Now,", the detective continues, "I'm also told you are friends with Elaine Shiver, and she accompanied you to this dance."

"Um, yes and no, sir."

Before I can explain the other detective chimes in. "It can't be yes and no, it's one or the other!"

"Well, yes I know her, and we are friends but, no we did not go to the dance together. I didn't see her there. I mean, she was supposed to come and may have later, but I didn't see her."

The younger detective looks harshly at me and allows the balding detective to continue. "Have you had any contact with her since the dance?"

What is going on? I ask myself. Is this about me and Trevor or Elaine? "No, sir, I haven't talked to her since she did my makeup for the dance. What's wrong? Is Elaine ok?"

They ignore my question, instead of asking another of me, "Do you have her cell phone number?"

"Yes sir."

"Call her on speaker right now, if you don't mind," the older detective asks.

I pull the cell phone Jonasan gave me from my pocket and press the necessary buttons to get to her contact. As the line rings without an answer, my anxiety starts to build.

"Hola más suelto, si no respondí, es porque no quiero hablar contigo. ¡Adiós!", I hear Elaine's recorded voice say. I remember the day she recorded it. She'd taken advantage of her knowledge of Spanish and her mother's disadvantage of not knowing it to create the snarky message. I think she told her mother it said a basic greeting when actually it says, "Hello looser, if I didn't answer, it's because I don't want to talk to you. Bye!"

After the beep and a nod from the officers, I leave a message for Elaine to call me as soon as she gets the message.

The detectives don't ask me anything about Trevor spiking my drink which is what I thought this may all be about at first. Instead, they hand me a card with the police department's numbers on it with instructions to call them if I hear from Elaine. Once they leave the room, Mr. Dye leans forward, resting his forearms on his desk.

"Now, Cathy, let's address your behavior at the school dance. I must say I am very disappointed you would involve yourself with such characters. Up until now, you have been a good student, giving me no reason to get involved." He looks at me as if I should know exactly what he's talking about, but I'm at a loss of both understanding and words.

"I will not tolerate false accusations against the upstanding students here. I have expressed this to Mr. Challis and given him three days at home to reflect on his actions Friday evening. Also, your drunken behavior will not be tolerated on school property. Now, it's common knowledge your mother is an addict and I guess I shouldn't be surprised you would follow in her footsteps, but I sternly warn you to keep that behavior away from this facility, or I will be forced to have you removed as a student here."

I sit in stunned silence. My face must be visibly red because it feels like it's on fire. The pit of my stomach is knotted so tightly I think I may be sick.

"As far as Elaine Shiver's disappearance, I fully expect you to divulge any information to me and I will pass it on to the detectives." He holds his hand out and looks at the business card in my sweating palm.

I hand it to him. He opens his center desk drawer and drops it inside.

"You are dismissed." He speaks coldly and turns his attention to the computer screen to his right.

He pretends I no longer exist, so I stand and leave the room. Ms. Bell, the elderly receptionist, sees me coming from his office and quickly turns her back and pretends she is busy with other things.

I walk down the empty hallway towards the next round of classes that have started but can't seem to make myself go into the room. Instead, I turn around and leave the building altogether. I pass Mr. Dye's office window as I'm leaving. We make eye contact, but he looks back to his computer not acknowledging I'm skipping afternoon classes.

Walking home, I tried to call Jonasan, but he didn't answer. I made it almost home but as I passed the grocery store where I'd received the Bible from the mysterious lady, I couldn't hold back any longer. The tears came hard and fast. Passing drivers stared but no one attempted to stop to make sure I was ok. By the time I made it home and locked my door, I felt alone and helpless. I sink to my knees and cry out to God.

"What's going on, Lord?" I sob as I wait to hear something, anything from Him.

I hear the rain coming down outside. Even the weather is crying with me, I think to myself. I lay down and pull the covers over my head.

8

Losing Them All

The next morning, I think about staying home from school but I'm hopeful Elaine has resurfaced or that I can talk to Jonasan.

Things at school are no better than the day before. I'm still getting glares and comments accusing me of somehow trapping poor Trevor Hayes in a scandal. He is back though. I overheard him telling his friends his dad is a lawyer and kept him out of school yesterday so Principal Dye could deal with them. I assume the 'them' he referred to is myself and Jonasan.

Elaine is still a no-show. I try calling her again but get no answer.

After school when I get off the bus, Steve runs towards me with a distressing look.

"Cathy, it's your mom! I think she's dead!" he tells me.

I drop my backpack and run to the trailer.

Inside, she is lying face up in the living room. I drop to my knees next to her.

"Mom! Wake up!" I shout. I lightly smack her on the cheek, trying not to hit her hard. Her face has too much damage already.

"Is she ok?" Steve stands behind me wringing his hands.

"I don't know. Did you call nine-one-one?" I ask. I try to stay calm.

"Yeah, they should be here soon." He walks around me and

kneels on the other side of my mom. "It was awful! The whole neighborhood heard her screaming! My dad wanted to come over here to help her, but he knew there was nothing he could do. My mom called the police. That man almost hit me when he sped away. I'm guessing someone told him the police were on the way."

I lay my ear against her boney chest and hear her heart beating faintly. She smells like alcohol and other chemicals I don't recognize.

I hear the ambulance arrive. A female medic pulls two pairs of gloves out of a bag she carries, handing one set to the male EMT. They don't speak until their purple gloves are on.

"Please step back!" the man says.

"Can you tell me what happened?" The female asks like this was the millionth time she's asked today.

I open my mouth to speak but Steve jumps ahead of me. "Her husband beat her up and..."

"He is not her husband!" I interject. I take a deep breath, give Steve an- I'm sorry- look and hold my hand up to reset the situation.

"Her boyfriend, Pete, did this." I clarify.

"How much meth has she done?" the man asks. He doesn't look at me. He pulls her eyelids open and swings a light from side to side in front of them.

"Sir, I have no idea. I just got home from school. It's plain to see she's on something but I don't know what or how much of anything she takes. It used to be Percocet until Pete got involved." I do my best to explain. I feel like such a horrible person. I'm her only family in the whole world and I know nothing about her anymore.

A police officer appears at the doorway. He talks to the female EMT in code and very hushed. He looks at me then approaches. "Are you two her next of kin?"

Next of kin? Tears fill my eyes and my heart sinks to my stomach. I look from Mom back at the cop and the room starts to spin. Steve braces my shoulders and helps me steady myself.

"Mom, Mom, no, Mom!" I sink to the floor next to her again.

"She's not dead ma'am but we are taking her to the hospital." the male medic tells me.

I look up at the cop. He addresses Steve. "I just need to know who family is so I can get her information," he says. His posture is void of compassion.

Steve looks at me and tells the officer, "I'm just a neighbor. We heard what was going on before she got here." He motions to me.

The EMTs bring the gurney inside and pick Mom up like a bag of potatoes and strap her to the bed.

"Can I ride with her?" I ask. I'll have no other way to the hospital if I don't go with them.

"No minors allowed in the back, sorry." the male EMT says. He doesn't sound sorry at all.

The officer scribbles on a notepad. "So, you are her daughter?"

"Yes."

I try to fill the cop in the best I can with what little I know. I can't answer about Pete's last name, the kind of van he drives, or the EMTs questions about her blood type or any known necessary medications. I can only tell them about the rods and pins in her back and legs before they shut the doors and leave.

The siren comes on and I jolt with the sudden noise. The ambulance pulls away and the cop leaves me with a business card.

"Are you ok?" Steve asks.

I'm not sure how to answer. I have so many emotions running through me all at once. Fear for my mom, shame because I wasn't here to protect her, and hate towards Pete. What else could go wrong? This has been like the worse week of my life!

For fear Pete may try to come back to the trailer once everything has calmed down, I stay at the junkyard tonight. I call Vanessa on my cell and ask for prayer for Mom. I call the hospital to check on her. All they will tell me is they are keeping her overnight. I use the cell phone light to read some Psalms. Vanessa gave me some suggestions on chapters she thought would help me.

When my battery gets to twenty percent, I turn it off so the alarm will be able to wake me up in the morning. Vanessa's prayers helped but more than anyone else, I want to see Jonasan. He still hasn't called or text me back.

I say a prayer for him, Mom, Elaine, and Shaday, before drifting off to sleep.

Thursday, Jonasan is back at school. A flood of relief washes over me when I see him in homeroom. Finally, a friend I can talk to about all this mess!

I sit at the desk next to him and whisper, "I'm so glad you're back. It's been a horror show around here and at home. Pete beat Mom almost to death. Elaine's missing, and two detectives came here to question me. Did you see her at the dance Friday? And Principal Dye is accusing me of being a drunk and trying to entrap Trevor! What did he say to you?"

He looks over at me and around the room to see if others are paying attention. "Um, I can't talk about it right now."

That's it! He said nothing else. Mr. Groce starts the class and Jonasan seems to avoid me at all cost the rest of the day. This continued the rest of the week.

I was hoping he would at least be normal at church Sunday, but he was a no-show for service.

Steve and I sit in our normal section, but it seems empty without Shaday and Jonasan there. Matthew stopped hanging out with us after the retreat months ago.

Pastor Mitchell takes the pulpit before worship starts, which is unusual.

"Good morning everyone. I have some troubling news to announce." He clears his throat and seems to be wrestling with his emotions. "It seems Jeffery and Teresa Pike were arrested by Albanian authorities three weeks ago for preaching. Mr. Jeff, as most of you know him, was beaten as well as Teresa. His injuries were more severe than hers and were left without medical treatment." He struggles to find the words. "Our brother, Jeffery, is with Jesus now.", he says before lowering his head to rub a tear away.

"No," I say. Steve and I look at one another.

There are sorrowful moans throughout the congregation.

"Teresa has been released by the authorities and is on a plane back to the States. Her mother says she suffered terrible violence at the hands of the guards, but they are relieved she is alive and headed home."

"Let us pray church. Father, our hearts are heavy with sorrow right now, but we know the Holy Spirit is our comforter. Thank you for the time we had with Jeffery. I trust as he stood before you, he was told of all the people he had impacted with the love of Christ. And when the day of reward comes for all those who have served you faithfully, our beloved Mr. Jeff will receive many." Pastor Mitchell starts to cry and unable to speak clearly.

I couldn't stop crying the rest of the service.

After church, I try to call Jonasan, but once again, he doesn't answer. I decide not to text him. This kind of news is better when spoken I think. A text seems too cold. I call the hospital to check on Mom.

"Regina Maze was released from the hospital just before noon today. That's all I can tell you, ma'am," the hospital employee says.

"Oh ok, well that's good. I'll see her at home then. Thank you." Finally, some good news.

"Hey." Steve gets my attention. "Have you been able to get in touch with Shaday?"

I shake my head. He wrings his hands and a look of distress reappears on his face. Now that I think about it, he's asked about Shaday a lot. He knows her better than I do. Seeing him this worried only heightens mine.

"I've been calling her sister every few days to check. She told me their grandmother passed away. Shaday left right after the funeral home took Ms. Jackson's body. Leesa said Shaday took all her clothes and such while everyone was at the funeral. She doesn't know where Shaday is staying. That's not like her, Cathy. Shaday adored her Grandma Cora!"

"You and Shaday must have been closer than I realized," I say.

He looks out across the parking lot. "Not close enough, I guess."

Before I can process his meaning and the expression of someone whose heart is breaking, he changes the subject.

"How is your mom?"

"I just called the hospital. They said she was released. I assume she's at home by now. I guess I'll see in a few minutes."

"Well, that's at least some good news."

"Yes, thank you, Lord."

I've got to help Mama get Papa in the van. See you later."

"Ok, bye."

I stare out the windows of the church vestibule, waiting for the church van to pull around.

When I get home, I walk into the trailer searching. I go to her bedroom. She's lying down.

"Mom?"

"Hey, baby."

"Are you ok?"

"I'll be fine."

I go to the side of her bed. I kneel so we are eye to eye.

"How did you get home?"

"Our neighbor Judy came to get me. I had to give her my last ten dollars for gas."

Did the cops arrest Pete?" I ask.

"No, it was my fault. No need getting the cops involved."

"Mom, it was not your fault! He is dangerous! You have to see that!"

"She smiles sleepily and rubs my cheek. "You are so much like your father."

I swallow back the tears.

"Don't worry, everything will be fine." She manages to say before she slips into sleep.

As the morning comes, I am hopeful this week will be better. Headed for the bus stop, I pass Steve on his porch.

"How is she?" he asks.

"Tired and still recovering but ok, I think. Will you just keep an eye out and call the cops if you see Pete's van?"

"Sure. I'll call you too if I see anything weird. Do you want me to go check on her later?"

"That would be awesome of you. Thank you."

"You got it," he says.

I think back to all the times I flipped him off and feel bad. The bus pulls up and I board, realizing Elaine is still not coming. I think about Mr. Jeff passing away. I would have never thought that would happen. What if something terrible has happened to Elaine as well? I try not to think about it, but instead, focus on the positives. I still have Mom and my church family. Although Jonasan is acting weird, at least he's alive. I lean my head over on the window, close my eyes and pray in the spirit quietly for all my friends.

I had managed to scrape together some change at home, so I wait my turn in the cafeteria line to buy a carton of milk. When I set it in front of the cashier, she punches some buttons then says, "Ok." She then turns her attention to the guy behind me.

"Um, don't you need my money?"

"I just took it off your account. Did you want to pay cash instead?" she asks.

"You mean I have money on my lunch account?"

"Yeah." She types in my name again. "It says right here, forty-three, eleven is your available balance."

"Where did it come from?"

Becoming frustrated with the questions and the line beginning to back up, she looks over her glasses at me. "I don't know. Do you think I'm able to remember how and when every student puts money on their account? Do you want the milk or not?"

"Yes, thanks… I guess."

I leave the line and head for a table when I see Jonasan sitting by himself. I'll bet he put the money on my account. I walk over to his table and take a seat directly in front of him.

"What's going on?" I demand.

He just looks at me through his hair.

"I'm not leaving till you talk to me!"

"Do you think you could lower your voice please?", he says hushedly.

I exhale, tap my finger on the table, and stare him down.

"Fine! If you will walk away, for now, I will call you after school."

My cell phone lights up with Jonasan's name displayed on the screen.

"Hello?"

"Hey, it's me," he says. As if I didn't know.

"Please tell me why you are avoiding me? What did I do?" I sound pitiful and that's not what I was going for.

"You haven't done anything wrong."

"Then why?"

"It's complicated, Cathy, and I really can't go into all of it right now. Just..."

"Just what? Just forget you said you loved me, and God told you to help me? Just deal with the stares and comments of everyone at school, alone? Just mourn for Mr. Jeff alone?"

"Mr. Jeff? What are you talking about?"

"Well, if you had been at church Sunday, you would know!"

I get worked up and feel like he's partly to blame. He should have to know what it feels like when people just stop talking and leave you to wonder, so I press the button that looks like a red telephone receiver, hanging-up on him.

Seconds later, my phone lights up again but I don't answer. Let's see how he likes it for a while!

I figured he would come crawling to me this time for answers at school the next day, but he doesn't. Fine! If he doesn't want to talk, so be it! I'm done begging for his attention!

Tuesday, when I get on the bus after school, my phone rings.

"Hey Steve, is Mom ok?"

"I think so, but there is a truck from one of those rental stores at your trailer. They have been unloading furniture into your place.

"What in the world?" I ask. "I'm on the bus now. I'll be home soon."

"Ok."

When I get home, men in khaki pants and matching shirts are taking a sofa inside. Mom is cleaning the kitchen as music plays in the background. It was just like when Dad was alive, and the most I'd seen her do in a long time. I smile and go to hug her, feeling like I am seeing the old her again.

She didn't hear me come in and jerked away when I touch her. She spins around, her eyes darting around quickly.

"Hey, it's me, Mom. Didn't mean to startle you," I say.

Her mouth twitches as she bites her lip then grinds her teeth. She turns back around towards the sink wiping it with a towel. "Oh, it's just you."

Something is off in the way she speaks to me; like she doesn't recognize me. She sporadically goes from wiping the sink, to wiping the stove, then bending over and scrubbing an imaginary spot on the linoleum. It dawns on me, she is tweaking! I back up a few steps watching her in disbelief.

"Ma'am, that's the last of it," the man says. His coworker removes plastic from the sofa. "The other furniture has been set up. I just need you to sign here." He holds a clipboard out to her.

Before I can find out how she plans to pay for the rented furniture, Pete steps inside as the movers' exit around him.

"Honey, I'm home!" He announces in a mocking manner holding open his arms like he is expecting a hug from his little woman.

He sees me and his expression changes. "And there's my baby girl."

In a long stride, he is against me, hugging me close to him. The way he touches me makes me want to vomit. My heart starts pounding and I push him. I give him the most aggressive stare I can muster.

"Awe, now you ain't gonna be one of those rebellious teenagers are ya?" he says. He oozes with sarcasm. "Not after all I've done for you. Why don't you go look in your bedroom?"

I head quickly for my bedroom more to get away from him than an act of obedience. From the doorway, I stare at the new bed in my room. Why is he furnishing our home? Then I realize, he's moving in!

Horrified by the thought, I didn't hear him come up behind me. He is suddenly whispering in my ear from behind. "I couldn't very well have you laying on that cold, hard, floor tonight, now could I?"

Fear rises inside me till it's all I know.

Mom calls from the kitchen. "Pete, Joey is here!"

He breathes on my neck for a couple more seconds, then returns down the hall. He didn't come right out and say it, but I know this bed was more for his pleasure than mine.

I am shaking so hard I can barely stand upright, but I force myself to go on in the room and lock the door behind me. I know come nighttime, I cannot be in this trailer, period!

I cram as many of my clothes as I can fit into my backpack. I hear an engine rev up and voices sound like they are coming from outside.

I need to move quickly while Pete is distracted. I crack open the door, peering down the hall. It's clear. I walk quickly but quietly just in case he didn't go outside. At the living room window, I slightly moved the curtain. Pete and some other man are bent over a muscle car looking at the engine. Pete calls out to Mom. "Give it gas, and don't stop till I tell you to!"

This is my chance. As soon as the engine roars, I bolt down the steps, not closing the door behind me for fear it might draw his attention. I run as fast as I can across the field to the junkyard.

I lock myself in the Buick and alternate between sobbing and praying in tongues. I can never go back. I shiver as the sun starts to set; I wish I had grabbed my blanket. I take the clothes from my backpack and layer them on.

When it's dark, off in the distance I hear Mom calling me. Later, I hear voices that seem closer than the trailer park. I listen closely and watch for any movement in the yard.

A flash of light darts across a pile of crushed cars only feet away from me. Gravel shifts under footsteps. I panic but force myself to stealthily squeeze through the hole in the back seat of the Buick. I tremble in the fetal position hoping he doesn't find me.

The interior of the Buick lights up as a flashlight shines through the windows. I hold my breath, fearing he might somehow hear my heart beating. Thankfully, he gives up. I hear him cursing, his voice becoming less intelligible as he moves farther from the junkyard towards the trailer park.

Even when the sun comes up, I stay in the trunk, praying. The sun warms the metal above me. I stop shivering enough to fall asleep.

The cell phone rings, startling and causing me to bang my head on the trunk. I look at the display.

"Hello?"

"Hey, Jonasan called asking why you were not at school this morning. He sounded worried. When I didn't see you this morning, I figured you had overslept considering the partying going on there last night. I told him that's probably what happened. Is it, are you ok?"

I know if I tell Steve I've run away, he will tell Jonasan and I don't want that. "I'm staying with a friend now. I'm good. See you at church Sunday."

"Are you sure? You sound funny."

"Yeah, I'm fine. I've got to go now, ok. See you soon.

Pete didn't come looking for me anymore, thankfully. I slept in the trunk every night though to be safe. I waited Wednesday, Thursday, and Friday, but Greg didn't open the shop until Saturday. He must have gone on another fishing trip. He does that sometimes.

I was reading my Bible when I heard his truck. I scoot across the bench seat and stand where Greg will see me.

He smiles when he sees me at first, but his face changes as he gets closer to me.

"You ok, Cathy?" It's the first time he hasn't called me "girl".

"Oh, Greg, I need your help." Before I can say anymore, I begin shaking and am overcome with emotion.

He ushers me into his office and guides me to the chair behind his desk.

I tell him everything, about Dad, Mom, the pills, Pete, and Tuesday.

"What am I going to do, Greg?"

"I would invite you to stay with me, but when my Linda passed, I sold the house. In between selling it and setting up the camper down by Chester's Lake, I stayed here some. There is a small room in the back. It's a mess right now, but there's a shower and a bed frame back there. I'll have to get a new mattress and some blankets. You can stay there as long as you need to."

"Oh, thank you, Greg!"

"You gotta promise me to be careful. I'll be trying to figure out what we can do differently. I guess you're old enough to decide if you want to stay in school or not, but I hope you will."

Thinking about the recent events, quitting school is tempting, but I know graduating will make things easier on me when I do turn eighteen.

"I want to go talk to my mom one more time, but I don't think it's safe for me to go over there alone."

He doesn't move or say anything at first, so I keep talking.

"It's my birthday. And I just want to see her for a few minutes." I look away, determined not to wallow in any self-pity.

"Sure kid." He unhooks the keys from his belt loop.

"Well, I didn't mean right this second. I know you have a business to run and I don't want to get in the way of that." I shake my head.

"Do I look busy to you?" he says.

Although we could walk the short distance, we get in Greg's old pick-up and drive to the trailer park.

Pete's van is in the driveway and there is music blaring throughout the neighborhood. I give Greg a wary eye.

"I got you, girl." He pats his side and I know he's letting me know he's carrying. "You do what you need to do."

I take a deep breath and walk through the door. There are about twenty people inside the living room and kitchen area. I can hear more laughing down the hallway where my room used to be. I look around trying to pick Mom out of the group.

"Well, looky who it is!", I hear Pete say. "The prodigal has come home. Come to daddy, Sweetheart. Give me a kiss." This gets lots of laughs from everyone except me and Greg.

I hold my hand up to let him know there will be no kissing or touching at all for that matter.

"Where's Mom?"

Pete rubs a large sore on his cheek and grinds his teeth together.

"Gina! Somebody here to see you woman!" he says. He looks from me to Greg and back again.

Mom comes from the bedroom. "There you are! We were worried sick, weren't we Pete?"

I look around at the partiers. "Yeah, I can tell."

"Where have you been? I went looking for you; worried, like your mom said," Pete says.

"Can we go outside and talk for a minute, Momma?" I ask.

"I guess," she says. She looks at Pete for approval.

Greg allows me to walk out first then Mom before he too comes down the steps.

We stand there for just a couple of seconds to see if Pete is going to try to come out too, but he doesn't. There is so much I want to tell her, but I don't think she'll listen. I must try anyway.

"Do you know what today is?"

"It's Saturday, I think." She looks at Greg for confirmation.

"Yeah, Mom, it's Saturday. Do you know what else it is?"

I can tell she is trying to remember what she must be forgetting but her arm seems to be pulling for her attention as well. She slaps it and looks on the ground for an insect that isn't there.

"It's my birthday. I'm sixteen now."

"Oh honey, I'm sorry I forgot. Being in the hospital just messed my days all up.

Pete looks out the door. "Y'all done gabbin' yet?"

"Mom, you don't have to live like this. We don't have to live like this. Let's go somewhere, away from here. Pete's trouble.

She looks a little anxious and shakes her head. "Oh no, I can't go anywhere. Doctor's orders. I have to stay close to my medicine."

I know I need to be quick. "Please, Mom, please go with me. I can get you some help." I was eager to get through to her. My desperation intensifies as Pete walks towards us.

"Gina, I think it's time for your medicine baby. Why don't you go on and get started? I'll be there shortly."

I turn my attention to him and with intense anger. "Why would she need to get started to take some medication? Are you pumping her full of drugs to keep her compliant?"

Mom lowers her head and walks away.

"Mom!" She acts like she doesn't hear me.

Pete looks me up and down and then at Greg. "You two exclusive or can anyone join this action?"

"You can just shut your filthy mouth right now!" Greg warns him.

Pete reaches out to rub my hair, but Greg pulls the nine from his side. Pete's eyes get wide and he holds his hands up in surrender. He smiles nervously at Greg. "Careful old man. I was just checking. You two have your fun. It's none of my business."

Pete turns and walks away. Once he's back inside, I start to breathe again. I look at Greg, who has put the gun away. "Come on girl, let's get you something to eat."

Greg slides back into the side of the booth he'd chosen as I take another small bite of my cheeseburger. He picks up the fork he'd unrolled from the napkin and digs into his food. I need to eat but my appetite is fighting me.

"We've got to stop by a friend's place when we leave here," he says. He sprinkles salt onto his meatloaf.

Must have something to do with the phone call he'd gotten and gone outside to take after ordering his food.

We ate in silence and neither of us spoke as we drove out to the country. I stay in the truck while he and a short chubby woman talk. She calls into the house and a man with down syndrome comes out with a German Shepard on a leash. He smiles broadly at me when he passes by. The dog is loaded onto the truck. Greg shakes her hand and hugs the young man.

When he gets into the truck he asks, "So what will you name him?"

"The dog?"

"Your dog to be more specific."

My eyes widen and I look at the panting dog through the rear window.

"Happy birthday, Cathy," he says.

"Oh Greg, I love him already. But…"

"No buts. I'll help you out with food and shots. All you need do is give him a name. Jerry has a thing about naming animals for some reason," he says. He nods towards the short fellow waving excitedly at us. "He thinks it's bad luck."

We make another stop by a store buying a mattress in a box, supplies for the dog, and a ton of stuff for me to make the back room a decent place to stay.

Several hours of moving old car parts to another area, dusting, sweeping, etc., the room is finished. Greg brings a small electric heater from his office.

"The nights are getting chilly, so you'll need this."

"I don't know how I'll ever repay you Greg, or even say thank you enough."

"No need to. It's the least I could do," he says. He looks around at how tidy the area is.

After Greg has locked the gate and left, I pet my dog.

"I think I'll name you Arc. After the archangel, Michael."

9

The Funeral

Jonasan fits right in with the crowd now. Everyone is dressed in black as we come to the church for the memorial service for Mr. Jeff. The church gave Teresa time to settle in at home and recover from her injuries before they presented her in public again. It's been weeks since he was killed, three weeks since we heard the news.

Jonasan and I look at each other but don't speak. It hurts me so badly. I want to understand why he won't talk to me. I take a seat behind the youth leaders. To my surprise, Jonasan sits next to me. My heart races with his nearness. His arm, rest on the seat and I look at his hand remembering when we held hands and how good it felt to touch him. I want to take his hand in mine and beg him to talk to me again the way he did that night.

Pastor Mitchell approaches the pulpit and the hum of conversation slowly lowers to silence.

"When God called me into ministry, I charged at my new role with all the excitement of a newborn believer who is full of zeal but deficient in maturity. I soon learned although it was a great honor to be in this position, it also came with moments so hard to bear, such as this one, it made me question if I wanted to be in the ministry. I don't stand here today simply performing a duty. I am also grieving at the death of my friend, Jeffery Pike."

"Knowing Jeff, he would tell me not to be sad. He is in glory right now with our Savior and there is no sad story to be told here. But I would have to remind him I will miss his support and encouragement. I know there are many here who feel the same."

Pastor Mitchell unfolds a piece of paper and smooths it out with his shaking hand.

"Before Jeff left us to serve as a missionary in Albania, he gave me this. I remember opening it and staring at my friend in disbelief. At the top, it reads, 'The obituary of Jeffery Dawson Pike written by himself'. I asked him why in the world he would write such a thing. He told me he didn't believe I would need it anytime soon and he would most likely give me updated versions as life happened. But as he was starting his family with Teresa, God impressed upon him the importance of preparing a future for them both and this included not leaving her to deal with the unnecessary task such as this one."

A loud sob came from the front row and the congregation reacts to it like an infection. Soft moans and cries spread throughout. I am one of them.

One of the harsh comments I'd overheard last Sunday was Teresa should be happy now. Jeff had left her the beneficiary to a large life insurance policy and a funeral plan that covered any cost. She would never have to work again a day in her life. I tried not to judge the gossiper too severely because just a few months ago, I would have probably said the same thing, having not been a fan of hers from the start. But the glaring truth right now isn't how fortunate she is to have all that money, but rather how fortunate she is to have had a love like Jeff's. The kindness of his forethought to not burden her in a time like this is astounding.

This also makes me think about my dad's death. He hadn't planned so well for his passing. Mom tried her best to make all the arrangements to honor him but in the end, all he got was a cremation and his remains crammed into a cardboard box. Even at that, there was a balance, that to this day remains unpaid. There is no grave to visit with flowers. No marker telling the world just how much his life had meant to his family.

Pastor Mitchell clears his throat and wipes away a tear before he begins.

I, Jeffery Dawson Pike, was born on Halloween to Fredrick and Ellen Pike. Being their only child, I was showered with love, affection, and limitless attention. They loved me despite my drug problem.

My eyes grow wide at hearing this. I never would have guessed he had done drugs.

I was drug to church every time the doors were open.

The sound of chuckles came from a few, as the punch line was delivered.

Although I wasn't a willing attendee of a church at first, the Lord answered my parent's prayer their little scuttlebutt would be saved.

More laughter.

Giving my life to Jesus Christ has, by far, been the best decision I have ever made and if any of you are hearing this and have not yet surrendered, please don't waste another minute. I ask my friend and Pastor, Bruce Mitchell, to pause from reading this to allow you to raise your hand and have someone pray with you to make your very own 'best decision' of your life.

Several couples stand to their feet and walk to the front. I recognize them all as the elders of the church.

Pastor Mitchell looks up from the pulpit, "These are our elders, and they are here to pray with anyone that would like to decide to surrender to Christ. The Shooks were standing among the other elders at the front looking over the crowd. One by one, each couple heading off in the direction of someone who had raised their hand. For some reason this made me cry even harder than anything else in the service. I know in my heart if Mr. Jeff can look down to see this, he is one of those celebrating with all of heaven.

When I gave my life to Jesus, I felt awkward and didn't want anyone to see me cry. Putting myself in such a vulnerable position was so unusual for me. I was used to holding a guard up and keeping people at a distance from my inner heart and thoughts. I know how hard it can be to admit you are a sinner and don't have it all together. But having been through that and on the other side to witness when someone gives their life, I see it so much differently.

I would put it up there with watching a baby being born. The preciousness of new life beginning never gets old or humdrum.

The Pastor gives a few minutes then turns his attention back to the letter his friend left behind.

In most obituaries I have heard, a list of people the deceased leaves behind is named along with their accomplishments in life. I don't feel the need to talk about things I've accomplished but rather what you all have meant to me in my life.

Without the love of my parents, other family, and friends, I don't know where I would be. All of you have nurtured me with your love and advice over the years and I am forever grateful. But I want to give a special shout-out to all the young people who have been a part of Bible study and Sunday school. Wow, there are no words to express just how much I love you guys. I feel so privileged to have had the opportunity to minister into your lives and hopeful I have impacted you as you have me.

Now, to my beautiful bride, Teresa. I hope I must rewrite this multiple times over the years as we have children and grandchildren and other wonderful life experiences. And finally, allow someone else to edit the last draft to include that we passed away peacefully, at home, and in each other's arms. But if that is not the case and this is the first and only draft that is read; I want you to know I have loved you more than any man could ever dream is possible. Second only to Christ, you are my everything. Please don't allow grief and sorrow to stop you from carrying on fulfilling the calling you have in your life. I want you to love again. Bring light into another man's life like you have done mine. Just know when you get to heaven, I will reclaim you forever, lol.

P.S. I believe I can say with full confidence heaven is more beautiful than I can describe. As all of you make your way to our eternal home, you'll find me at the feet of Jesus worshiping Him. I look forward to hearing about all the souls that come to Christ through your ministries and witness.

Your brother in Christ Jesus, Jeffery

A.K.A. Mr. Jeff

Pastor Mitchell folds the paper again as the music begins. The lights dim and the big screen behind the pulpit that usually displays the lyrics during worship lights up with an old photograph of Mr. Jeffery as a baby. Even as an infant, his smile lit up his whole face. Another photo swipes across the screen showing him as a toddler in nothing more than a diaper eating a fist full of birthday cake.

As each life moment flashes across the screen, there are mixed sounds of sorrow and awes at the memorials of time captured on film. In each one he grows a little older but that same brightness about his soul is ever-present even when he wasn't smiling for the camera. One of the last photos is the one Shaday had snapped the first night I came to Bible study. Mr. Jeff is posing in a cheesy fashion which he must have done quickly because I don't remember seeing him do that. Matthew's face is distorted like he was in the process of saying something and the photo caught it. Steve is blushing and looking embarrassed, unaware a photo is about to take place. I too, look uninformed because my eyes were closed, my mouth open in mid-sentence, my hair was a mess and there were crusty smears of blood dried around my nose.

"Oh... my... goodness," I say. I cover my face with my hand on my forehead. I remember Shaday offering to give me a makeover. I needed one, judging by this picture.

Suddenly, there is a commotion from the front row. I uncover my face and turn my attention to where Teresa had been sitting. Her mother and father are bent over trying to revive their daughter who has passed out. I look up to the stage and see Mr. Jeff smiling lovingly at his new bride in their wedding photo.

Pastor Mitchell gives a signal to the video guy to stop the slide show then looks back at the worship band and signals them to keep playing. He rushes down the stage and motions to the youth leaders to come and assist him. They gather around Teresa and begin to pray. He looks to the congregation and mimics praying hands, to let us know we should do the same. Everyone in the church link hands with people on either side of them.

Jonasan takes my hand in his. Tears spring to my eyes as a rush of emotions warms my face.

People softly pray for a moment, but the room is tense.

Suddenly, Jonasan lifts his voice with a song we sing frequently on Sundays. It was a song Mr. Jeff led us in sometimes. I had no idea he could sing so well. Other's join in and before long the whole auditorium is filled with the voices singing praise to God.

I look around, taking in the wonder of the a-cappella performance. I blink my eyes a couple of times but the haze filling the air doesn't clear. I wipe my eyes with the tissue I've had wadded in my palm, yet the smoke is slowly descending upon us as we worship. I look behind me where the seats are elevated slightly and as the cloud lands on people, they fall to their knees. Just as the cloud reaches me, I smell a fragrance in the air like I've never smelled before. The weight of the smoke touches me, and it feels like warm oil flowing over my whole body. I drop to my knees hard but there is no pain. Jonasan and others around me lower too till the whole room is on their knees. A great silence comes over us all and the peace that envelopes us is more glorious than anything I've ever experienced.

I don't know how long we were like this, but no one seemed sore from the prolonged position. As the cloud lifted people started to rouse and move around again. The worship band had all landed on their backs on the floor and were now starting to get up slowly. Teresa is being helped to her feet and back to her seat by Mr. Paul.

There wasn't any more that could be said or experienced after that, so the service gently ended. I make my way to Vanessa.

"What was that?" I ask. "I know it was from God but what do you call it?"

She smiles at me reliving the incredible presence we'd all felt. "That was the Glory Cloud."

"You mean the actual glory that surrounds God?" I ask.

"Yes. Just a tiny glimpse of it."

"Cathy?"

I heard her tiny frail voice behind me and intuitively know who it is.

I turn to face Teresa. She is so fragile and pale. Her veil has been taken off and I can see more of her now. Her dress looks baggy on her skinny frame.

"Hey, Teresa." I reach over and hug her. I can feel the bones of her shoulders.

"I'm sorry I haven't gotten this to you until now." She holds out an envelope with my name scribbled on the outside.

I don't want to press her for what it is right now, so I accept it. "Thank you."

Mr. Duncan touches her shoulders, and she turns to be led by him to their car. I decide to wait till I'm home to see what she's given me.

Jonasan and Steve are talking with Vanessa and another woman. As I approach the group, I hear the end of a conversation.

"Well, we love having him here," Vanessa says to the dark-haired woman. Then looking at Jonasan she says, "And you don't need to be a stranger." As I reach the group, she looks at me while still talking to him. "We all miss you very much.

He turns his attention to me and blushes slightly.

"Mrs. Challis, have you met Cathy?" Vanessa asks.

"Cathy?" She looks at Jonasan then at me. She holds out her hand. "It's nice to meet you."

I shake her hand but can't help but notice the stiff exchange. Could his parents be the reason he isn't speaking to me anymore? Do they not approve of me?

"Nice to meet you too, ma'am," I say.

"Johnny, I think we should be going now." his mother tells him.

He looks irritated but complies.

I watch him walk away. Deep longing tortures me with every step he takes.

By the end of the day, I am exhausted, I can't wait to get into bed. I empty my pockets before removing my clothes and find the letter bearing my name.

I open the envelope to see what Teresa has given me. Inside is a letter with the same scribbled handwriting. I look at the bottom and see the writer's signature, Jeffery Pike.

I stare at the letter for a while before I can bring myself to read it.

Dear Cathy,

I felt prompted by the Spirit to write to you. While in prayer this morning, God told me you needed some encouragement. I'm not sure what you may be facing right now, but I want you to remember, greater is He that is in you, than he that is in the world. Your weapons are not carnal but mighty through God. Trust God will see you through all trials and make you the victor.

Things here are going well. Teresa has been learning how to cook traditional Albanian dishes from the ladies that meet with us at the underground church. Just between you and I, though she tries her best, the food upsets my stomach terribly. When she first started cooking it, I had a hard time ministering because I had to go to the restroom every few minutes. I think I'm finally getting used to it though.

Although we must be careful, most of the Albanians have been kind to us. A large part of the population is Muslim, and they don't like us telling people Jesus is the only way to God. They hold him as a good man or maybe a prophet, but not the son of God. We meet secretly to keep them from becoming violent.

We have had many wonderful experiences. In the first two weeks, twenty-two people gave their life to Jesus and true to his word, signs, and wonders followed. I have seen God heal many illnesses and disfigurements. Cathy, I even saw a woman's finger grow back right in front of my eyes! I'm so excited about all God is doing here. It is my goal to be so on fire for the Lord, all of Albania comes to Jesus.

And, Cathy, I have you to thank. You are the one who inspired me to make this leap of faith. Years ago, I heard the Lord call me to missions, but I was afraid I would fail so I never went. As you would ask all those questions, it would cause me to get back into the Word like never before. Seeing your life change before my very eyes made me hunger for more.

I told Teresa about my desire to go and she agreed. I know how hard it is to be away from her family and really, this is my dream, not hers. But she has been so wonderful about it all. I could never ask for a better wife than her. I know the Lord gave her to me to be the support I need.

I hope to fill you all to the brim with stories of miracles I've witnessed when we come home for Christmas. Until then, keep up the Bible study and the prayers for us.

Yours in Christ,

Jeffery Pike

He had gone because of me! All this time I've been blaming Teresa. I lay the letter aside and lay back on the bed. A mix of feelings swirl in my thoughts. I feel ashamed of myself for being so critical of Teresa. I miss my friends Elaine, Shaday, and Jonasan. And more than just being his friend, I miss the way he looked at me. When he touched me, it was with chaste affection unlike Trevor, who had grabbed at me lustfully with only his wants considered.

I pray for all of them, even Trevor before I fall asleep.

10

The Word as a Weapon

It was like Shaday had described it!

The Evangelist and Prophet, Lester James, read Joel chapter two in the King James Version, verses twenty-eight through thirty-two. *And it shall come to pass afterward, that I will pour out my spirit upon all flesh; and your sons and your daughters shall prophesy, your old men shall dream dreams, your young men shall see visions: And also, upon the servants and upon the handmaids in those days will I pour out my spirit. And I will shew wonders in the heavens and in the earth, blood, and fire, and pillars of smoke. The sun shall be turned into darkness, and the moon into blood, before the great and terrible day of the Lord come. And it shall come to pass, that whosoever shall call on the name of the Lord shall be delivered: for in mount Zion and in Jerusalem shall be deliverance, as the Lord hath said, and in the remnant whom the Lord shall call.*

He spoke with such authority and passion, every word felt as though it blazed through my soul. I sit on the edge of my seat as he described the villages, cities, and rural farming towns he'd preached in all over the world. He told of miracles, prophecies, and healings so great, it was almost hard to put into words, he said.

The revival brought people from other churches and all races. The sanctuary was packed with the walls lined with men, generous enough to give up their seats. Jonasan is one of them. I try not to look at him but catch myself doing it anyway. He is always looking back at me.

The black men and women stand from time to time to wave a handkerchief wildly in the air while shouting out phrases of encouragement or agreement.

Every so often, the keyboardist traveling with Brother James would pound out an organ sound to emphasize what he is declaring. This brings people to their feet, into the aisles where they jump, dance, and even run!

"God has sent me here to prepare you for a mighty move of God! He has already begun to pour out His spirit upon the youth of the world. I have been to many states in America and across the seas into foreign nations and I keep hearing the same thing from the youth; God is telling them to reach out to others in their age group. 'I keep having dreams and visions, Brother James' they tell me."

The organ burbled to a stop.

"Hallelujah!" Voices call out.

My heart is pounding as he speaks. I could have been the only one in the room as far as I knew. The way he spoke of the dreams and a mighty move of God. Hadn't Jonasan said the angel told him about a coming move?

He pauses for a while. "Yes, Father, I hear You," he says.

The organ cries as it builds. James paces the stage, scanning the crowd. Sharply he turns, pointing in the audience!

"You, there! The young man with the shaved head," The evangelist points to a young boy from Vanessa's class named Jason. Jason points to himself with wide eyes.

"Yes, you young man. The Lord God would have me tell you He has seen the anger in your heart. He knows the pain you feel so intensely, you feel driven to do things you know is wrong. God says for you to trust in Him. He is The Just One. He will bring recompense to you and your sister. Hold on to your faith and don't let the enemy of your soul trick you into taking matters into your own hands, son. God is with you and He will never leave you."

Jason begins to sob uncontrollably and drops back into his

chair. People around him pat him on the back while shouting praises to Jesus.

Vanessa leans over and says, "His father is very abusive. People have tried to help get him and his sister out of the home, but his dad is good at lying and hiding things."

"How does Lester James know that?" I ask.

"The Lord showed him. There's no other way he could know," she tells me.

"You sir!" The minister points to another man in the crowd. "Please come to the front."

As the man, I'm not familiar with, jogs towards the preacher, the keyboard player makes the keys dance. I listen amazed as the music seems to run with the man. He stands with his hands raised at the front.

"The Lord has instructed me to tell you He loves you very much. He has seen your selfless acts of kindness and enjoyed your worship. He has one thing against you, however. You are not obeying his voice to go where He has told you to go. Some souls need to hear the word the Lord has given you. Stop procrastinating and go in the Name of the Lord Jesus!", as Lester James finishes what he has heard from the Lord, he waves his hand swiftly in front of the man. Like an invisible lightning bolt hit him, he begins to shake and falls back onto the floor.

"Oh, my goodness! Is he ok?" I ask Vanessa.

"Yes Honey, he is more than ok, I promise you," she says.

"Young Lady, look at me," I hear him say.

I look to see where he is pointing now and it's someone sitting in our section. I follow the pointing of his finger and look around to see who would stand.

"You Sister. The one in the blue shirt," he says.

Vanessa looks at me. I look down at my blue shirt and almost faint.

I look at him with wide eyes wondering what he's about to tell the whole church about me. My palms start pouring sweat and my heart is trying to hide behind my spine.

"Yes, you, daughter of the Most-High. You have been having

dreams about your calling, haven't you?" he asks. A kind smile alights his severe face.

I nod.

"Please come up here, sister." He points to the front carpet area where the other man still lays, twitching.

I slowly get out of my seat and walk to the front on trembling legs. I'm not sure what to expect. Am I going to be shoved onto the hard floor by his unseen powers too?

Please don't let it hurt, God is all I can hope for and think to myself.

"Ha, ha, ha, the power of God doesn't hurt, sweet girl!" Brother James answers my unspoken request.

"I see one of your angels, young lady. She whispers to you. God wants you to know He is with you through every storm. You *are* never and *have* never been alone." The minister says theatrically as he comes down the side steps and approaches me.

"He has a mighty work for you and him. Together you will be a force of good in the Name of the Lord God Almighty." He stops and scans the crowd again. "Come here, young man."

I look back. Jonasan rakes his hair away from his face as he comes to meet us. He moves next to me facing the evangelist. How could this man know we were connected? We were nowhere near each other and since he came out onto the stage, I haven't looked Jonasan's way.

"You have been misunderstood by many so-called Christians. But God has seen your heart. And He tells me you are like David, a man after God's own heart." As he speaks the word heart, he lightly puts his finger on Jonasan's chest. Jonasan's arms spread wide. He descends backward like he is falling into a swimming pool. He lays on the floor crying and praising God.

The red-faced, sweating preacher turns his attention back to me. "The silver liquid you have seen in your dreams is the anointing of God. He is pouring it on you tonight and you will never be the same. Stay in His word. Use it as a weapon on the enemy and stay in prayer not letting circumstances sway you. Receive!" He shouts and ever so slightly touches my forehead.

It was like time stood still.

I felt his fingertip touch my skin but even stronger than that, I felt warm liquid gush out onto me, drenching me from head to toe. Suddenly, I felt the carpet beneath me, but I'd had no sensation of falling. I never felt my weight hit the floor with any impact. It was as though I settled onto the floor like a feather. A joy and inner peace I cannot describe sets every molecule in my body alive and vibrating. I know if my cells had voices, they would be glorifying God just as my lips do right now in tongues.

I lay there for a few minutes, feeling the weight of the oil-like anointing of God. I swim in His presence. Vanessa says my name and touches my hand. I open my eyes which are still filled with tears of joy.

"Can you sit up, Lovie?" she asks me.

Though I still feel weighed down, I accept her hand and pull myself up. I suppose I should go back to my seat so the preacher can carry on with his message.

I accept the tissue Vanessa offers me. I stand to my feet as smoothly as I can, wondering if the whole church is watching me. I glance up at the seats to see if I'm correct only to find they are all empty. Only a few people remain in the auditorium and they are chit-chatting the way people do after church service.

I look at Vanessa. "Where did everyone go? Is it over?"

She smiles. "Yes, Honey, it's over for tonight."

"I thought it would last longer than a few minutes," I tell her.

"Cathy, you have been lying here for the whole service. Over an hour!" she says. "Both of you." She looks around me to Jonasan who has been helped up by Buddy.

"Wow! Will this happen every night of the revival?" I ask.

Probably not to you personally but I'm sure God isn't done speaking to His people about His plans for us all. Unless He has more for you, you will mostly get to sit back and watch others be blessed which is almost as glorious." She laughs.

The following night, Lester James directs us all back to Joel, chapter three this time. He instructs us to read along with him verse three, still in KJV: *"And they have cast lots for my people; and have given a boy for an harlot, and sold a girl for wine, that they might drink."*

"The Lord told me to warn those who don't know and to confirm those who do know there are demon spirits like Incubus and Succubus of old. They are demonic spirits that trade in sex. They are working alongside demon spirits of Pharmacia, to seduce our youth into drugs. Their goal is to strip them of the destiny God has planned for them."

Evangelist James goes through the Word like a craftsman who has perfected his trade. He shows in the Word of God how these things work and how to defeat them. I take lots of notes and feel encouraged with each spoken word of the Lord.

"I thought you said it would be a week?" I question Vanessa.

"Well, that was the plan, but Brother James said the Lord told him he was needed elsewhere," she says. With her sigh, she seems as disappointed as I am it's over after only three days.

"I was getting so much out of it."

"Yeah, I always enjoy a good meeting, but man, they sure can wear you out!" She rotates her head and rubs the back of her neck, followed by a yawn.

I don't feel tired in the least. I feel energized and ready for what comes next.

Arc, my German Shepard, lays curled up on his dog bed. I lay on my bed in the small room at the junkyard, my Bible by my side as I read and take notes. Arc snores as I reach down with one hand and stroke his fur.

The confirmation I received at the revival has supercharged my study.

While thinking about what I just read, I remember back to the little old lady who I now believe was one of my angels in disguise. *"Cathy, read this for what it is; it holds your life and future. Don't read it like it's just a book because it isn't. It is alive with the very words of God. Through it, He will speak and if you will listen and obey, He will protect you and you will do His mighty works."*

Wouldn't it be great if there was a translation of the Bible that inserted your name in parts relevant to you and read like a declaration for you to say over your own life, I think. That gives me an idea...

I turn to a clean sheet of paper in my notebook. I flip back to the beginning of Ephesians. With pen in hand and my index finger on the page of my Bible running line by line, I write a statement of everything I see the Apostle Paul said.

Before long, I have written every part of Ephesians that speaks to what is now mine through Jesus. It's very eye-opening to see it this way. The words no longer sound like something that was for someone else but written for me.

I look over some of the verses and say them out loud once again before putting the notebook and Bible to the side.

"He has blessed me with ALL spiritual blessing in the heavenly places in Christ!"

"I am sealed by the Holy Spirit of promise."

"He loves me with a great love."

"I am filled with the fullness of God because He can do abundantly more than I could ever ask or think."

"I understand what the will of God is for my life."

It feels good to hear His Truths spoken over my life and gives me confidence for the future. Although I had to look up some of the words on Google, seeing what they mean just make the scriptures more personal. I feel like I am finally seeing what my angel was telling me. I think about the dreams I've been having more frequently. I believe God wants me to help other teenagers that don't have such a great life. I'm not sure how it's going to all work, but I just know it will.

I scratch the top of Arc's head, telling him what a good boy he is. When I pull my arm back, I catch a whiff of my armpit. "Oh, gross!"

Arc looks up at me.

"Not you pal, that is all me!"

Before getting in the shower, I decide to let Arc out to do his business before locking up for bed.

I try to be quick, knowing Arc will be needing back in soon. When finished, I turn off the water and dry off, wrapping a towel around my body.

I hear a noise in the front office. "Hold on Arc!" I call out.

Opening the door between my room and the office, a shadowy figure is standing in the outside doorway. I hear Arc barking as he runs towards the building, but the intruder slams the office door before Arc has made it. A rush of adrenaline forces me from my surprised state. I try to close my door and slide the lock in place, but the man prevents the door from closing. I push against it with all my strength, but I am no match for the intruder shoving back.

The door opens with a bang and hurls me backward. I slip on the moist floor and fall hard on my back, slamming my head against the concrete. My vision blurs and sparks of light pop, along with a dull pain in my head. I try to get to my feet, but once again, I'm not fast enough. The trespasser grabs my foot and yanks me towards him, causing the loosely encircled towel around me to fall away and roll up under my weight. I will myself to focus again.

Pete!

His eyes are wild, and he looks high. The apparent tweaking causes his teeth to grind together and his head turns, responding to a spasm in his neck. He looks at me getting right up in my face. His breath is horrendous with alcohol and rotting teeth.

"You're good and clean for me now aren't you girl?" He runs his eyes down my body.

In all the struggle, I am completely naked on the floor.

Inside I scream for help, but my vocal cords are paralyzed. I can barely manage to draw air into my lungs as terror grips me. The realization hits, he is about to rape me. It sounds weird, but the first thing I think about is my wedding day. As I lay on my back dizzy, it looks like my innocence will be taken, not by the man I love and want to share all I am with, but with Pete, violently and painfully.

Finding my voice, I beg while trying to push him away from me. "No, no, no, please stop!" I cry.

He pins my flailing arms to the floor with both his hands and pushes his weight against my pelvis.

"Oh no, you little tease! You owe me! And they said I could have you! You must have teased the wrong person." He laughs and brings my wrists together, pinning them with one hand. With his free hand, he runs a finger along my jawline. "I tried to be good to you and your mother," His finger traces down the middle of my exposed chest. "And what're the thanks I get? You run away, then turn your momma against me, but she'll get hers." He looks me in the eye. "Now, it's payday!" He maneuvers the zipper on his camouflage pants with his free hand.

I try to struggle but he is so much stronger than me.

This can't be happening. Somebody, please help me, I cry inside.

"Greater is He that is in you than he that is in the world." I hear on the inside.

The words are loud and clear in my spirit.

"Our weapons are not carnal but mighty through God." I hear again.

I know I must stop the fear and fight, using the only weapon I have right now. With all the spiritual strength inside me, I look Pete straight in the eyes and scream to the top of my lungs. "JESUS!!!!"

"Hush and stop squirming you little..."

"I bind you in the name of Jesus! You foul spirit of darkness, I cast you out in the name of Jesus!" I declare so loudly and forcefully; I empty my lungs of air.

Pete looks surprised, releases my wrist, and arches back like he sees something behind me. I take advantage of my limited freedom and pull my right knee up to my chest and kick as hard as I can towards the undone part of his pants. He grabs his crotch and falls completely back through the doorway. I scramble to my feet as fast as my shaky legs will let me and stumble to the office door. I frantically grab at the two doorknobs I see, due to the double vision. Pete moans and leans to his knees starting to get up while cradling his wounded manhood.

Arc continues to bark at the door. As soon as I open it, he bolts inside and lunges toward Pete. All of Arc's seventy-eight pounds propels Pete back into my room. The volume of Arc snarling and growling paired with Pete's cussing and screaming are not helping my already frazzled nerves. I pick up the junkyard phone and punch in, nine-one-one. It seems Arc has things under control now, but I don't want to take any chances. I shut and lock the door leading to the back room while telling the operator my situation, simultaneously putting on one of Greg's jackets he leaves here. I slide under the desk with the operator telling me help is on the way.

"Thank you, Jesus. Thank you, Jesus. Oh, thank you, Jesus." I pant out feeling like it is taking forever for the police to show up. I try to stop shaking but it's no use.

I hear Pete slam against the door, still fighting with Arc. I jerk and try to become smaller under the desk.

Eventually, I hear a siren then the cops come in yelling orders.

I peek over the desk while on my knees. The cop's flashlight blinds me. I point wordlessly towards the back room.

"Get this dog off me, man!" Pete cries.

One of the cops yells a command at Arc and immediately I hear him stop growling. There is a lot of knocking around on the walls. I assume Pete is being subdued and handcuffed.

"Ma'am, are you ok? I'm Officer Meyers with the police department. You are safe now. I need you to step out from behind the desk."

It takes all the courage I can muster to come out of my hiding place.

"It's ok ma'am." The officer assures me.

He pulls a handset from his shoulder to his mouth and requests two ambulances: one for the perp and one for the victim.

Victim. I'm not a victim. I am more than a conqueror; I think to myself while trembling.

"Here ma'am, have a seat. What's your name?"

"Cathy Maze." I stutter.

"Cathy, do you live here?"

"I… My mom… Pete…" I stammer trying to explain. My head is throbbing, and my focus is still off.

Soon an ambulance arrives. When the EMT enters the room, I recognize him as one of the two who'd responded to the trailer when Pete beat Mom. The stone-faced male is carrying the bag this time. He drops it at my feet and reaches out to touch me.

I jerk back in terror and start to hyperventilate.

"Goodness gracious, Terrell!" The cop chastises the medic while pulling him away from me by his shoulder. "Can't you see she has been handled roughly enough? Get Deb in here!"

The medic doesn't seem to like being manhandled but leaves the room. The cop lowers his head back to his notepad, shaking his head in annoyance.

I like this officer much better than the one who had responded to the trailer park that day.

The female medic, I now know as Deb comes into the room. She looks at the officer and sighs. "Sorry Meyers, Doug just doesn't think sometimes."

"You got that right!" He looks at me and motions with his ink pen. "This is Cathy. I want you to be very gentle with her. I'm going to go outside and make some calls.

She moves carefully in my direction and lowers her voice to a calming tone. "Hey, Cathy. I'm Deb. Let's see what's going on here." She covers her hands with latex gloves and pulls a small flashlight from her pocket. After waving it in front of my eyes she asks, "Did you hit your head, honey?"

I reach up and touch the back of my head. A sting ripples through my scalp. My hair is still slightly wet from the shower but there is warm dampness there too. I pull my hand back to see my fingers are stained with blood.

The sight of blood reminds me of something Pete had said. 'She'll get hers.', he had said referring to Mom.

I stand up quickly and run outside to the police officer. "Sir! Sir! Please!"

He lowers his cell phone and looks at me.

"Can you please go check on my mother? He said something about my mom. She may be in danger! She lives just across the field in trailer number twelve!"

Instinctively I start to head towards the opening in the fence, but Officer Meyers stops me. "Woah, I'll go check on your mom, but you need to let the EMTs look you over. And you might want some clothes on too."

I look down realizing I'm still only wearing Greg's coat.

I go back inside and refuse a trip to the hospital. I try to get them to follow officer Meyers to my mom's, but they say they can't go unless dispatched there officially. They sit in the ambulance outside for a short time then leave. Shortly after, Officer Meyers returns but waits in his patrol car till another car arrives.

A tall thin woman with a clipboard comes to the door with officer Meyers.

Oh, God, please let her be ok. I pray silently.

"Miss. Maze, this is Patricia Wilder." The officer introduces her.

She holds out her hand and I take it, although with a puzzled look.

"Is she ok?" I ask officer Meyers.

At first, he seems confused then remembers he went to check on my mom. "There was no one home, ma'am. The place was a mess, but she wasn't there.

Patricia interjects, "Cathy the reason I am here is that it has come to our attention at Family and Children Services you are only fifteen, living here without adult supervision." She looks around with a grimace.

"I'm actually sixteen."

She smiles like I just reasoned with her in baby talk. "Hmm, well, that still makes you a minor and not of legal age to be living on your own. I need you to come with...."

Our attention is redirected to Greg's truck coming to a screeching halt just outside.

He rushes from the vehicle toward us quicker than I'd ever seen him move.

"Just hold on there a minute you two.", he calls out as he approaches. He holds a piece of paper in the air and continues, "She ain't going nowhere with you. She's in my custody now."

"And who are you, sir?" Patricia asks with disdain.

"Ma'am this is Mr. Jiles, he owns this scrapyard." Officer Meyers explains to her as he holds his hand out to greet Greg. They seem to know and be friendly with one another.

Greg shakes the cop's hand with one hand and gives the paper to Ms. Wilder with the other. She unfolds it and reads the document.

"Now, as you can see, Cathy's mom, Regina Maze has signed full custody over to me. It was made legal just this evening at the courthouse," he tells the DFAC's worker.

He then looks at me. "Your Momma's ok, girl. She had to go but said to tell you she loves you very much."

I don't know if I believe she said that or not but just hearing it and she is ok is enough to make me weep like a little girl again. The gravity of what happened tonight weighs on me like a ton of bricks. My legs give way and I sink to the floor, finally feeling able to breathe.

11

Dreams and Answers

Although Greg was now my legal guardian, Ms. Wilder made it clear I couldn't live on my own.

"I got that covered too. She will live with me," Greg tells Ms. Wilder.

Officer Meyers interjects. "Now Greg, I happen to know where you live and I can tell you, that won't work."

"You don't know as much about me as you think Charlie. As a matter of fact, I bought a house two days ago, furniture too. I was going to come here in the morning to bring Cathy home."

I look at Greg. My bottom lip trembles.

"I think she's answered all your questions, so I'm going to take her home now," Greg tells them.

I watch Mrs. Wilder and the police officer leave through the gate. Greg examines the chain and lock, determining he'll have to get a new one tomorrow.

My mind is still reeling. Did Greg say he bought a house? Surely he didn't do that for me? I think about the custody papers. He has gone through a lot of trouble during this time to help me. I brush a tear away and the thought, *you don't deserve this.*

We pull up to the house in Hill Top Meadows. My jaw drops.

"How did you do this? Are you... rich?"

"I got a few bucks," he says. "I didn't have time to get a whole lot of stuff. We have beds to sleep in and a table to eat at, but that's about it for now. I thought I might let you help me in that department if you don't mind."

"These houses are like, for really rich people Greg. Surely there were less expensive homes available."

"Well, this one is gated and has some fancy security system. I think I'll need your help with that too."

I take my garbage bag of things from the truck. Arc waits patiently for my command.

"Come Arc."

Greg unlocks the door letting us in. He takes me down a hallway, showing me my room. I've never seen a bedroom this big. It was as big as our whole trailer almost.

I set the bag down and begin to cry again.

"I'm sorry, Greg. You didn't ask for this."

"Actually, I did," he says.

I look at him, waiting for him to explain.

"I been praying for a long time God would send me people I could share life with, like kids and grandkids, nieces and nephews, people I can love and them love me back. That's the thing I hated most about Stan dying so young. Linda and I didn't get the chance to get grandkids. Linda was an orphan and didn't have any family and all mine have all died off over the years. I don't have folks anymore to have Thanksgiving dinner or Christmas with. I miss that."

I look around at the large master suite he's given me as he talks.

"Also, I went to your momma and asked her if I could have custody of you."

I look at him intently. Why would he do that? I mean, I'm glad he did. There's no telling where Ms. Wilder would have taken me, but what prompted him suddenly to do it now?

"Why?" I ask.

He pauses looking like he wants to tell me but not sure if he should.

"After we went to see her on your birthday, I got a call from someone. They told me you were in danger and I should take measures to help you in any way I could. That's why I called and got you the dog."

"Who called you?"

"I don't know his name. It was a man though and he sounded official, like a cop or something. Wasn't any I know from the local force. I know them all by name and can recognize their voices usually. This man sounded more important than just an average policeman."

My brow wrinkles with questions. Who would have known to call Greg? So many more questions arise, but my train of thought is paused as he continues.

"I started watching your mom's place and when that thug left, I took my chance to go talk to her. It took some doing but I finally was able to get her to understand she needed to do this for you. She was scared and told me she knew that man would kill her if he beat her one more time. I convinced her to let me buy her a plane ticket to some of her family in Washington state so she could get cleaned up."

"Wait, what? Did you say family in Washington?"

"That's what she said."

"She told me we didn't have any family!" I say. This night hasn't stopped with the surprises and betrayal.

Greg had nothing more he could tell me. I decide what I needed was to spend some time praying in the spirit for answers. The last time I looked at my phone, it was a little past one a.m. I must have fallen asleep because a few hours later, I awoke from the most breathtaking dream of them all.

"Vanessa?" I say over my cell phone.

"Hey Hun, what's up?"

"I need to talk to you."

"Do you want me to come over to your place?"

"Well, I'm not living there anymore. A lot happened. I haven't been staying at the trailer. Here's my new address."

I can hear the questions rolling in her mind. I know they would be in mine. But she waits till she can see me face to face. Her questions double when she sees the house.

I tell about all I'd been hiding. Pete moving in, me running away, and Greg letting me stay in the room at the junkyard. "When I got out of the shower, I heard a noise and before I could lock the door, Pete was in there trying to... uh... attack me." I pause feeling the familiar chill run through my blood.

"Oh, honey! Did he... are you..." She stops not wanting to even say the words.

"No, he didn't rape me. He tried but I was able to get away from him. I don't know how because he had me pinned to the floor and I was totally at his whim. The only thing I can figure is when I screamed the name of Jesus, it startled him so much he... I don't know... like, he got off me like he'd seen something! I was able to kick him and get to the phone to call for help. Arc kept him busy till the police got there. Oh, I have a dog now too."

Arc gets up from his bed and lays down at my feet, seeming to know I was talking about him, or maybe he sensed my unease talking about what happened last night.

"Thank you, Jesus." She whispers to the Lord. She reaches out to touch my hand. "I'm so thankful you are ok. Did you come here because of that?"

"Kinda, the police officer saw I was alone and called DFACS about it. The lady they sent said I couldn't be there alone because I'm still a minor. Thankfully, Greg had gone to my mom and gotten her to sign custody of me over to him. Vanessa, he bought this house so I would have a place to live. He lives here too of course, but he said when I'm ready to be on my own, this house would be mine!"

"Wow, that had to be God setting that up because of the timing," she says.

I nod my head realizing I hadn't thought of it that way earlier.

"Oh, V, so much has happened and come to light I don't even know where to start!" I tell her feeling exasperated. "It turns out some anonymous man called Greg and told him I was in danger. That's why he got me Arc and went to Mom about custody. Also, my mom has always told me we have no family. She said they were all dead before I was born, but when Greg offered to help her, she told him she had family in Washington State! Why would she lie to me?" I shake my head before putting my face in my hands.

Vanessa reaches out and pulls me close to her like I imagine a big sister would do if I'd had one.

"Sweetheart, in my experience, when a person lies about extended family it's for a good reason. Maybe their parents didn't approve of their marriage and disowned them. She must have wanted to protect you from some hurt."

"Pete said something too that has been bothering me." I sit back and look at her. "He told me, 'they said I could have you! You must have teased the wrong person.'." I shake my head questioningly at her. "I don't know what he's talking about."

She pinches her chin like she does when she's thinking. "And Greg said someone called him and said you were in danger? These two things have to be related."

"And I think they are. Do you remember what that evangelist said to me; about me having the dream about the liquid silver? Well, I couldn't remember all the dream but last night I had it again. I was surrounded by the darkness again like in the first dream. At first, it was just me and a few others. Suddenly, this liquid silver poured from Heaven and coated us, making us strong. We ran into the darkness and found other teens who were being held captive by the darkness and we pulled them out into the light we carried with us. Soon they too had the coating of silver light and would rescue others. Before long there was a massive army of us, chasing away the darkness."

"Cathy- girl, that is a dream straight from Heaven if I ever heard one!", Vanessa says looking visibly overtaken by goosebumps. She rubs her arms with wide eyes.

"I've been thinking for some time this is what God is calling me to, but I don't know where to start. I mean, who am I? I'm just a poor nobody. I don't have anything."

"No, no, no, Honey! Remember, you've got God, and if God is for you…." She waits for me to finish.

"Who can be against me. I know but..."

"No, you've got to start somewhere. It doesn't mean you need to run off and put yourself in danger but start somewhere. Talk to Pastor Mitchell and the Shooks. They can direct you.

"Cathy, I'm sorry hun, but I have to leave. My mother and I are going to Calhoun to do some shopping." Vanessa kisses me on the cheek and hugs me. "I'm so glad you are ok.

I walk Vanessa to the door. When I open it, Jonasan is standing there with his finger about to press the doorbell.

I'm shocked to see him here. I knew he lived in this neighborhood, but how did he know I did too now?

"Did he hurt you?" His voice trembles.

I shake my head.

"How do you know about it though?"

He sighs. "Can I come in?"

"Sure." I back away from the entrance so he can come inside.

"Bye Jonasan," Vanessa says as she leaves.

He looks around the empty house then sits at the small table in one of the two chairs. I join him.

I wait for him to start but he doesn't. "So, why are you here?"

"I wanted to make sure you were ok."

I feel my frustration growing. I don't want to be angry anymore. Questioning him hatefully will not solve anything. Whatever the reason for him to distance himself, it is what it is.

"I'm ok. I have a headache from hitting my head on the concrete, but other than that, I'll live." I gently touch the small gash, thankful once again I didn't need stitches, and nothing worse happened.

"I'm sorry."

"It's not your fault."

"Yes, it is."

"Look, I know you feel like you were told to protect me but be realistic. You can't protect me from life. Besides, I don't know how you plan to always be there when we aren't even talking." I feel myself getting defensive and I don't want to do that. I take a deep breath to reset.

"All this is because of me."

I roll my eyes, tiring of his self-blame. "Yes, of course, you caused my mom to become an addict! You moved Pete into our home and caused him to attack me! For goodness sake, Jonasan, stop being ridiculous. Do you want to know what is your fault? Telling me you loved me and then shutting me off. I could understand if you changed your mind, but at least have the decency to tell me!" I rub my temples as the pounding in my head intensifies.

"I didn't change my mind. I do love you," he says.

"Well, you have a weird way of showing it!"

"I know it looks that way, but I have been trying to protect you. I thought if I stayed away from you, Trevor would turn his attention somewhere else." He looks sad. "The only problem is, I think he did turn his attention to another person and he still found a way to punish me."

"What are you talking about? I thought we were talking about Pete, not Trevor."

"They are connected."

"What? How is that possible?"

"Pete is a low-level thug that works for people Trevor has connections with. When he was unsuccessful at the dance, he told Pete, he could have you. I was hoping he would direct his revenge towards me and not you, but I was wrong."

"Pete did say, 'They said I could have you! You must have teased the wrong person.'," I tell Jonasan.

Things were adding up now. "Wait, you said you think Trevor directed his attention to someone else. Who?"

"I don't know for sure. It's just a theory. I don't want to say unless we find out for sure."

"Will you please stop talking in code and tell me what is going on!" I grab the sides of my head. The pain is intense.

"Cathy! Are you alright?"

"I need something for my head again." I stand to go to the kitchen for the aspirin and some water. The room twist throwing me off balance. Suddenly, I lose control of my legs. They seem to lock in place, and I fall forward. I think to put my hands out to catch myself only to find my arms in the same condition. The searing pain shoots through my head like a bullet. I can feel myself jerking on the floor.

Jonasan is by my side instantly. He is speaking to me, but my ears are humming, and his words are lost to me. Then there is only darkness as I lose consciousness.

Have you ever sat in a crowded restaurant and listened to the background noise? The clanging of dishes, the hissing of meat searing, the slight sound of the door opening as patrons enter and exit, and the hum of many voices speaking without being distinct. That's how I perceived my surroundings. I was present to hear but unable to participate. I stared into a black fog with the occasional burst of light. I differentiated the voices by the color their tone would create. The most brilliant and luring light was the blue one. Whenever it would burst into view or streak across my consciousness, I felt everything was right.

Time was irrelevant to me. I didn't think in measures of it. I only waited for the blue light to sing to me again. But like most things, a change began and before long my perception had altered. The black fog lifted and was replaced with a brightness that stabbed at my head. Voices were no longer visible but resounded with a scratching buzz. The irritation of it is what brought me back.

"I have to think of her now. I can't allow her to be put in a dangerous situation." One distorted voice says.

"I've done my best and she is still in danger. I think we should do the opposite." The more pleasant voice replies.

"Hey guys, I think she may be coming around. Her eyes are moving." That voice seems comforting.

"Cathy? Girl, can you hear me?" I know that voice. That's... that's...

"Greg?" My mouth and throat are dry. Speaking is difficult.

"I'm here girl." I feel someone rubbing my right hand.

"Cathy, it's Vanessa, Sweetheart. I'm here and Jonasan's here too."

I try to open my eyes. Nothing seems to want to work properly. I feel like I'm in a dream state. I settle there and wait. I'm not sure what I'm waiting for but until it comes, I sleep.

Laying on my back, I stare at the tall tree that gives us shade. I twirl a loose thread around my finger, pulling it free from the old blanket. Mom and Dad talk about needing new tires for the car, they debate about getting used ones or getting them new.

"Cathy." I hear the gentle voice say to me.

I smile. It's my Father. Not my dad, but my Father.

I stand to my feet looking downhill at the pond. A jogger runs by a man feeding ducks. A couple of young boys ride their bikes, racing one another. I smile at the various activity. People relaxing and spending time with family and friends.

"Turn and see," the Father says.

I turn, looking uphill, and see the looming storm. It's closer than I remember. The darkness tries to draw me in, but I am held by the Father.

"What am I supposed to do?"

Lettie walks up beside me. She smiles. "It's time."

"I don't know how to start.", I tell her.

"Just take one step at a time. You will have to step into the darkness but carry Him with you and it won't touch you. Learn to hear and respond. Find who you can, but remember, it's ultimately their choice."

Suddenly, I'm inside the darkness. There are so many noises it's hard to tell where they are coming from. Should I go left, or right? Should I stay here, or go?

I pray in the spirit and listen with my heart.

"Cathy!"

I hear to the right of me. With my eyes still closed I turn and see with my spirit. I go towards the cry.

"Mom? Is that you?"

"Mom is that you?" Something mocks me.

Don't go that way the inner voice says.

"God, please help me!" Another voice calls out in the distance.

"Shaday?" I call out.

Pray and she will find you, the inner voice tells me.

I pray intensely. Scriptures come to mind as I speak from a place of faith. Soon I see Shaday emerging from the darkness toward the light I carry with me.

I hear another cry for mercy coming out of the thick blackness.

This time invite them to the light the Spirit says.

"Come and hear the good news. Come and see the Father loves you and He is waiting," I call out.

I see a young boy straining to see.

"Here! Come here. I can show you the way out!" I announce above the sound of the storm.

He sees me and runs in my direction.

I think about Elaine. "Lettie, is Elaine in here? Can you lead me to her so I can help her out too?"

"She's not here anymore."

"What do you mean?"

Lettie looks up for a moment then back at me. "It's time to wake up, dear."

"But what about the others? What about Elaine? Where is she?"

"It's time to wake up and get started," she says. She begins to fade. "Cathy? Cathy? Can you hear me?"

"But where am I? How do I get out?"

"Cathy, Sweetheart, wake up." I hear her voice though I can no longer see her.

"Cathy?" Vanessa says.

I open my eyes and see her leaning over me. I'm lying down. I'm not in the storm anymore. I'm not outside either. I look around at the unfamiliar setting trying to figure out where I am and how I got here.

"There you are. Here, drink some water. I know your throat has got to be dry." She says while bringing a straw to my lips.

I pull the ice-cold water into my mouth. It's both refreshing and a shock to my senses at the same time.

"I'm going to raise your head a little so you can wake up easier, ok?" Vanessa prewarns me.

The bed hums as my head is brought up. A wave of dizziness flows from my head to my stomach.

"Ok, that's enough, please," I say. My voice is hoarse. I flex my fingers and toes. They work thankfully. "Where am I?"

"The hospital, Lovie. You had a convulsion due to your head injury. You've been out of it for a few days. The doctors sedated you so your brain could heal better."

"How did I get a brain injury?"

"When you hit your head on the concrete during Pete's attack. Do you not remember?"

It seemed familiar but like a story, I had read and not something I'd experienced.

Vanessa types on her phone. "I'm texting Jonasan to let him know you're awake. He'll call Greg too. They left to get something to eat and a shower."

She pulls a chair closer to the side of my bed. "They have been up here almost constantly the whole time. That Greg is a character! And he really cares about you.", she says reclining in the chair and crossing her legs.

Bits and pieces start coming back to me. "Why did it take so long for me to have issues from the attack. I was fine, just a bad headache, that's all."

"Apparently, it did a little more damage than you thought. The headache was caused by your brain swelling. It's a good thing Jonasan was there with you to call for help."

Vanessa looks around on the edge of the bed for something. She picks up a remote attached to the bed.

"Can I help you?" A woman's voice asks from a speaker behind my head.

"Yes, she's awake and talking now. The nurse told me to let you know when that happened," Vanessa tells the hospital staff.

"Ok, I'll let the nurse know."

Several minutes later a man wearing purple scrubs comes into the room. "Knock, knock!", he says while tapping on the door and coming on in. He smiles as he puts on some latex gloves from the box on the wall. "So, how's our girl doing?"

I don't feel the need to answer. His question seems redundant.

He plugs his ears with a stethoscope, lays the cold metal end on the bend of my arm while pressing uncomfortably on my wrist. He follows a set of procedures making sure all signs point to my progress.

"Are you hungry Cathy? I can have a tray brought up for you if you think you can tolerate it," he says.

I nod. I don't feel hungry, but if I've been asleep for a few days, I probably need to eat.

"Ok, I'll let them know." His focus is drawn to Vanessa's feet. "Oh girl, I like those shoes! Where did you get those?" His sudden voice pitch alludes to his probable sexuality.

Vanessa looks at her shoes and seems saddened. "I got them in Calhoun at the outlet mall."

"M-hm, I'm going to have to drive over there this weekend, honey," the nurse says. He throws his gloves away and washes his hands in the tiny sink. As he dries his hands, he tells me, "I'll bring that tray in here as soon as they get it up here. You just rest."

Vanessa stares into space for a moment, then catches me looking at her. She flashes a fake smile.

"What's wrong, V?"

"Nothing honey, I'm just tired."

I know she's lying to me but I'm a little too tired to argue with her. I close my eyes and slip into a light sleep that is interrupted when I hear someone come into the room.

Jonasan walks in quietly. His hair is wet and hangs uncombed in front of his face. A few loose strands cling to his nose. He looks towards the window drawing my attention there too. Vanessa stands at the window, looking into the night sky.

"Hey," he says. He takes turns smiling at each of us.

Behind him, the nurse comes in with a tray of food. Sitting up feels strange. I can feel the prolonged position in my muscles. I nibble on the food as Jonasan and Vanessa talk about nothing important. It feels like there is an elephant in the room no one wants to bring attention to.

Greg comes in more hurried than Jonasan had. His eyes dart to everyone in the room with a silent greeting.

"Hey, Cathy. You feeling better?" he asks.

"Yes. Just a little sore from laying here so long. How's Arc? Is he missing me?"

"You better believe it! I've been letting that friend of yours..." He looks at Vanessa, "What's his name?"

"Steve," she tells him.

"Yeah, Steve. He's been coming over to the house making sure Arc has food and water and gets a walk outside several times a day."

Vanessa looks at me, "Steve got his driver's license. He's been volunteering to run errands for everyone." She smiles. Her phone vibrates. She checks the screen. It's minute, but sadness flashes across her face again. She rejects the call.

"You should go home for a while. I'll be staying here tonight," Jonasan tells Vanessa.

"Yeah, I think I will head home. I could use a shower too."

She leans to kiss my forehead. "I love you, Sweetheart. I hope you're home by Sunday so you can come to church. Everyone has been asking for you."

I smile at her. "Goodnight. Thank you for being here."

"You're welcome." She turns her attention to Greg. "You should go home too."

"Yes, Greg. I'm fine. Go be with Arc and let him know I'll be home soon."

He looks at me and Jonasan. Jonasan nods.

"Alright then, if you don't want me here, I'll go." He winks letting me know he's just kidding. "I'll walk with you, Miss Vanessa."

After they leave it's quiet between Jonasan and me for a while. Looking at the food tray and knowing I couldn't hold one more bite. "You should eat the rest of this. I can't and it shouldn't go to waste."

"I grabbed something to eat on the way home to take a shower. I'm good."

"It's too quiet in here. Can we turn on the tv?" I ask.

He takes the remote Vanessa had used to call the nurses' station and turns on the television. "What do you want to watch?"

"Put on the news or something dull. I just want the background noise. I don't care about watching anything."

An election ad comes on for the governor's race. The salesman-looking candidate puts his arm around a blonde woman, I assume is his wife. They both hold a fake smile while his voice in the background says, "This is Cameron O'Doyle and I approve this message."

"That guy's a jerk," Jonasan says.

"You know him?"

"I met him once. He's a phony and a pervert."

"How so?"

He shakes his head. "Just another part of my past."

My eyes widen. "You mean you and that guy…?"

"No! Not me, never! But he does like little kids. Boys or girls just as long as they are prepubescent."

"Oh gross! You saw this with your own eyes?" I ask astounded.

"Well, not him doing the deed but word got around at the events what he was in to. I avoided people like him at all cost."

The conversation takes me back to the night of the dance. I'd been upset with him for not warning me about Trevor. I still don't understand but have decided to let it go. He's probably right anyway, I wouldn't have believed him.

The news anchor reports on local events. I watch the way his mouth curves when he says something with an 's'. It's interesting to find little idiosyncrasies like this about people. A picture appears on the upper corner of the screen and a flash of recognition catches my attention.

"Elaine!" I yell hoarsely.

"The sixteen-year-old high school student never made it to the dance that night, however. Gill McNeese has more. Gill?" says the anchor.

"That's right, Shawn, behind me is the shallow grave where the young girl's body was discovered by a city worker, late this afternoon…."

"NO!" I cry out.

Jonasan turns the tv off. He lays down next to me on the bed. I moan into his chest as he holds me.

"Jonasan. She's dead!" I sob into his chest.

The sound of my cries gets the attention of the nurses and soon several of them are in the room. Jonasan explains with as little details as possible why I'm upset. A short time later, the male nurse gives me a mild sedative in the I.V. to calm me down.

I fall asleep in Jonasan's arms.

12

A First Kiss and a New Role

"That boy's folks invited us for dinner tonight," Greg says. The hospital can no longer be seen from the side mirror. "I told them you may not feel up to it yet, but said I'd ask."

"A home-cooked meal would be nice, and it would keep us from having to do the cooking and cleaning." I smile at him. I don't know if I feel up to the pressure of socializing with Jonasan's parents, but it would help Greg. He shouldn't have to wait on me hand and foot and I'm still too weak to be cooking.

"Alright then, I'll let 'em know."

The house is still new to me but feels more like home than the hospital. The shower gel and shampoo are the kinds I like and I'm not washing with a rag, thousands have used it before me. That felt gross!

I want to wear something nice to their house, but I still don't have much in the way of clothes. Greg has already spent so much money on the house and says we are going furniture shopping as soon as I feel up to it. Asking for a trip to the thrift store might be too much. I decide on my best jeans and a shirt Vanessa gave me.

Whether he doesn't have anything nice either or wanted to make me feel better, Greg wore unstained jeans and a button-up shirt as well. I laughed to myself as we walked to their house. We look like two country bumpkins in this fancy neighborhood. He tried to drive us there, but I needed the fresh air.

I look around at the fine things in their home. I had thought to get some ideas about what to put in our place, but after seeing the crystal vases, marble tables, and fine art in every square inch, I think Greg will need Mrs. Challis' help furnishing our place instead of me. My idea of fine art was anything you could get at Rent A Center instead of the Dollar General Store.

"Mr. Jiles, would you like a beer or a drink from the bar?" Mrs. Challis asks.

"I'll take some sweet tea if you have it," he says.

Mr. Challis hands her the lowball glass half full of brown liquid. "Sweet tea sounds good."

Jonasan looks how I feel.

I sit on one end of the couch and he on the other. Greg takes the matching leather chair on the right of Mr. Challis when offered it.

"Do you smoke cigars, Mr. Jiles?" John Challis asks.

"No sir, I gave up all vises when my Linda got sick."

I wonder to myself, will Mrs. Challis set an extra place at the table for the awkwardness in the room. It is so tangible; it's taken on a life of its own.

"Would you like to see my room?" Jonasan asks me. I'm guessing he feels the awkwardness too.

Greg gives him a stern look. His father looks surprised.

"Sure."

I follow him down a hall like ours, only lined with painted family photos and decorative metal branches. I try to imagine what I may see and steady my facial expression not to show disgust at the probable black walls, black bedding, and posters of gothic art.

I didn't prepare well enough.

The walls are a light tan with wide white crown molding. The carpet is white underneath a massive designer rug. The four-poster bed and other furniture are a stone grey. Something about his blanket catches my attention. I move closer to get a better look.

"Oh, wow! Are that military fatigues?"

"Yeah, they were my Poppy's. He was a Marine. When he died,

my Nan made this quilt for me." He rubs one of the patches that read 'Challis'.

"That is so cool," I tell him.

Instead of demonic symbols and gore art on the walls, he has Disciple and other band posters, a framed collage of his grandfather's Marine dress-whites with several medals attached.

On the nightstand, by his bed, something familiar catches my eye.

"Hey, I have that same lotion. It's my favorite. I wear it all the time," I tell him.

He gets oddly silent and looks uncomfortable.

"I'm surprised you like it. It has a feminine smell to me." It's not an expensive lotion. Before giving my life to Jesus, I use to shoplift it from the dollar store. I take a tissue from the box next to the lotion and wipe my nose.

"Where does that door lead?"

"That's my closet."

"May I?"

"It's nothing you haven't seen already. Go ahead."

My closet is bigger, but it looks pitiful with the three outfits hanging inside. His is packed!

"There's all the black." I smile at him.

"Told ya."

Being in the tight space with him and the smell of his cologne in the air, I stay there longer than I guess I should, but it makes me feel like I'm being hugged by him. I don't want to leave.

I'm counting the pairs of shoes when I feel his hand brush against mine. I look toward him but not in his eyes. I tilt my hand out in case his touch wasn't accidental. I'm rewarded with his fingers searching for mine. I open my hand letting him know I want him to take it. He does and my heart dances wildly.

"Johnny? Are you in here?" Mrs. Challis says.

My face flushes at almost being discovered in the intimate moment and longing stabs at me when he pulls away quickly to step back in the open room.

"Yeah, Mom. I was just showing Cathy my room."

Though I can't see her, I notice the pause before she responds. "Dinner is ready."

"Ok, we're coming." He looks inside at me.

The awkwardness is no better at the table. John and Susan try to make conversation, but it is a struggle to find anything we have in common.

After several minutes of nothing but silverware clinking against the china as we take another bite of the awesome food I can't pronounce, Jonasan drops his fork onto the plate and looks frustrated.

"Ok! I can't take this. Greg, Cathy, my parents invited you here because we think you deserve to know what we know."

He looks at his dad. "My dad works for the FBI. He isn't on Elaine's case, but he has access to the investigation."

When his dad still doesn't speak up, he continues. "After the dance, I told them about stuff I knew. They knew I was angry and had gotten into some trouble, but they didn't know the why behind it all. I think you deserve to know too.

Mrs. Challis lowers her head. She gets the same expression of sadness as Jonasan does at times.

"At my old school, I hung around the popular kids. Trevor's cousin, Keela Hayes, was my girlfriend, or that's what I thought. We used to party a lot. The kinds of parties we went to were a mix of all ages. Everyone was there for two things, drugs and sex."

Mrs. Challis shifts uncomfortably in her seat.

"I thought it was cool to hang out with college professors, politicians, athletes, musicians, and all the cool kids from area high schools and colleges. I didn't have a problem with what people did with each other until I started noticing some young kids being brought in. When I say young, I mean like, under ten."

He stops to drink some water.

"When I started asking questions, Keela invited me to, what she called, an opportunity. She said I could make a lot of money recruiting runaways and foster kids. I was appalled and let her know I was not going to be a part of that. She laughed at me and in the course of trying to shame me about being 'so innocent' as she called it, she told me she'd had many abortions including one since she and I were together."

He gathers his emotions to finish.

"It was more than I knew how to handle. All I could think about was that she murdered my kid." He lowers his head, unable to say more.

Mrs. Challis looks at her son. "It was out of his character to get into trouble or be so emotional. He would come home and tell us he hated God. I didn't know what was happening and couldn't let him feel that way. I knew someone out there had to show him a different way. That's why I kept insisting he go to all those churches."

"I don't mean to pry, but why don't you go to church?" I ask her and Mr. Challis.

They look at one another. "I've never gone to church myself," Mr. Challis says. "It was mostly Susan who wanted Johnny to go."

"John believes in God. He just doesn't believe in organized religion." She looks at me. "I used to go to church as a girl but in my teens, I developed a fear of crowds. I had to sit in the car during your youth leader's funeral. I only came inside once many had left."

That's why she looked severe. It had nothing to do with not liking me at all.

"I have to say though, I felt more peace in that church than others I've attempted to visit. After seeing the change in Johnny, I've been thinking about trying to come and see how it goes."

"If this case goes well, I might have to visit as well to thank God personally. It's going to be a tough one to crack," John Challis says.

His comment brings us back to Elaine's case.

"What have they figured out so far?" I ask.

"The investigators on the case tell me they have a witness that says she saw Elaine get into another student's car and leave the dance with him. They are trying to corroborate that now."

"Whose car did she leave in?" I ask.

He looks at Jonasan then me again. "I really can't say until we know more."

With disappointment on my face, he sighs. "However, I will tell you Quinton Petroski is rolling like a log down a steep hill. He's giving us lots of leads to follow."

My brow wrinkles. "Who?"

"Oh sorry, his street name is Pete," Mr. Challis informs me.

Something occurs to me I wouldn't have guessed before today. "Mr. Challis, did you call Greg and tell him to help me?"

He looks at Greg who seems to be beyond words through all of this. "Yes. After Johnny told us what he had gone through with the girlfriend and his suspicions about her cousin, I asked around and found out about the investigation into several disappearances of some local kids." He pauses. "Let's just say this is bigger than just your friend Elaine." He looks at Jonasan and back to me. "Your friend Shahlay may be involved too."

"It's Shaday, Dad."

"Yes, excuse me. We think she's with a man called Reggie. Petroski threw his name around and mentioned your friend."

Greg finally speaks. "My only concern is keeping Cathy safe. What's the plan?"

No one leaves me alone anymore. Greg has cut his work hours short. When we aren't on Christmas break from school, Jonasan stays by my side all day. I no longer ride a bus to and from school, but with him. Vanessa works but comes by frequently to check on me.

She takes me shopping a couple of days before Christmas.

"Now we have more furniture in the new house, Greg said we should invite some people over. I was thinking about having a Christmas party. Will you and Buddy come?", I ask her.

She looks away pretending a pair of jeans caught her attention. "I would love to come."

"What about Buddy? You haven't mentioned him lately. Is everything ok?"

"If I tell you, will you keep it just between us?" she asks.

"Sure." I touch her arm.

Her eyes glass over with tears. “Do you remember me saying my mom and I were going shopping in Calhoun the day you collapsed?”

I think back, my memory still gets a little fuzzy sometimes. “Yeah, and didn’t you tell the nurse you got the shoes he liked in Calhoun?”

She nods. “Well... We saw Buddy in Calhoun while we were having lunch. He didn’t see us. Before I could get his attention and find out what brought him there, I saw him with another man. They were obviously more than friends if you know what I mean.” She covers her face and begins to cry harder now.

She’s taller than me but I manage to get my arms around her shoulders. She bends and cries on my shirt.

“Oh V, I’m so sorry. How long had this been going on?”

She searches for a tissue in her purse then wipes her nose. “He said he’d always felt different and he’d tried to hide it for years. He met that man and said he just couldn’t resist the temptation any longer.”

She laughs sarcastically. “I thought he was the perfect gentleman because he never tried to kiss me or pressure me into anything. Turns out, he loved my sense of fashion more than me.” She laughs again through her tears.

Tuesday when we arrive at Bible study, we are all surprised to see Pastor Mitchell there. Elder Andrew Shook comes to the podium as usual but he only releases the kids ten and younger to go with Pastor Mitchell’s wife, Deborah. The rest of us stay in the sanctuary and are addressed by the Pastor.

“In light of the revival meeting last month, I spent a lot of time in prayer. The Lord brought out in the meeting things I have neglected to see. Adults sometimes seem to think the younger generation has little to offer, but I should have known better. The Word of God is full of young people being used by God in mighty ways.”

Someone from the back shouts, "Woohoo! We love you, Pastor!" It is followed by more shouts of agreement and clapping.

Pastor Mitchell smiles. "Thank you, guys. I love you too. So, I'm going to turn it over to Elders Andrew and Trena. They have some questions for you all."

The two men trade places and Trena joins her husband at the pulpit.

"We were reminded God uses different ways to speak and show us things. The Word of God tells us not to believe everything we see or hear, but to try the spirit and see if it is from God.", Mr. Shook pauses. "How many of you have had one or more dreams you felt were odd or significant in some way?"

A few hands go up all over the sanctuary including mine and Steve's.

"Ok, how many of you have had other strange events?" he asks.

Only one or two hands go up.

Mrs. Shook steps forward to interject. "Cathy dear, would you mind telling everyone about your encounter with the angel?"

I wasn't expecting this, but I'm not embarrassed. For a split second, I think about how I would have felt about speaking to a crowd a few short months ago. Wow, how things can change so quickly.

I tell them about the lady at the grocery store, giving me the Bible, and the things she said. I also talk about seeing her in a dream later and how I've come to believe this is one of my angels sent to minister to me. When I finish, I look at Trena, who gives me a nod and I take my seat again.

"So, with what Cathy had to say, does anyone think they have had similar things happen to them?"

This time many more hands go up and I can see why she had me tell my story.

Pastor Mitchell comes back to the microphone and asked those who had raised their hand to go to their youth leader and tell them their experience.

As the kids stand, most who have a story are about fourteen

and up. Since Miss. Vanessa would be overwhelmed, Mr. Paul and Ms. Jane help interview her kids.

After the kids have left the church. Pastor Mitchell ask Jonasan, Steve, Matthew, and me to stay behind.

We all take a paper and read some of the experiences the kids have had.

"Lonnie says a woman approached her in the park and told her to pray for harvesters to be sent into the fields. When she asked the woman why farmers needed help so badly, the woman smiled and said all God's children need each other," Ms. Jane read.

Mr. Paul speaks. "I took one from Jennifer. She's only eleven. She said she and her mom were shopping in the mall, a man stopped them in the food court and said Jennifer was a special child who would win many to God soon. He told Jennifer's mom to make sure they stay in the church."

"This kid said a homeless man tried to pay him a dollar to follow him behind a building, but he was scared and didn't go," Trena says. "I told him that was the right thing to do, he should never take money or follow strangers anywhere. I assured him if God sends an angel to him, they won't try to lure him to danger."

I read one I pulled from the stack. "Benji said he dreamed he was in a jungle and a tall man in shiny clothes led him to a small house. Inside was a group of children praying in English. He said the tall man told him they were praying in tongues and didn't know they were speaking English. Benji said one of the kids was telling about the future. He said the kid spoke Benji's full name and called him an instrument of God's compassion." I stop because I'm tearing up. "Wow, just wow!"

"I know," Vanessa pats my knee.

"So, what are we going to do?" Jonasan asks.

"We need to design a program to help these kids know how to hear and follow God's voice," Pastor Mitchell says. "And we need to assign them a mentor to follow."

We all look around the room. Most eyes land on the Shooks or Mr. Paul. But all eyes refocus when Pastor Mitchell says, "I believe the Father has made it clear Cathy is that leader."

You could have knocked me on the floor, and I would have been less taken by surprise!

"Me?" I point to myself.

"You won't be alone," the Pastor adds.

"That's right," Jonasan says. He takes my hand, squeezing it.

"We will all be here to guide you." Pastor Mitchell gestures around the room with many agreeing nods.

Moving forward, Bible studies focus on hearing God's voice. A Thursday night meeting is added for the youth leaders to pray. Those of us from Mr. Jeff's class are now in training to be directors.

After prayer, Jonasan drives to our subdivision. When we pull into my driveway, all the lights are off, indicating Greg isn't here.

"That's unusual," I say.

"Give me your key and stay in the car," he commands.

"You're not going in there alone either! Let me call Greg's cell and see where he is before you go all John Wick!"

I put the call on speaker, and we wait for Greg to answer.

"Yellow!" Greg says.

"Hey Old Man, where are you?" I ask. I make sure to use a teasing tone.

"I left you a note on the table. Me and Charlie Meyers are bowling." He yells out to Charlie, "You were robbed! I saw it, yes I did."

"Mulligan!" we hear Officer Meyers holler.

"Who is Mulligan?" I ask.

"That's an old Irish phrase meaning a do-over," he tells me.

"Mulligan!" I shout into the phone.

"Cathy agrees, Charlie."

"Ok, well I'm going to go. You have fun," I say. I feel the warmth of emotion. Would mine and Dad's relationship be like this if he had lived?

"I'm still going to walk you in," Jonasan insist.

I roll my eyes but smile too.

We enter and cut on the lights. I see Greg's note on the table. He's old school. A text would have been better, but he doesn't think of these things.

Jonasan stands awkwardly in the living room. His stance makes me question what he may be thinking. I start to ask but decide not to.

"Your TV is bigger than ours," he says, making conversation.

I stand beside him. "When we went to get some things for the house, we walked by a wall of TVs and Greg almost drooled on himself. All the money he's spent the last few months has been for me. I insisted he get something for himself."

"And surround sound too, I see."

"Watch this." With a few taps on my phone, music begins to play. "I can..."

Jonasan caresses my face with a hand and stares into my eyes, cutting off my train of thought. He leans in slowly and gently kisses my lips. He pulls away and looks into my eyes. Desire and longing flare inside me. I pull his head to mine and release all the passion I've had for him for months now.

His phone rings.

Reluctantly he pulls it from his pocket and looks at the caller ID.

"It's my mom," he says. "Hey, Mom."

I go to the bathroom. I squeeze a little bit of toothpaste in my mouth and refresh my deodorant. I give myself a once-over in the mirror and steady my breathing. This could be it; I think.

When I get back to the living room, he is standing close to the foyer.

"I should go," he says.

I try not to let the disappointment show on my face but I'm afraid I'm an open book. I feel confused. Why would he kiss me if he weren't interested?

"Why?" I don't disclose my question is twofold.

He looks at the floor. It isn't fair he can hide his face behind the dark curtain of hair. "I respect you... and Greg, but mostly God. It's just not right, you know."

He hooks the car keys on his thumb. "I'll text you later, K?"

I lock the door behind him and wonder if what I've heard about cold showers works; guess I'll find out.

I knock on the first door of the apartment building. I feel unsure of what to expect but confident at the same time with the Shooks and the members of our Tuesday night class with me.

The door opens and a cloud of cigarette smoke billows out. The woman looks at us suspiciously and says, "Yeah?"

"Hi, I'm Cathy. These are some of my friends and we wanted to come by and invite your family to our church. If you have kids in the home, we would like to also invite them to a special event we are having next month on the eighth."

Before I could give her any further information she yells out, "Jessica! Door!"

Before she reaches the door, we hear them argue about who it is and what they want. She pulls back the door wearing a bikini and it is nowhere near swimming weather. I see out of the corner of my eye Daniel, one of the kids from our newly combined class, perks up. Andrew lays his hand on his shoulder and smiles at him in a cautioning way.

"Hi, Jessica. I'm Cathy. My friends and I would like to invite your family to church and to a special event we are having on the eighth of next month." I tell her my spill again as Daniel's twin sister, Danielle hands her a flyer trying not to look at her any more than she has to.

Jessica notices Daniel's reaction so she stretches her arm up the door frame, crosses her legs, and turns her hip out. She pretends to look over the flyer while eyeing Daniel over the page.

"How much does it cost?" she asks. The flyer announces in giant letters across the top the event is FREE!

"It's fre-EE." Daniel's voice pitches high. A side effect of puberty.

He clears his throat and looks away.

"Yes, it's free and there will be food and live music. Will you come?" I press for an answer so we can move on.

"Oh, yeah..." She looks at Daniel. "I'll be there."

"Great! If you need a ride to the event, the church bus line is on the form. Call within that time frame listed and we'll come to get you. Bye, Jessica," I say. I hold my hand out to shake hers. She looks at my hand and shuts the door.

We move on to the next apartment while Andrew holds Daniel back to have a heart-to-heart with him about the trap of the female body.

"Who is it?!" The person yells out sternly from the other side despite having a peephole on the front door.

I do my introduction to the closed door which feels awkward and impersonal. Just open the door I think to myself.

"I don't want any!" The person calls out.

"Oh, we aren't selling anything, it's a free invitation," I say loudly to the door.

"Not interested, go away!"

I have been prepared for things like this by the youth leaders. Before the season changed, we spent several afternoons at the church between services discussing past experiences with witnessing and what to do and not do. How to handle rejection and in the cases such as the first, how to handle overly excepting people.

"Thank you for your time anyway," I say.

We move on.

Some of the easier conversations were with the kids who were playing outside. One kid named Theo kept wiping his running nose on the sleeve of his light jacket. The right arm was covered in green snot. Nyah, another girl from the class, had a hard time with that one.

"Oh, gross!" she said. She began gagging and had to look away.

"Come on Nyah, let's take a walk." Trena leads her away to talk to another group of kids.

We were cussed at, laughed at, had doors slammed in our faces or not opened at all. Some people weren't home, and some pretended not to be home. But overall, there were a few positive interactions, and I was hopeful for a good turnout.

"Oh, my feet hurt!" complained one of the kids.

"I'm starving!" whined another.

I look at Jonasan. We feel the same. For the one-hundredth time, I ask myself if I want the responsibility as the leader. I guess I should say something wise and profound to rally my troops, but what I want are a cheeseburger and a hot bath.

"Come on guys, just a few more houses. This is the last canvas day before the event. We can't give up now and deprive these people the chance to hear God loves them."

"Well, all I gotta say is I better get extra fries today," Nyah says.

"And a milkshake!" Benji licks his lips.

My stomach rumbles as I picture the hot, salty fries dipped into an ice cream cone.

"What we need is some music to pump us up." Jonasan taps on his phone.

When the lights go up and the game is on

Are you ready for me 'cause I'm ready for you?

When the bell rings out and the fight is on

Are you ready for me 'cause I'm ready for you?

Disciple sings Game On over the small speaker.

He pauses the song when we approach the houses. Weirdly, it gives us something to look forward to and does boost morale.

"The last house, oh praise God!" I let my true thoughts slip.

Nyah knocks on the door saying the words we all know by heart now.

I was watching Nyah thinking about the soon coming food. The person who answered the door listens and takes the flyer from Nyah.

"Cathy?" the person at the door says.

I look up and realize it's Rebecca Sprule.

"Hey, Rebecca. How are you?"

"I'm ok."

Everything is not ok with her; I hear in my spirit. Before I have a chance to ask her something to help me know how to pray, a man comes to the door opening it wider.

"Who's this Becky?" the man asks.

"It's someone I knew at school. Her church is inviting us to an event they are having next Saturday," she says.

"Oh, how nice. Can anyone come or is it just for you kids?" he asks.

"Everyone is welcome to come. The event is geared towards the youth, but no one is excluded," I tell him.

"Well, that's great. I think we'll go, what do you say Becky? You want to go?" He looks over the flyer.

She hesitates. "Yeah, sounds like fun."

I feel the tug again in my spirit, but I don't know what to do about it. I wonder what it is about her. On the outside, everything looks ordinary but on the inside of me, the Holy Spirit is buzzing like an alarm bell. Since they will be coming to the event, I decided to pray about it and hope to have the opportunity to speak to her there.

13

Bliss and Nightmares

Greg drops me off at the church at seven in the morning. I think about the long day ahead. As if canvasing wasn't tiring enough, this is looking like an even harder day. If I were having to do this myself, I would sit down in the parking lot and cry now. Thankfully, Deborah Mitchell has taken the reins and is telling the vendors where to set up the inflatables and food stands.

"How can I help?" I ask her.

She looks at her clipboard. "Matthew is setting up the green room for the bands. Can you help him? I've seen his bedroom at home. I think it will need a woman's touch." She laughs.

I chuckle. "Gotcha!"

The designated green room is Mr. Jeff's old classroom. It hasn't been used in a while. Everyone gets too sad when we try to do anything else in there.

I open the door. Matthew is kneeling at Mr. Jeff's chair, praying. I decide to back out and give him a few minutes. While waiting, I check my phone and decide to text Jonasan.

(Me) U up?

(JC) No!

(Me) Liar

(JC) Must…get…sleep.

(Me) Boo Hoo! That's tough, Buttercup!

(JC) What time U want 2 B there?

(Me) Im THERE already!

(JC) UG! UR a machine! I can't keep up.

The door to Mr. Jeff's room opens and Matthew is startled to see me there. I put my phone away.

"I came to lend a hand."

He looks down the hall. "Where's your dark shadow? I didn't think you did anything without him pulling the string," he says.

"Matthew let's not do this. You are my brother in Christ. I don't want us to be weird around each other. Besides, that was so long ago."

"I just don't get it! What do you see in him you don't see in me?"

"There's nothing wrong with you. We just didn't click. And I think God has it planned for Jonasan and me. I mean, I've not heard a voice from heaven saying, 'thou must marry Jonasan', but I feel it in here." I point to my heart.

"I think he just wants in your pants. And when he has gotten what he wants, he'll move on to the next church looking for someone new."

"That's a harsh thing to say. What makes you think he would do that?"

"I did a little digging. I might be homeschooled but that doesn't mean I don't have a network of friends. I happen to know at his last school, he got a girl drunk then took advantage of her. When she got pregnant, he forced her to have an abortion and then dumped her."

"Your facts are distorted. You don't know as much as you think you do."

"Oh yeah, then why did he spend time in juvie?"

I look at Matthew with a blank face, but inside I feel like I've been slapped. Why wouldn't Jonasan tell me that part?

"I'm just here to help get the green room set up. I don't want to talk about his past. Besides, he isn't here to refute your accusations."

"Why don't I just leave you to it? I'll find something else to do. I don't need your help!" he says.

I hate conflict! It ruins my mood. I spend the next hour praying in tongues trying to quiet the turmoil in my head.

Jonasan finds me around noon. "Pastor Deborah says you should take a lunch break. She doesn't want anyone fainting at the event from low blood sugar. Want me to take you to the Burger House?"

"So, you are going to show up and take a lunch break before any work is done?" I tease him.

"Hey, Pastor Deborah's orders." He shrugs.

We see Matthew on the way out.

"Hey Matthew, come go with us to get lunch! I'm buying!" Jonasan calls out to him.

"No thanks, I'd rather starve."

"Woah, what is that all about?" Jonasan asks.

"I'll tell you at the restaurant."

The Burger House is packed. Jonasan stands in the long line while I sit at a table. I keep looking at the time, worrying about all there is yet to do at the church. Eventually, he sets our tray of food in front of us. I open and squeeze out no less than seven packs of ketchup onto the paper liner on the tray.

Jonasan watches me with a smirk. "I think you eat more ketchup than anyone I've ever known."

I draw the remnants from the packet into my mouth. "Mm, yummy."

He shakes his head and sips on his drink. "So, what was up with Matthew? You said you would tell me later."

"He is still mad I didn't pick him. He tried to persuade me you were a horrible person. He knows about Keela but thinks she was a victim in the whole thing. He said you spent time in Juvenile Detention."

He looks at his burger but puts his hands in his lap. "I did."

It's quiet between us for a moment.

"Why?" I ask.

"When Keela told me about the abortion, I lost it. I slapped her. Then I threw a brick through her windshield. I was charged with assault and destruction of property."

I don't condone physical violence, but I have never held the belief men should never hit women. I think under some circumstances a man might need to protect himself. A couple that used to live in the trailer park was evicted for domestic violence. I saw her smacking his head and calling him names. He took it for a long time until he shoved her backward. She scraped her elbow on a rock. He's the one who went to jail. Later when he returned, she beat him almost to death. Why he didn't leave, I don't know. I always thought he should have defended himself. Maybe not by hitting her but leaving.

"It was a really bad time for me. I don't like thinking about it, much less talking about that time. I wasn't trying to hide it from you, I was, well… ashamed, I guess. Does it make a difference in what you think of me?"

"No. I can see why you would have lost your head. But…"

I swirl a fry in the ketchup like a miniature Zen garden.

"But what?"

"How do you know you wouldn't respond that way to someone else? Like…me?"

"I don't know how to answer that," he says.

We don't look at each other for a little. He picks up his burger and begins to eat. Does it make a difference in how I see him? Do I still trust him? I can't imagine a scenario where he would be driven to act that way again. He's only been protective and gentle, never forceful, but does that mean he would never hit me when angry? I think about Trevor. I could easily see him escalate to being violent without cause.

He swallows the bite of the burger in his mouth.

"Where do you see us going?" he asks.

I've always heard guys don't like it when you talk about love and especially marriage. They think you're psycho and usually run as fast as they can. But he did let it slip and even confirmed he loves me. Whether his definition of love is vastly different than mine or not, I want him to know how I feel, and I hope he will be honest with me.

"Knowing that about you does cause me to wonder. But I also know I love you more than I've ever loved anyone. If you were to ask me, I'd marry you today." I blush. It feels like I'm risking a lot by telling him this, but I also think about Vanessa. If she and Buddy had had this conversation, would she have seen he wasn't in love with her as she thought?

He wipes his face with a napkin and stands. My heart sinks. Oh well, I had to know.

I stare at the table wondering how I will get back to the church. How will I continue today with my heartbreaking?

I see him go down to the floor from the corner of my eye. I look to see what he dropped. Before my line of sight makes it to the floor, I see he is on one knee with a ring pinched in his fingers.

"I knew I would know the right time when it came. Although we can't do anything until we are eighteen, I have known since that day in the woods I would give my life for you. Leaving you after that kiss in your living room, was the most difficult thing I've ever had to do. I want to share everything with you."

I cover part of my face so I can still see him but hide as I ugly cry.

"Cathy Jolene Maze, will you marry me?"

I grab him by the neck. "Yes, yes, yes, forever yes!"

Applause erupts around us, but we are too caught up in our joy to notice anything else going on.

He slips the ring on my finger.

On the ride back to the church, I remember another time when I had counted the months, weeks, days, and minutes till I would turn eighteen. Even though it is closer now than then, it feels further away. I stare at the ring until I put it away. As he locks it inside the glove compartment, a question comes to mind.

"How did you know my middle name is Jolene?"

"I asked Greg. It's listed on the custody papers he has."

"Ah, sneaky."

As the time for the event gets underway, I am no longer tired, even though I moved chairs, stocked bathrooms with extra TP, and much more. I floated around on a cloud the whole time. We decided in the car to only tell certain ones. Those who don't know us well would probably try to convince us our feelings would change, and we shouldn't be making plans at this young age.

I see many we'd invited, and we have a packed house. The music is lit with the first group being our very own praise and worship church band followed by another band from Georgia called Rushing Wind. But the main act of the night has Jonasan acting like a giddy schoolboy. When he found out Mr. Paul, now super close friends with Jonasan, knew someone in the band, Disciple, and they had agreed to come play, Jonasan was beside himself.

Just after the music gets started, Vanessa instructs the security team to do a sweep. To avoid any teenagers from sneaking off into a dark corner somewhere and using this as an opportunity to have a make-out session, they check all the 'hot spots' as they call it. The elders that volunteered, walk around and keep an eye out for unruly children since most of them came without parents. The youth leaders watch the crowd and listen to the Holy Spirit for ministry opportunities such as someone crying or trying to hide in the crowd, looking lost. They want everyone to enjoy themselves and no one to feel they are invisible and each person to know they are loved, and they matter to God.

Rebecca still has not arrived.

After Rushing Wind plays, there is an intermission. All the food trucks offer free food and drinks. Despite Pastor Mitchell not wanting to give the kids sugar, Pastor Deborah told him we should at least do cotton candy. Pastor Mitchell stands at the doors to stop kids from taking it inside; worried it will end up on the carpet.

Mr. Paul comes over to where Jonasan and I are sitting. "Hey, you want to meet the guys in Disciple?"

"Dude!" Jonasan says.

We follow Paul to the green room. The visiting bands are treated to slightly better food and comfortable chairs. We walk in to find the two bands praying together so we hang back and bow our heads respectfully.

After the 'amen', we go in and Paul introduces us to them. The lead singer of Disciple, Kevin Young, doesn't have hair as dark as Jonasan's but it is long except on the right side, where he has shaved it. I see Jonasan touch the side of his head getting an idea.

Jonasan gets his photo with Disciple and I get mine with Rushing Wind. I enjoyed them before the break.

"Hey, I hate to cut this short, but intermission is about over," Paul says. Then to Disciple's lead singer, "Kevin, the sound guy said you are ready for a soundcheck. We'll talk more after the show."

"Thanks, man, hey, it's good to see you again," Kevin says. They shake hands.

Jonasan and I head back to help round up the kids while Disciple heads for the stage.

Just before we get to the doors, Jonasan and I hear one of the security team scolding someone. We walk around the corner and see Daniel and that girl, Jessica, with Lance, the head security guy.

"What's going on?" I feel like I already know the answer.

"I caught this two making-out down the hall in a supply closet. Do you know them?" He looks exasperated.

"I know him," I say. I point to Daniel. "You should know better, Daniel," I say.

"Thanks, Lance, we can get them back where they need to be," Jonasan tells him.

"Jessica, is it? Are you ok?" I ask her.

"I wasn't attacking her, Cathy, we were just kissing!" Daniel defends himself.

"Calm down. We're just trying to help," Jonasan says.

"I didn't figure you were, Daniel. I'm just trying to find out why the two of you think it would be okay to do this at church. Come on, you had to know the security team would be watching. And besides, you both should have more self-respect." I remember my temptation a few weeks ago. I sound like a hypocrite. However, I had asked for this event, so I feel responsible that no one ends up pregnant or with rape charges.

Jessica rolls her eyes and huffs out a short laugh. "Whatever," she mumbles.

"Hooking up seems like a lot of fun on the surface," Jonasan tells them, "but on the inside," he points to his heart, "you get messed up when you give yourself to someone when not committed in marriage.

"Ok, well, can I just go back to listen to the music?" Jessica asks. She looks embarrassed.

"That will be up to the Shook's," I say.

"No!" Daniel pleads. "You don't have to tell them, do you?"

"We can't keep it from them. You know Lance will tell them we volunteered to get you guys back to the event," Jonasan explains.

"What's the big deal? All we were doing is a little kissing!" Jessica whines, ending her sentence with the Lord's name.

It rubs me the wrong way how she uses Jesus' name as a cuss word. I remember Jonasan telling me Christians didn't like it when you say His name that way. I understand now why.

We lead the two of them into the auditorium to the Shooks. I don't know what they said to them, but Jessica didn't look humiliated and she seems to enjoy the rest of the event.

During a break, Disciple's lead singer, Kevin, took out his Bible and ministered to the kids. In the end, he gave an altar call and fifty-three kids gave their life to Jesus. Jessica was one of them.

It struck me again Rebecca never showed up.

Steve moves into my view with a big grin on his face. "Look who I found." He shifts to the side a little and Shaday appears behind him.

I reach over and grab her, hugging her tightly.

"Whoa, girl, I gotta keep breathing!" she says. Though her protest is weak.

"I'm so glad you are here! I have been praying for you." I say. I'm on the verge of tears.

"Yeah well, I saw one of the flyers and it sounded like fun," she says.

I think about the dream I'd had where I was in the darkness and I heard her. *Pray and she will find you, the inner voice told me.*

The band comes back on stage and they do a final set of a medley of several songs from previous albums. Jonasan was able to tell me from what album each song came from as he yelled in my ear over the music.

The rest of the event went well. No other kids were found wandering where they shouldn't be, and all the kids got home safely.

"Where are you staying, Shaday?" My instincts tell me she is on the run.

She doesn't answer right away and tries to change the subject.

"Come home with me. Greg won't mind and we have an extra room. You'll have to sleep with me tonight because we don't have a bed in the spare room yet. It'll be fun, like a sleepover.

I think back to a time when I would have never had a friend over. I think about Elaine and swallow the lump in my throat.

After a little persuasion, she agrees. Steve insists on bringing her over in his parent's van.

On the drive home, I lay my head over onto Jonasan's arm. The event was a big success, but we are all worn out. Being so close to him makes me think about Jessica and Daniel. Jonasan had mentioned emotional damage sex before marriage can have on you.

"Do you feel like you're damaged?" I ask. I'm too tired to beat around the bush.

"What do you mean?"

"You told Daniel and Jessica sex before marriage messes with you. Is that the reason you didn't want to be with me?"

"Oh, I wanted to be with you, still do, but my reason for not going any further was my relationship with God. But I know the problems it can cause. And sometimes I do feel like I wasted something precious on the wrong person."

I look up at him, wanting to convey my love for him isn't less knowing he's been with another girl. "I won't be disappointed you're not a virgin when our time comes."

"I kind of know that but, I don't know, I wonder about it sometimes. I talked to Paul, told him some feelings I had and the confusion I felt."

He looks at me then back to the road. "Would you like to know how he explained it to me?"

I nod.

"It's deep in a spiritual way but helped me a lot. Anyway, he said men are circumcised to show their covenant to God, and women bleed the first time to show covenant with her husband. God is the covering of the man, and the husband is the covering of the woman. That way the flow of blessing is singular and not divided and weakened. We are strongest together. The chain of authority God designed is not so men can dominate women, but they cover them, like a protector. And we don't protect you because you are inferior to us, but because you are valuable, and we need you. When I had sex with Keela, although she wasn't a virgin, I was, and I entered a covenant with her whether we realized it or not. I think that's why it was harder on me than her; it was like going through a divorce on an emotional level. And because God created us to be faithful to covenant, that type of break leaves a scar that doesn't go away easily. Now, thankfully, the blood of Jesus heals every hurt and I wouldn't say I feel damaged, as you put it, but I feel sad I tarnished that first experience."

We pull up to Greg's house which will be mine when I turn eighteen.

"Greg! I'm home."

"Alright then, I'm gonna turn in. I got a bunch of scrap coming early before time for church."

"Before you go, is it ok I invited a friend to stay with us for a while? She has nowhere to go."

"If you trust her, I trust her. It's your house after all." He winks at me and heads down the hall.

"Has Arc been out?" I ask.

"Yep, just a few minutes ago."

"Alright, love you, good night." I'd never said that to him before.

He caught it too. He smiles at me. Just before walking into the bedroom, he says, "Love you too, girl."

Jonasan calls his mom to let her know he is at our house. Hearing him talk to her makes me miss my mom. I wish I could call her. I hope she has gotten help. I've wondered if the 'family in Washington State' was a lie. Why would she tell me we had none if there were people she could go to for help?

Steve pulls up with Shaday. When the guys leave, I show her around the house and make sure she has the code to turn the alarm off to the house and the gate code to get into the subdivision. After I take a quick shower to wash away the long day, we sit on my bed and talk. I try to gently enter the conversation about where she's been all this time. So, I start off telling her about Jonasan and me, showing off my engagement ring I'd been hiding all day.

She looks at the ring but seems unimpressed.

"I heard about your Gramma. I'm sorry," I say.

"Thanks."

"Where did you go? Steve called your sister and she said you left home before the funeral."

"I just needed some time, you know," she says.

"I wish you would have told me."

"What could you do? It ain't like you was doin' any better."

Her words are true but still sting a little.

"I at least reached out for help and kept coming to church. You had us worried!"

"You wouldn't understand," she tells me.

"How do you know? You don't know everything about me either. I've had my share of problems."

"I know more than you think I do, I'm sure."

Something about the way she says it tells me she's right.

"Please, enlighten me then."

"I know about that football player that tried to git you. And when he didn't, he took your friend instead."

My heart leaps in horror and my mouth feels dry.

"Are you saying Elaine left the dance with Trevor Hayes?"

"Um-hm, and I know you listed as free game for embarrassing him."

I think about Pete saying, 'they said I could have you'. "What do you mean 'free game'?"

She looks away.

"Day, if I'm in danger, I would hope you would tell me."

I try to give her time but it's hard. I want her to spill it already.

"You remember all that nice stuff I had?"

"Do you mean the iPhone and Apple watch?"

"Yeah, I got that stuff from Reggie. He a lot older than me so I didn't tell nobody about him and me. When Gramma died, I went to stay with him. I wudin' gonna let Leesa treat me like her maid. Things were ok for a while, then one night at a party, he told me he need me to help out some friends of his. I was thinking like, cleaning they house or something, but he told me to do other stuff, like sex stuff. When I told him no, he beat me bad. He said he'd kill me if I ever talked back to him or tried to leave."

She stares ahead numbly.

I touch her hand. "Oh, my goodness, 'Day, how did you get away?"

"He been under a lot of pressure from higher-ups. Seems like that Trevor boy has got a lot of pull. I think his dad is part of it too. Anyway, they been on Reggie about making sure you learn a lesson. Since you got away from Pete, they don't feel like you suffered enough, so I told him I could get him close to you."

I look at her trying to understand what she's saying. Before I can fully wrap my head around it, I see a large black man coming down the hall. I stand to run to my door, but Shaday trips me.

"Greg!" I'm hoping he isn't a heavy sleeper and has heard me.

He opens his bedroom door just as Reggie gets to it. Greg has a gun in hand but so does Reggie. I hear the pop. Then two more.

I struggle to get up, but terror has me immobile.

"Get up!" Reggie yells at me.

"Greg!"

Reggie grabs my hair and pulls me to my feet. He turns me around, throwing me on the bed face down. Shaday moves backward.

"Stop fightin'!" he tells me. "Here, hold this." He tells Shaday.

Reggie yanks my pajama bottoms down. I attempt to roll over in hopes I can kick him the way I did Pete. Before I can maneuver, I hear three quick blasts. The noise causes my ears to ring but doesn't stop me from trying to flee. When I get turned around, I see Reggie sitting against my dresser. His eyes are dim and unfocused. Shaday is still pointing the gun at him and pulling the trigger. With every dry fire, she whispers through her tears.

"I'm sorry. I'm sorry. I'm sorry."

I run to Greg.

"Greg!"

He's struggling to breathe but alive. I see his cell phone on the nightstand.

"Nine-one-one, what's your emergency?" a male voice asks.

"I need an ambulance! My dad, he's been shot! He can't breathe!"

"Ma'am, what's your address?"

Greg's eyes get still. His chest isn't rising and falling.

"No! Don't you die! I can't lose you again, Dad, please! Breathe!"

He pulls in a sharp breath. I give the operator the address then lay the cell aside while I try to stop the bleeding.

"God, tell me what to do!"

He stops breathing again.

"I call you healed in Jesus' name! Live!"

I wipe the tears and snot from my nose.

"Please God, don't let him die!"

I think about the account of Jesus raising Lazarus from the dead. "Greg! Come forth! Greg! Listen to me, listen to me, please."

I sink to the floor beside him. I lay my ear to the side of his chest hoping to hear what my eyes haven't seen. Instead, I hear a siren and watch the red and blue lights flash through the curtains.

"I'm sorry, Cathy." Shaday says "Can you hear me, Cathy? Cathy?"

I jerk awake.

"Greg!" I scream and cry.

"He already gone to work. You been having a bad dream," she tells me.

I look at the floor in front of my dresser.

"I have 'em too. I been so scared Reggie would find me. I went on and on about it last night thinkin' how good you was listenin', then I seen you had went to sleep on me. I guess you was tired after that thing yesterday."

I look beside the bed where my cell rests on the charger. I take it and call the shop.

"Hey girl, what ya need?"

I burst into tears. Arc is instantly by my side.

"Cathy? What's wrong?"

I'm hysterical and nothing makes sense. Arc whines and turns in circles.

"I'll be there in a minute!" he says. The line clicks.

Shaday rubs my back, trying to calm me, but I still feel leery of her.

"Front door ajar." the security system says.

I hold my breath as a figure coming down the hall.

"What's wrong?" asks Jonasan. His eyes are wide and he's panting.

"She had a nightmare and can't seem to know it ain't real."

"Jon-a-san, Greg was..." I point towards Greg's room then to the floor in front of my dresser. "Reggie..." I struggle to explain.

In a couple of long strides, he's holding me.

"Shh, I'm here now. It's ok."

When Greg arrives, I recount the dream to them. "I should have known something was off when Arc didn't appear. It just seemed so real though. Shaday, did you tell me Elaine left the dance with Trevor or was that only in the dream?"

"I told you I heard about the dance and Reggie knew that Hayes boy somehow. Iównt know if he took your friend, though.

"Greg called me to check on you. He didn't know why you were crying just told me to get here quick. I ran here as fast as I could."

I notice he's wearing flannel pajama pants and a blue t-shirt. I look him over. It's the first time I've seen him in something other than black. He blushes and looks uncomfortable.

"Now I know you're ok, I got to get back to the yard. That load should be there soon if he ain't already looking for me."

"What time is it?" I ask.

Greg looks at his watch. "Ten minutes to eight."

"I need to start getting ready for church. I guess we all do." I say.

After church, Vanessa drives Shaday and me over to Rebecca Sprule's house. I want to touch base with her and see if she will come to the evening service with us.

I knock on the door and wait. After a moment, Rebecca's father answers the door. He looks rough. There are dark circles under his eyes which are bloodshot.

"Hello sir, I was by here Saturday a week ago and invited Rebecca to an event we were having last night. Since you both had shown interest in coming and I didn't see you there, I just wanted to stop by and make sure you both know you are welcome to come anytime. You don't have to wait for another event," I say.

He doesn't answer for a few seconds and I wonder if he's forgotten about last week.

"I'm sorry miss. Um.... my Becky.... took her own life Friday." He looks next to him like he's staring at her ghost standing in the doorway, just as she was the day, I last spoke with them. "She's dead." He seems to forget where he is and what he's doing.

I'm so caught off guard I feel like I may fall backward.

"I'm so sorry, Mr. Sprule!" It's all I can think to say.

"Thank you, ma'am," He closes the door.

I walk back to the car feeling like I weigh five hundred pounds heavier. This is what the Holy Spirit was alerting me to. I knew something was wrong I just didn't know what.

Feeling the pressure of guilt weighing on my soul, it occurs to me I could have prayed about it, but I didn't. I could have asked her more questions. Maybe she would have said something that would have told me what to do next. I left Rebecca's house with that feeling from the Holy Spirit and I did nothing. I know from experience and a great message Pastor Mitchell preached a few Sundays ago; I can't let guilt move in now. All I can do is learn from this and act next time.

Our Tuesday night group decided to go to the funeral to pray for the family and show our support. They read the note she left behind at the service. She'd been bullied to the point of quitting school and the bullies continued to harass her on social media. She felt she had nowhere to go, her note had said.

After the funeral, Shaday doesn't seem herself. Come to think, she has been distant since Sunday morning. Although somewhat shy and sad looking at times, Saturday, she'd seemed open.

"What's wrong, Day?"

"I'm ok." She takes another bite of her Coco Puff cereal, our late-night snack.

"Are you sure? You have seemed…even sadder than when you first came over. Has Greg or I done something?"

She rolls a puff over with the tip of her spoon.

"Greg's an old country boy. If he called you girl, that's just his way of talking. He isn't racist."

"No, it ain't nothing Greg said."

The inflection of her voice tells me to keep going. "Is it something I said?"

"Not pacifically."

I don't correct her mispronunciation of the word, specifically. "Spit it out, Day. We've been friends long enough for you to be honest with me."

"I just hurt by the way you thought of me in your dream. Do you really think I would do that? That I'd sic Reggie on you like a dog?"

"No! It was just a dream. I don't know why my mind went in

that direction. If I didn't trust you or thought you would do that, I wouldn't have invited you here."

She begins to cry. "Just so you know, I'm grateful to y'all for givin' me a place to be. Me and my sister just don't chill."

We hug and cry it out for a while. Arc joins us on the living room floor. He whines and lays his head on Shaday's leg.

14

Reunions and Accidents

As usual, we get lots of stares, but we no longer care. I look at the school cafeteria line and sigh when I see the length of it. Jonasan slides his pack of ketchup to me.

"Thanks, Babe."

He looks at me from the corner of his eye. For a minute, I'm lost in them. I'm still getting used to the shorter cut. The longer strands in front lay in jagged points to the side while making both his eyes visible. It was breath-taking to have one of those brilliant green eyes looking at me, now it's spellbinding to see them both at once.

"What? Can I not call you Babe?"

"It's fine. You've just never called me that. It was…strange."

"Do you prefer a different term of endearment?" I ask, smiling widely.

"Not at all. Carry on…my lady."

We both laugh.

"…disgusting!" We catch the tail end of her sentence as Mandy Tucker walks by. To be sure we knew she was talking about us, she looks over her shoulder and down her nose in our direction.

I lay my head on his shoulder and whisper. "I love you so much it's disgusting."

"Same here, Babe."

Although I don't look at him, I know he's smiling at me.

The PA system makes a high-pitched squeal. Everyone winces or covers their ears. We hear Ms. Bell clear her throat.

"Would the following students please come to the office?" Paper shuffles and hushed voices are in the background. "Trevor Hayes, Nicolas Carver, Mandy Tucker, Jonathan Challis, and Cathy Maze. Is that all?" Ms. Bell can be heard asking someone.

Jonasan and I look at one another. Although she pronounced his name incorrectly, he's the only Challis in the school. All eyes are on the five of us as we empty our trays and head out of the lunchroom. No doubt had the popular kids not been included in the summons, there would be lots of comments as we exit, but instead, there is a hush.

On the way to the office, down B hall where all the windows are, we see Principal Dye being put, handcuffed, into a black SUV. Trevor, Nick, and Mandy look at one another. In turn, Jonasan and I give one another a questioning stare.

The blinds inside the office have been closed which is unusual. We enter the room one by one and find our parents, or in my case guardian, waiting for us along with men in suits and ties. Other people are in Mr. Dye's office removing computers and thumb drives.

Jonasan's dad isn't there but his mom. She motions for us to remain silent.

"What's going on?" Trevor asks his father. He sounds nervous.

"Just stay quiet! I'll handle this," he's told.

"Daddy? I don't know what's happening, do you?" Mandy says.

I've never seen her act anything but vile. To see her pout like a little girl to her father is so out of character, I almost laugh, but catch myself.

Greg stands with his arms crossed looking severe. I quietly stand next to him. I look at him to see if I can glean anything from his eyes. He winks at me and I know, whatever is going on, will be ok.

An older man steps from the Principal's office and watches the boxes being carried out. He looks at Ms. Bell. "No one is to go into the office without proper clearance."

"Call me when the forensics team arrives.", he says to another agent standing by the door.

He looks at the parents. "You are to follow us downtown. You may call your lawyers to meet you there. Anyone who isn't present when I enter the building will have a warrant issued for their arrest. Do I make myself clear?"

All the parents' nod.

"What's this all about?" I ask Greg once in his truck.

"Mr. Challis told me the case for that friend of yours is about to be wrapped up. He told me the case is a lot bigger than just her and we should hold anything we hear close to the belt.

Once at the Federal Building, we were all separated. I had to tell why I was at the dance with Trevor, what happened once there, and if I'd had any further conversations with him. I was asked about Elaine in the same manner.

When Greg and I got home, I watched down the road to see when his mom's car would pull into the driveway. Late into the evening, I saw her pull in with his Charger behind her. He got out and walked to our house.

"That took a while," I say.

"We stopped by Dad's office and talked to him. He'd watched the interview from the other side of the mirror but didn't want to let on he knew us to their lawyers. Also, we had to go by the school for my car."

"I see."

He kicks at a few sprigs of grass growing up on the sidewalk. "I had to tell them about Keela and all that stuff."

I rub his arm.

The next morning:

(JC) R U Up?

....

(JC) Answer your phone!

(Me) Im up. Whtz goin on?

(JC) Get D up. Im coming over.

He rushes through the door. "Turn on the news!" he says. "Where's Shaday?"

"She's coming, it just takes her time to get out of bed," I say. I turn on the television.

Greg mostly watches the news so it's already on the channel.

"Boy, this better be good to git me up this early.", Shaday tells him.

The advertisement goes off. The news anchor calmly talks about a breaking story he'd mentioned before the commercial.

"Local high school principal, Lenard Dye, was taken into custody by the Federal Bureau of Investigations Friday afternoon. Dye is linked to child pornography and a sex trafficking ring that has been under investigation for some time. Our own Marsha Tanner has more."

"That's right, Glen, I'm standing in front of the West End High School where Lenard Dye has been the acting Principal for nine years. A source at the FBI says Dye was removed from the school Friday and placed under arrest. The computers and files were confiscated as well. Here's what a student at the high school had to say."

Allison Parks appears on the screen. "It was, like, so scary. They, like, stormed into the office and like, told me and Tara to, like, go back to class. But, like, it was lunch period so, we absolutely ran to get Mrs. Muñoz. She's like, the guidance counselor. We saw him being led out in like, real handcuffs! I took a video on my phone. I'll show it to you if you want. Like, for real."

"How is she in high school?" I say. She's not the only one. There are a lot of kids at the school who can't complete a sentence or a thought without saying 'like' several times.

"Many others have been implicated, including Quintin Petroski,

Reginald Jeeter, and Defense attorney Ralph Hayes." Their mug shots appear on the screen.

"That's Trevor's father." Jonasan and I say at the same time.

"We are told by our source more surprising arrests are to follow in the coming days. Back to you, Glen."

"Thanks, Marsha. We'll keep you updated here on Channel Twelve news. Be sure to like us on social media and subscribe to our channel for behind-the-scenes extras."

I turn off the TV.

"Does that mean they got Reggie?" Shaday asks.

"Yes," Jonasan tells her.

A tear rolls down her cheek. "He can't hurt nobody no more?"

"Well, he'll have to stand trial, but my dad told me they're not letting any of them make bail because of the flight risk."

"Oh, thank you, Jesus." She whispers.

"Day, I think you should tell the FBI what you went through and know about him. It might help," I tell her.

The more surprising arrest did follow in the next few days. Many wealthy and political figures were either arrested or implicated. Suspicious murders and suicides started taking place and Mr. Challis let us in on the FBI's suspicion they were close to someone big.

I felt relieved at least partly, Elaine's death had opened the door for the arrest. Until then, they had no concrete evidence to go on and couldn't close in on the ring leaders. I'm sure it's little comfort to her family though. Their daughter was gone forever for such a senseless reason.

"Surprise!" They all scream as I walk outside to wait for Jonasan.

I jump and look around at all the faces.

I feel like the only question I seem to ask anymore is 'what's going on'. I never seem to be in the loop of the events in my own life. To avoid saying it one more time, I just stare at them all, waiting for an explanation.

"Cathy, we love you very much. You have been such a blessing to us all. You helped me when I had broken up with Buddy," Vanessa says. She leaves out the reason they split.

"You gave me a place to live and a shoulder to cry on," Shaday says.

"You became family to a lonely old man," Greg says. His lip quivers and he clears his throat.

"You've helped the church grow and not just in the youth department. We are seeing more parents of these kids because you are teaching them to take the message of Jesus to their homes and schools," Pastor Mitchell says.

"You helped me see I didn't have to hide behind a false persona. And I was worthy of love and forgiveness," Jonasan says.

Their lovely words have me crying, but I still don't know why they are here yelling 'surprise' in our front yard.

Almost like they read my mind, they part, and sitting in the driveway is a new car with a giant red bow on top. Greg comes to my side and puts his arm around me.

"It's yours from us all!" Vanessa says.

"No way!"

"Yes way," Shaday says.

Jonasan tosses the keys in the air in my direction, but Greg catches them.

"We got to get you a license first, girl."

A backyard BBQ ensues. I watch Greg at the grill talking basting techniques with Mr. Paul and John Challis. Several women have gathered to talk about shoe finds and a possible shopping day for the ladies. Even Susan Challis sits among them. She looks slightly out of her comfort zone but becoming more at ease by the minute. Jonasan talks to Steve, Benji, and Daniel. I watch him with puppy love longings as I'd called it once upon a time.

Greg's cell phone rings next to my lemonade. I don't recognize the number but why would I? Everyone we know is here. I run the phone to him and take the spatula.

"Give that to me," Mr. Paul says. "You shouldn't be cooking at your party." He playfully snatches it.

I hold my hands up in surrender. "Ok, ok."

I see Greg go back inside as I reclaim my seat to continue people-watching.

"Cathy?"

I turn with a smile to greet another guest wondering who could have possibly not already been here.

It took a minute to realize it was her. She looks so good. Healthy, just like when Dad was alive.

"Mom!" I say. I throw my arms around her.

I introduce her to everyone before we sit to catch up. Everyone keeps a distance so we can have some privacy. I tell her everything.

"I'm so sorry." She cries. "I was gone long before I'd left you physically."

"Greg told me we have family in Washington. You'd told me since I was small, we had no family. So, what is it? Do we have family or not?"

"We do. It's a long story."

"Greg! How long on the burgers?" I yell out to him.

"Well, I burned the first batch, so we are starting over," he confesses.

"Greg's being kind, everyone," Mr. Paul announces. "It was my fault. I turned the burner up too high. I concede to the grill-master." Paul walks backward as he bows repeatedly to Greg.

I look at Mom. "We have time."

"I met your dad when I was fourteen. He was sixteen. His mother married my daddy. Your grandfather was a mean man. He'd done things to me too horrible to tell you right now. The abuse stopped for a while when he married Loraine, but eventually, he just abused us both. Your dad would try to stop him, but my daddy was a big man, used to fighting. Before long, your dad and I fell in love. Things happened between us and I got pregnant. When the old man found out, he decided to beat you out of me. Your dad took one of the old man's guns and shot him. We ran away, stealing a car from a lady in town that rarely stepped out of her house. We knew she probably wouldn't miss it for a few days. We made it here. Your dad was able to get a job getting paid under the table so he wouldn't have to use his social security number. I tried to get a job but couldn't find one that would pay me the same way."

"You see, we thought he had killed my daddy and was sure the police would find us if we didn't hide. The day of the accident, a cop tried to pull us over for a broken taillight. Your dad just knew he would go to prison for the rest of his life. So, he tried to outrun the police. At some point, he lost control. Before he died, he made me promise not to tell his baby girl he was a murderer."

Tears stream down my face.

"When Mr. Jiles came to me, Pete had come close to beating me again but was called by someone he worked for. He was so mad you had run away, for some reason. Mr. Jiles offered to get me help, so I took it, knowing it was our only chance. I wasn't just thinking of myself. I was thinking about you too."

"When I got to my hometown, Loraine was still alive and living with her sister. She told me the old man had survived the gunshot wound and wouldn't tell the cops who'd done it. Later he was stabbed to death in a bar for cheating with a married woman."

"I cried for the longest time when I found out we'd been trying to hide all that time for nothing. Your dad lost his life for nothing." Regina shakes her head. "I'm so sorry, Cathy, for all I've put you through."

I move from my seat and hug her. "I forgive you, Momma. I ask you to forgive me too. I was mean to you."

She shakes her head but I stop her before she can protest.

Shaday runs past us into the house.

"I'm going to go check on my friend," I tell Mom.

Shaday's bedroom door is open. I hear her crying on the other side of her bathroom door, so I tap twice.

"Shaday, are you ok?"

The door flings open. "Oh, Cathy!" she says. She throws herself on me.

"What's wrong, Day?"

"Steve is leaving."

"I'm sure you'll see him later. He seldom misses church."

"No! He's leaving for good! He's going to Bible College in Texas next month." She sobs.

"I'm not sure I understand why you're so upset."

"We been talking a lot since I been back."

"Uh-huh."

"And we got back close like before only more so."

"Ok..."

"And...and...I think I love him, Cathy!"

"Wow! I did not see that coming."

"I liked him before but just thought we couldn't be a thang, you know."

"I guess I do. Or not really. I'm trying to follow you, I promise."

We hear Steve say from the doorway. "I love you too, Shaday."

I turn to look at him. She and I both stare waiting for him to either repeat himself or something.

"I've loved you since I met you," he tells her.

"Then why you leaving?"

"I have a call on my life. Bible College will help me get there. It's only four years."

"It's only four years," Shaday says, mockingly. "If you love me like I love you, you wouldn't be able to take four years away from me."

"I can't, that's why I want you to go with me. We can't just live together, that wouldn't be right, so you'd have to marry me if you'll have me."

Her tears dry instantly. My mouth drops open.

I'm jarred from my stupor by the bathroom door slamming shut. Inside I hear Shaday crying. I look at Steve and shrug. He comes to the door and begins talking to her. I decide this is none of my business and go back out to the party. I'm sure they will work this out.

When I step back outside, Jonasan and Vanessa question me.

"Is she okay? What happened?" Vanessa asks.

"I think Steve said something to hurt her feelings," Jonasan says.

"No, it's more complicated than that. It appears Steve is going to Bible college soon and he wants Shaday to go with him."

They look at me puzzled.

"I know, I know, it shocked me too. It seems they've fallen in love at some point. But Shaday is acting weird. She's saying one thing but responding differently. I don't know what she's thinking."

Shaday stayed locked in her bathroom for the rest of the day. Steve eventually left.

"I wish Mom would have stayed, but I understand why she had to go back. I want her to stay clean and if she thinks Washington is the best place for that, I understand," I tell Greg.

"I told her I would help her stay in town a couple more days, but she's afraid of running into old acquaintances."

He tops off my glass of sweet tea.

"What should we do about your friend in there, girl?" Greg asks me.

I spoon leftover potato salad into my mouth and shrug.

"Are you gonna try to talk to her some more?"

"I don't know what to say. She'll have to give me something to work with. All I could get out of her before was- I love him, he's leaving- and when he kinda proposes, she locks herself in the bathroom and won't talk. This is above my pay grade. She needs someone with more wisdom than me."

I put my spoon in the dishwasher and replace the lid on the salad.

"When do my driving lessons begin?" I change the subject and smile at his expression.

"What? You don't want to teach me?"

He rinses his coffee mug and places it upside down in the dishwasher.

"I guess I could get Jonasan to teach me."

"That boy doesn't use his blinker and he drives way too fast."

I fold my arms and stare impatiently at him.

"Oh alright! I'll take you out tomorrow, but we're going in my truck. Those matchboxes they call cars these days are nothing but fiberglass. You hit a squirrel in that thing, and it'll be totaled!"

"Yay!"

Shaday appears around the corner.

"You hungry? We have lots of leftovers," Greg tells her.

Her eyes are swollen, and she looks zombiesque. "There any barbeque chicken lef'?"

"You want it hot or cold?" Greg pulls the tinfoil-covered plate from the refrigerator.

"I ownt' care."

I watch her as Greg pulls the covered dishes out and sets them around the counter. She watches him with a distant look in her eye. I want to understand what she is thinking. I would have thought after she confessed love, Steve confirming his feelings, would have made her happy.

She chooses a few sides and tears into the food with gusto. I should let her come to me if she wants to tell me what's going on in her head.

Greg raises an eyebrow at me. My body language says what I've decided to do. He sighs.

"Miss. Jackson, what you planning on doing about that boy?"

She loads the fork with roasted potatoes and shoves it in her mouth. Once she has chewed as long as she can, she swallows and washes it down with tea.

"I'm gonna let him go on to Texas and find him a nice white girl," she says.

"Whoa! Where is that coming from? 'A nice white girl'? Day, why would you say that? You know Steve doesn't think of you as a 'black girl', he seemed genuine to me today," I say.

"I know. And I don't mean it like it sound, but… I ain't no good for anybody no more. Reggie done stripped me of all that."

I look at Greg for help.

"Here's the way I see it. Are you born again?" he asks.

"Yeah, I redone it at church last week."

"The Good Book says when you accept Jesus, the old you

passed away and behold, you have become a new creature. So, you ain't that girl Reggie hurt no more."

She stares at her plate.

"And summarizing Galatians 3:27 and 28 says, we have put on Christ, so we ain't known by our race, social standing, or gender now. We are one in Christ. You back talkin' the Good Book?"

"I know it says that, but how do I feel that in here?"

I lay my hand on hers. "I know it's hard to see ourselves the way the Bible describes us when all we can see, and think are the bad things. But you've got to accept it by faith. I think the first step towards healing is letting Steve love you. Whether you marry right now or not is something you both should pray about. Maybe waiting till he's back from college is best. You don't have to rush into anything."

She nods and we all put the subject to bed for the night.

"Greg's taking me after we go by the DMV for the permit."

Jonasan looks at me with a sideways glance. I think sometimes he forgets his hair isn't hiding his facial expressions anymore.

"What?"

"Just wondering why you didn't ask me."

I know why but saying it out loud is awkward, though it's silly to feel this way.

"Although he isn't, I think of Greg like my dad, you know. It feels like a right of passage to have him teach me."

"That makes sense. I didn't think of it that way." Jonasan takes my hand and smiles at me.

A cool breeze visits the outdoor seating area, lifting my hair into my eyes. The end-of-period-bell rings. We gather our trash from lunch, tossing it as we enter the school. Things have settled somewhat here since Trevor and Nick were charged. Word is, they both made a plea deal. Although charged as adults, Trevor's charges are more severe. Nick will go to juvie for a while. Trevor may go to prison.

"Dad gave me an update on Principal Dye last night." He

whispers. He stops talking when someone comes within earshot, then continues when it's clear. "He said they found hundreds of videos and pictures on the computers they seized of him molesting boys as young as five."

"Lord, help them," I say. I'm learning more and more to pray without ceasing as the Bible says. Pastor Mitchell said a preacher named, Smith Wigglesworth, once said he didn't pray more than fifteen minutes at a time, but rarely went more than fifteen minutes without praying. I have a new goal.

"He tried to make a plea deal but some of the images were so gross, they refused. He's looking at going away for the rest of his life. My dad said Mr. Dye may get killed in prison. A lot of pedophiles are beaten to death by other criminals."

"I'm not sure if a person who is capable of doing something as vile as hurting a childlike that even has a conscience anymore, but if he can repent, I hope he gives his life to Jesus."

Just as we reach our next class, Jonasan adds his opinion. "I hope he burns in hell! If I'd heard him talk to you the way he did, I would have helped him get there faster."

Though I understand how he can feel this way, I don't think it's how we should feel. I don't tell him this. I still have a hard time not wishing eternal damnation on Pete and Reggie. Although my experience with Reggie was just a dream, knowing he'd done worse to Shaday, was enough.

Later, Greg stomps his imaginary brake pedal as I drive the country roads.

"Alright now, you see that van with all the flashing lights ahead?"

"Yeah."

"That's a mail carrier. You need to slow down, cause they'll be stopping at some boxes. If you can see down the road apiece, it's ok to pass 'em, but don't do it otherwise. Be patient and they'll turn right on one of these side roads in a bit."

Three mailboxes down, there is a road to the right. The vehicle labeled with "Frequent Stops" signs makes the right turn.

"How did you know they would turn?"

"Mail routes are set up to avoid left-hand turns."

"You are a wealth of information, old man." I smile.

We drove a large circle and was about a mile from the house when I see blue lights flashing in my rear-view mirror.

"What did I do wrong?"

"Don't know. I thought you were doing good. Just stay calm and let me talk. I probably know 'em anyways."

The cop approaches the truck. "License, registration, and proof of insurance."

Greg hands me the documents after I pull out my learner's permit.

"What'd she do officer?"

"Just sit tight, I'll be back in a minute or two." The cop walks back to his cruiser.

"Do you know him?" I ask.

"No, not him. He must be a new one or one of them that don't like folks. Every once in a while, you'll get one that thrives on the power. You have to watch out for them. Mind your p's and q's."

"I've dealt with him before, but I don't know his name. He was the one who answered the call when Pete nearly beat Mom to death. He's not very professional if you ask me."

The police officer approaches again. "Ma'am, can you step out of the vehicle?"

I start to pull the door handle. Greg stops me.

"Why did you pull us over officer?"

"Sir, I need you to put your hands on the dash and stop interfering!"

"Why don't you get Corporal Williams on your radio, tell him Greg Jiles is asking for a reason for this stop then we can go from there."

The truck door is opened by the officer. He reaches in and releases my seat belt.

"Officer Carnes, you are violating our rights and I demand you call for backup and your supervisor!" Greg addresses the cop by his last name now that his nameplate is visible.

Carnes grips my arm above the elbow and pulls me from my

seat. I stumble to the side of the road, not knowing what to do. Under my breath, I pray.

"Lord Jesus, help us."

Greg opens his door and gets out.

Officer Carnes pulls his weapon and aims it at Greg. "Sir, get back in the vehicle!"

The cop looks over his shoulder down the road behind us. He takes a few steps positioning himself farther from the road and closer to his cruiser.

"I ain't gonna let you have her on that street! That ain't safe!"

I look to where the officer had and see a white truck speeding toward us. I know it isn't going to stop. There isn't time for me to move.

"Get down on the ground, NOW!" Carnes shouts at Greg.

"Jesus." I close my eyes and whisper His name.

There is a horrible crunching sound then tires squealing away.

I open my eyes and from across the road I see what is left of Greg's truck, turned over on its side. Officer Carnes looks at me with wide eyes then gets in his cruiser and speeds off after the truck.

"Greg!" I look both ways and cross the road to get to the flipped truck. "Greg!"

"I'm alright, girl. I'm over here."

I follow his voice to a mud hole where he's landed.

"How did you get over here?" I ask. He was by the truck when the crash happened.

"I'm not exactly sure. One minute I was standing right there and the next thing I know, it felt like somebody pushed me."

He looks at me and to the road, I just crossed. "How did you get over there?"

I look there too. "I don't know either. I closed my eyes and said Jesus because I saw it coming and knew I couldn't do anything. When I opened my eyes, I was there."

"I think we just had some heavenly intervention," Greg says.

A few people pull over who saw the accident if you can call it that. Officer Meyers arrives followed by an ambulance.

The EMTs check us over not finding a scratch on us.

"Charlie, did Carnes call this in?" Greg asks.

"Yeah, he said he was chasing the driver of the hit and run." He looks at the demolished truck. "How did you not get hurt?"

"Well, that's a mystery. But what ain't a mystery is the fact Carnes stepped way outside his legal limits, and I want to file a complaint."

Charlie Meyers slaps Greg on the shoulder. "Get in line buddy. Hey, here comes the tow."

Charlie drives us home with instructions on who to follow up with at the station about Carnes.

I look at my new car sitting in the driveway. "At least we're not without a ride."

"The Lord does provide," Greg says.

15

It's Hidden For You, Not From You

"Cathy, you in here?" Shaday knocks on my door.

"Yeah. Come on in."

"You prayin' again?"

"I can't seem to feel satisfied with stopping. I've prayed for everyone I know practically and every situation that comes to mind and I still have the urge to pray, so I start all over again."

"Why you reckon you feel that way?"

"I don't know. We have prayer tonight at church. I'm going to talk to them and see if they can tell me why I feel like this."

Shaday nods then change the subject. "Steve's parents are having him a going-away party."

"Did you guys ever work things out?"

"Kinda. He wants us to get married, but I just ain't sure yet. I'll be eighteen in a couple of months. I been thinking a lot about what I'm gonna do with my life. I can't sponge off you and Greg forever."

I raise my eyebrow at her and purse my lips.

"I know y'all don't see it that way, but that's what an outsider would call it. So, I think I might go get my GED and maybe go to

Bible college too. I was real smart in school. I just had my mind and eyes on other things, you know."

"I think that's a good plan, Day. When's Steve's party?"

"He flyin' out Tuesday so they gonna do it Monday evening at five. He asked if you were coming. I told him you probably was."

"Well, of course! I wouldn't miss that. I'll text him today and tell him to count me in."

"I can just tell him. He coming over here to take me to the learning center to find out what I need to do. I'll leave you to praying again. Say some for me."

"Always."

When prayer at church has concluded for the evening, I talk with the elders and pastors for guidance.

"While praying today, a thought came to me. John 10:10 in the KJV, says the thief comes to steal, kill, and destroy. Ever since I started following Jesus a year and a half ago, I have had more trouble than seems normal. And when Lester James was here, he said the enemy was trying to stop me. I think the Spirit of God is leading me to pray so much because I'm in a fight. What do you all think?"

"I think you're spot on," Pastor Mitchell says.

"I wondered if fasting would get the Lord to tell me what I should do?"

The Shooks look at the Pastors.

Pastor Deborah is the one to speak up. "Cathy, do you know what the Word says about fasting?"

"Not every verse by heart, but I have read them. I've read the whole Bible."

"God never tells us to fast so we can get something from Him. Fasting doesn't move God, it moves us. When we are not hearing the Lord speak, it's because our ears are not tuned in properly. Fasting helps get us focused."

"I'm not sure I completely understand."

Trena Shook pats my hand. "It's like looking through binoculars.

If the view is blurry, you need to adjust the focus. Does that make sense?"

"But I'm at God's mercy. If He wants to tell me something, how can I help or prevent Him?"

"First Corinthians, I believe in the King James Version, chapter three, verse nine it says, we are laborers together with God. Remember, He is a gentleman and never forces Himself in your life. He does know how to get our attention, but Jesus told us there is some asking, seeking, and knocking we do. Sometimes we can just ask God for the answers. Other times we must seek; meaning they'll be some digging involved. And still, other times, we knock and wait for Him to open the door," Mrs. Shook says.

Pastor Deborah moves to sit next to me. "I think this is a time for you to pursue answers but be mindful of your part and God's part. God isn't moved by you. He is in position. You move towards Him. I would suggest you write down what's in your heart. Your desires, vision, and goals can be a big indicator of where God is leading you. Also, don't think you have to know every single detail of the plan before you take a step in faith. However, because of your age, you do need to clear things with Mr. Jiles before you take off and do something. I'm glad you came to us as well. We don't pretend to know it all, but God has put us here as a resource."

"I feel in my spirit you should take some time to do as Deborah said. Don't jump off into fasting too quickly. Have a direction in mind. Most of the time the answer is already in here. We just need to stop second-guessing ourselves and follow His leading. But if you truly feel you need to shut out things around you to get alone with God, then by all means, fast a few days. But at your young age, I wouldn't go more than three days," Pastor Mitchell says.

Vanessa and I give one more round of hugs and goodbyes to the Pastors and Elders.

The alarm on my car beeps when I press the unlock button on the key.

"I can't thank you enough for doing this," I tell her again for the fifth time today.

"As I said, it's no problem. I had a learner's permit once. My mom worked all the time and couldn't ride with me much. I was fortunate enough to have Aunt Geely around. Besides, I would be coming to your house anyway to pick you up since Jonasan is out of town with his parents."

"I miss him so much! You know we spent most of the school year together besides the time when all that Trevor mess was going on. Now school is out for the summer, I feel like I never see him. His dad has been keeping him on a tight leash. He's trying to get Jonasan to join the military. I don't want that."

"How is the case with the Hayes boy going by the way?"

"Mr. Challis says this stuff takes time. Trevor's dad hired a whole team of lawyers to represent them both. They are trying to get evidence thrown out and discredit that girl from school that saw Elaine get in his car. I'm just trusting God to bring justice for Elaine and peace to her family. As far as the other cases, Pete turned state's evidence on a bunch of high-profile people, so they have him hid for protection. I heard Reggie was talking about doing the same, but I don't know if he did or not."

"I'll bet you and Shaday wish this was done already." Vanessa puts one hand on the dash and takes the grab handle with the other.

"Am I scaring you?"

"Just a little. That car was stopping, and you didn't seem to be slowing down enough. It's ok. You're not doing badly; I just get a little nervous when I'm not in control."

A police cruiser pulls from a parking lot behind me. Vanessa sees me watching my rear-view mirror intently and turns her head to look behind us.

"Don't be so nervous. You're doing good. Just watch your speed and you'll be fine."

"It's not that. Greg and I had an incident with a cop a couple of days ago. Greg filed a formal complaint against him. He was suspended but it's caused me to be leery of police now."

"You didn't tell me this! What kind of incident?"

"He pulled me over and wouldn't give us a reason. He yanked me out of the truck, pulled his gun on Greg, and V, I think he was positioning me to be hit by another vehicle. This white truck came barreling towards us. That cop had to see it coming and instead of pulling me out of the way with him. He casually steps out of the way like he had set the whole scene up."

"What?"

"Yeah, but the Lord helped us. Greg was pushed into the ditch and I was instantly set across the road out of the way. Neither of us saw who or what moved us, but we are sure it was one or more angels."

"Oh, my goodness! You weren't kidding when you said the enemy was trying to stop you. So, what happened when the cop saw it didn't work?"

"He got in his car and went after the person, or so he says. It looked to me like he was running away."

The police car behind me turns into a convenience store parking lot. I relax. Moments later, I punch in the access code for the subdivision and wait for the gate to open. Vanessa's car sits in the driveway. I open the garage door and see Greg's new truck in the spot I was headed for. Vanessa moves her car so I can get into the other garage.

Once parked, I walk to her car to tell her goodbye and thanks again before she leaves.

Before heading to bed, I take the advice I was given and write down any goals, vision for the future, or dreams I have.

Help other teens.

Be a light in the darkness?

Teach the Word.

Marry Jonasan! ♡

I look at the shortlist. I know I want to help teens and being a light in the darkness is part of that. I guess teaching the Word would be too. But, where to start or how to help them is the part I am unsure about. What can I do?

I decide to sleep on it. Tomorrow I will think about how and when I may fast and what my goals are.

I slip on Jonasan's flannel pajama pants I made him leave with me before he left for the Bahamas. He tried to get his parents to take me along, but that didn't sit well with them or Greg. They found out he proposed to me and I'd accepted. His mother almost fainted when she found out the ring he gave me was his grandmother's. Now they feel like we need some time apart for whatever reason. We told them we were waiting till we were eighteen but that wasn't long enough for them.

I get in bed, unlock my phone and stare at his picture. He turned seventeen last month. My birthday is in three months.

"One year, three months, and nine days," I say to his photo.

I turn off the light and fall asleep.

The male nurse sits behind the front lobby desk putting on mascara. I walk up and clear my throat.

"Hey, I'm here to see my grandmother," I tell him.

He looks at me suspiciously. "Let me see them."

I back up and show him my shoes.

"Not in my lifetime, honey!" he says. He dramatically rotates his head and snaps his fingers.

I look down and see my shoes are covered in dirt. "How about these?" Suddenly I'm wearing a different pair of shoes though I'd done nothing to change them. The old, dirty pair are gone.

He peers at them. "That's better. Go ahead." He waves his hand dismissively at me.

I walk down a long hallway looking in the rooms as I pass. Each room is furnished with a bed, a nightstand, and a chair, but there are no residents inside. I keep checking each room looking for my grandmother. When I have searched my way back to the front desk, I see Vanessa, who is now the receptionist.

"Where is she?"

"She's in the basement, Lovie," Vanessa tells me.

"Where is the basement?"

"It's hidden for you, not from you."

Before I can ask her what she means a gust of wind blows the front doors open. I run outside to see where the wind came from.

A black tornado as wide as the whole city is headed straight for us. Jonasan is suddenly beside me in a solid black tuxedo.

"We need to get all these people in the basement!" I yell above the storm.

He holds a sign above his head so all who pass will see it.

I walk in front of him to read it, but it has no words on it. It's a black and white picture of a dark alley with a single streetlamp illuminating a door. There is a bright red cross above the door, the only thing in color.

Soon the inside of the building is flooded with teens. They tremble in a huddled mass. The windows rattle causing them to shrink back in fear.

"He'll find me!" Shaday screams in terror.

I look outside at the storm. Breaking off from the swirling wind are dark, smoke-like creatures with red eyes beating on the doors and windows.

"Find the basement!" I yell out to Jonasan.

We begin searching behind every door. I open a door to one room and see another one on the back wall. I open it. It's another room. Door after door is opened to find hidden rooms with clothes, shoes, medical supplies, food. On and on it goes but I can't seem to find the basement. I come to the last door. It's sealed tight and secured with locks. I hear Arc whining on the other side of the door.

"I'm coming Arc."

I unlatch one lock, but another appears on the door. Behind me, I hear the rescued teens in fear and Arc on the other side pleading desperately to be let out. The locks seem to multiply. I can't seem to keep up.

"Jonasan, help me!"

He runs over and takes me in his arms. I stare into his eyes. I've missed him so much. Suddenly, all I want is to kiss him and let him hold me. I lift my head to his. To my surprise, he licks my cheek then my nose, leaving behind his saliva.

I wake abruptly. Arc whimpers and licks my face again.

"Ok ok, I'm awake. I guess you gotta go out, huh?"

I wipe the sleep from my eyes on the way past the kitchen. I unlock the patio door and set the dog free to relieve himself.

On the counter is a note from Greg telling me he would be home around three. Below his scribbled writing is Shaday's bubble style saying she was with Steve and wouldn't be home till the evening.

I let Arc back inside and go back to bed. I see the list I'd made last night. I pick up the pen laying beside it on my nightstand. I draw a curly bracket to the side of all the lines and write on the right of it; 'find a nursing home with a basement. It's hidden for me, not from me!'

I don't remember going back to sleep but later Greg wakes me again.

"You still in bed, girl? You feelin' ok?"

I yawn and sit up. "Yeah, I'm fine, just had vivid dreams again. I don't sleep well when I have them. Hey, do you know of any empty nursing homes in town?"

"I ain't that old!"

I laugh. "No, it was something I dreamed. It's given me an idea."

"Let me think. I don't know of any empty ones. Those places usually stay full. You rarely see one unoccupied. But I know the zoning commissioner, I'll get him a quick call and see if he can tell me anything."

"Thanks, Dad."

I didn't realize I'd said it at first. It wasn't till Greg left the room it dawned on me. After getting dressed, I found him in the kitchen, still on the phone.

I get the milk from the frig, the cereal, a bowl, and a spoon. I prepare my breakfast. I look at the time on the microwave. I guess this is more like an early supper.

"Ok, we'll do that. I haven't been fishing in a while. I'll get back to you in a few days. Ok, tell Ruth I said hello. Alright, bye, Clarence."

I cram my mouth full, dripping milk onto my chin.

"Clarence said there is a nursing home that was just built down past Strunk Avenue. It's empty right now because the company just filed for bankruptcy. They are not sure what's gonna happen with it yet."

He waits patiently for me to chew and swallow.

"Do you think we could drive past it later?"

"'Course," he says. He walks to the living room and picks up the tv remote.

"Hey, before you turn that on, can I ask you another question?"

"I'm all ears."

Leaving my cereal on the counter, I join him on the couch.

"Did you notice I called you 'Dad' earlier?"

He nods.

"Would it bother you if I called you Dad all the time?"

He touches my hand. "I would count it an honor."

Suddenly, I'm crying. I wasn't expecting the flood of emotion. When I try to stop, it only makes it worse. I snort and hiccup while wiping at my nose with my sleeve.

He pulls me to him. With my ear on his chest, I hear the deep bass of his voice telling me not to cry. I'm reminded even more of my dad and cry that much harder.

I peek through a window of the would-be nursing home. There is no furniture, and the walls are yet to be painted. I step back over the mud to the sidewalk.

"What ya looking for?" Greg asks me.

"I don't know yet. It's just an idea I got from the dream I had last night."

"Which was...?"

I squint at the evening sun. "I'm thinking this or a building like this would be perfect for a teen safe-house."

He turns his head questioningly at me then looks at the building.

"I wonder if this place has a basement?" I ask.

"Was that in your dream too?"

"Yeah, but it could have just been one of those weird nuances you sometimes have in dreams."

"A basement would be good for a storm shelter," he says.

I stare at him surprised. "Exactly! That was part of the dream. I was looking for my grandmother at first and then needed a place to escape a storm."

"How would you get a place like this though? Something like this would cost millions to buy or build."

"I don't know. Guess I'll have to ask God about that."

16

The Miracle

Shaday paces the floor, looking out the window every few seconds. "Where is she?"

"You know how Vanessa is, she gets sidetracked sometimes. I'm sure we'll make it on time."

Shaday runs to the door and I know Vanessa has pulled in.

"Sorry, ladies." She tells us on our way. "There was a commotion downtown and parts of the city are shut down. I had to find another way around."

I focus on my speed, knowing that's something Vanessa watches for.

"What kinda commotion?" Shaday asks.

"I'm not sure. Cops were blocking Peeler Street, Dunbar, and Highland."

"That's the ways leading to the police station." Shaday reminds us.

"Most of the state buildings too," Vanessa adds.

"Well, let's not mention it to the Zablockis', I don't want to distract from his send-off," I tell them. I know how bad news can spoil everyone's mood. Or at least mine. Maybe I'm being selfish, I don't know.

I pull into the trailer park, glancing over to lot twelve. It looks different with the potted plants lining the porch and the tricycle blocking the driveway. It looks happier. Before turning to follow the girls inside, I look across the field to Greg's junkyard. I'm surprised to see the place looking a lot barer than I remember. There is a large arm with a magnet at the end, collecting crushed vehicles and dumping them in a truck.

"You comin'?" Shaday asks, bringing me back to the celebration at hand.

I hug Steve once inside and make my way to Mr. and Mrs. Zablockis to hug them as well.

"Are you happy Steve is following his dream or sad he's leaving?" Wow, Cathy, way to be a buzzkill, I think of myself.

"We are v-veryy honored to… have son that love God," Mr. Zablockis says. His thick Latvian accent, ever-present, and the Parkinson's hindering him as well.

"Yes, though I will miss him so," Mrs. Zablockis adds.

The small mobile home fills up fast leaving little room to maneuver. When Steve's mom pulls the cake from the refrigerator, someone bumps her, and the cake lands upside down on the floor.

Mrs. Zablockis does well at holding back her emotions, but I can tell she is disappointed.

"Hey, don't worry about it," I tell her, "I'll run down to the grocery store and get another one. What do you want it to say?"

"No, no, no, it fine. I had to order ahead. No time to get, but we don't need. All friends and family is only thing required, right Stefans."

"Absolutely, Mamma! Don't worry about it, Cathy."

"No, I want to. It's been a while since I've walked anywhere. I think I'll enjoy it." I grab some money from my purse, not wanting to laden myself with any more than necessary.

When I step outside, I notice how warm it's gotten in there. All the bodies are heating the place. The cooler air is refreshing. Walking out of the trailer park onto the curve of Bowdon Lane, I remember when the days were shorter, having to rush to get home before sundown.

Crossing the parking lot, I look to where Lettie had given me the Bible. The automatic doors open blowing a blast of cold air in my face. A little modern technology to keep insects from flying in.

I head to the bakery and scan the premade options laid out. I pick out the least girly and tell the hair-netted lady what I'd like it to read. While I wait for her to spell it out in the green icing, I rock back and forth on my heels.

Suddenly, I feel the presence of the Spirit of God so strongly I almost fall to the floor.

I take a deep breath and pray in tongues softly to myself.

I am here Lord. I will obey.

'You will do His mighty works.', I hear my angel's voice in my memory.

"AAAHHHH!"

The scream is so sharp and terrible I jerk. It is the kind of scream nightmares were made of.

"Go."

Instantly I'm walking past aisles, looking down to see where the moans are coming from. I see other people heading toward the produce section.

I push my way through and see Bill, the manager, holding a woman by her shoulders. He is telling her to breathe. She's pale and looks as though she may faint from her emotional state.

The lady reaches for something on the floor. I make myself taller by standing on my toes and peer over someone's shoulder to see a lifeless toddler beside an empty grocery cart.

"Ma'am don't move him! We have called an ambulance and they are on their way!" the manager says to her.

The grief-stricken woman doesn't listen, she picks up her baby anyway.

With everything in me, I know what to do. The crowd in front of me seems to part instantly, allowing me to approach the grieving woman.

"Give him to me," I tell her. I speak from a place of authority; a holy boldness resounding throughout my being as I kneel in front of her.

The woman looks at me through her tears.

"Please." I feel the love of Jesus cascading all around me. It reminds me of the dreams I've had where the liquid silver, the anointing, would pour over me, empowering me to be His hands, feet, and voice.

Unashamed, I pray in the Spirit. Listening to Him. I hear the words of Jesus in my mind. I can of myself do nothing. I only do what I see the Father do and only speak what I hear the Father say.

I align myself with His declaration. As soon as I hear the words, I look at the boy's face and speak. "I command this child's body to be healed and his spirit to return in the name of Jesus! Little boy, I said live! In the name of Jesus Christ. Be made whole and live!"

I touch his forehead, feeling the virtue flow out of me into his small frame. My other hand is supporting his neck. I feel the misplaced vertebrae move back to where they were created to be.

I hear someone just over my shoulder, blow. I feel the breath pass by me into the child's face. He takes a deep breath. I know I'm the only one to see Lettie walk from behind me. She smiles at me.

His eyes close and he is still again but only for a second. Opening his eyes, he gazes at me, trying to figure out who I am.

The mother's eyes grow wide and her back straightens. The crowded gazers visibly take a collective step back and hushed awe comes over them. The atmosphere has changed. I see the glory cloud hovering with us on the floor.

The toddler takes in another breath and starts to cry. He raises his head searching for his mother. When he sees her, he reaches out and clutches at her with his tiny fist.

I hand him across to his mother and she buries her face into her baby's neck and starts sobbing again.

"Thank you. Thank you. Oh, God, thank you so much!" The woman tells me repeatedly.

"Are you a Christian?" I ask.

"I haven't been to mass since I was a girl. I... I've been wrong," she tells me.

"He still loves you. He sent me here to help you find your way back."

Other Angels appear, walking through the crown, laying their hands on some and whispering to others. I can see their readiness to accept Jesus. I stand to address the crowd. I never again want to waste an opportunity to share the love of Jesus with someone.

"God sent Jesus to restore us to himself and to rescue us from sin, death, and hell. Believe and confess him as Lord and you shall be saved."

No one responds so I continue. "God loves you. Not just humanity, but you, individually. He knows you better than you know yourself."

"I believe and accept Jesus as my Lord and Savior," the mother says.

Others agree and I hear their confessions of faith. I watch as more Angels arrive, ready to minister to those who have just become born again. The angels fade from my sight, though I know they are still there. The atmosphere changes and I feel the anointing lift. A man walks away quickly, and I realize it's Rebecca's dad, Mr. Sprule. I follow him, trying to catch up.

"Mr. Sprule!" I call out.

He pauses then turns around to wait for me.

"Are you ok?" I ask him.

He wipes his face with the back of his hand. "Where was God when my Becky was taking her own life?" His words are laced with anger.

I don't know how to answer him.

"She was a sweet girl. She didn't deserve to be treated that way by those bullies!" His chest heaves as he struggles with the raw emotions.

"I don't have all the answers. I can think of some nice-sounding things to tell you, but I have the feeling it wouldn't help. I think what you need to know in all this is God loves you. He knows the pain of losing a child. Because of His son's death, you can go to the Father and be healed of the heartbreak you feel. I know, He's healed me of heartbreak and fear."

I touch his arm.

"Give Him your heart and let Him heal it," I say tenderly.

He starts to sob heavily and nodding his head in agreement.

I pray with him to receive Christ and watch another miracle take place before my eyes; that of a spirit being reborn and made new.

The EMTs emerge from the store with the mother and her son. They board the ambulance and drive away without the need for a siren.

I remember the cake abruptly and return to the bakery.

"I thought you left the store. I was about to scrape the words off and fix it to put back in the case." Gilda, I see her name tag reads, smiles as she passes the cake to me. "What was all that ruckus over in produce?"

"God was doing what He does best. Do you know Jesus, Gilda?" I ask. I'm on a roll now.

When I get back to the trailer park, I see a familiar Dodge Charger parked haphazardly.

"Jonasan!" My heart revs up.

I shove the cake to the first person I see so my arms are free to embrace him.

"Why are you back? I mean, don't get me wrong, I'm so happy you are, but I thought you'd be gone another two days."

"Somethings happened. They called Dad back to work."

Laughter burst out from among Steve and those reading the cake.

"True dat!" Shaday says.

Steve reads the cake out loud for those who can't see past the crowd. "It says, 'Don't get nervous Steve'."

Steve explains it to a couple, but most everyone else knows what the cake is referring to.

"Is it about Elaine's case or the others they were investigating?" I ask Jonasan.

"Yes." He looks around. "Let's go to my car."

"You aren't leaving are you, Jonasan?" Steve calls out.

"No, we'll be back. I just missed my Sweetheart." He winks at Steve.

I jab him in the ribs but smile.

Jonasan starts the car and turns up the radio a bit. "Pete was found dead this morning."

"What happened? I thought he was in protective custody?"

"He was. Someone tried to make it look like he OD'd on heroin. I don't know why they think he didn't do it to himself, but they are calling it a homicide from what Dad says. Also..."

A child runs by the car squealing in play, startling us both.

He continues after a deep breath. "Reggie was found beaten to death in his cell last night."

My eyes widen.

"From what Dad knows, he was promising to give up someone big for a deal. The prosecutors were supposed to meet with him today."

"So, what does this mean? Does it affect Elaine's case?"

"I don't know yet. Dad's seeing what he can find out. It does mean this is not over by a long shot. I want you to do me a favor."

"Of course."

"Don't go anywhere alone!"

"Why would I still be a target? None of their convictions hang in my hands."

"But mine does and they may try to hurt you to get to me."

I nod.

We go back to the party and pretend nothing is different, but inside I hear the Spirit of The Lord say to me, "The storm is here."

Printed in the United States
by Baker & Taylor Publisher Services

Printed in the United States
by Baker & Taylor Publisher Services